BEYOND

by

I.L. Middleton

This is a work of fiction. Names, characters, places, and incidents are either the product of the author's imagination or are used fictitiously, and any resemblance to actual persons, living or dead; events; or locales is entirely coincidental.

All Rights Reserved
Copyright © 2024 by I.L. Middleton

No part of this book may be reproduced or transmitted, downloaded, distributed, reverse engineered, or stored in or introduced into any information storage and retrieval system, in any form or by any means, including photocopying and recording, whether electronic or mechanical, now known or hereinafter invented without permission in writing from the publisher.

Dorrance Publishing Co
585 Alpha Drive
Suite 103
Pittsburgh, PA 15238
Visit our website at *www.dorrancebookstore.com*

ISBN: 979-8-89127-799-1
eISBN: 979-8-89127-297-2

For you, dad. For continuing to inspire me even from beyond.

PROLOGUE

IT BEGINS

One month. One long, dreadfully drawn-out month had passed since the accident. One month since the unexplainable happened. One month since the truck crashed through the already broken-down guardrail and into the river, submerging quickly.

It was surreal. There was no other way to explain the chain of events. No way to bring sense to escaping such a tragedy. There was no way out. The pressure from the rushing water was coming in fast as soon as the truck hit the water. The seatbelt was jammed. There was no getting out of it. At least…no reasonable way.

And yet, somehow, she did. Because here she was, a month after the accident, on her birthday no less, visiting the scene where her life had literally turned on its axis and changed forever. How she made it…how she was pulled out of the truck in which she was trapped, no one had a clue. The worst of it, her gran didn't make it.

She was wracked with guilt. So many what ifs invaded her mind every day since the accident. She should have paid better attention to the road. She shouldn't have insisted on going out at all that day. It was clear the more she thought back. Her gran had seemed apprehensive at the mere mention of deviating from their initial plans. There was something bothering her gran that day. But she was too focused on going out and taking in new scenery and capturing the best photo for a scholarship submission.

She stood at the edge of the river, looking over at the now nonexistent guardrail and prepping her camera. Taking photos, capturing memories, the raw emotion of places/people, offered her some form of peace.

And yet her mind wandered to moments before the accident...

ABBA's "Dancing Queen" blared through the car, she and her gran were laughing, singing along. ABBA was her gran's go to. Classic even, she'd argue, and no one could convince her otherwise.

It was the first day in some weeks Beaufort had not seen rain. A perfect day to grab the camera and just drive. Drive to any place which brought Lucy inspiration. And the day had been incredible. They'd found new places they didn't realize were even in the town, and they'd lived there their entire lives. It was starting to get dark when they'd called it a day.

She wiped away the tears which formed from the laughter their singing antics caused, and turned down the music as the song came to an end.

"That one never gets old," her gran said, smiling at her.

"'You say that every time." She smiled.

"Because it's true...each and every time," Gran stated matter-of-factly. "Oh Lucy, thank you for today. It was so wonderful."

"You say it as though we won't have many others, Gran." Lucy glanced in Gran's direction, worried. "Are you okay?"

"I'll be just fine, dear," Gran told her, though her eyes did not seem to agree. They held secrets...something she was holding back. "I've actually been meaning to talk to you for some time Lucy."

"What's on your mind?" She turned the music off altogether, giving Gran her full attention while also minding the road.

"Your birthday is fast approaching," Gran started.

"It does that every year, Gran." She laughed.

"Yes, but you're turning 18," Gran continued, hesitantly. There was much to discuss. There was so much Lucy didn't know about their family, their lineage.

"Eighteen's not that big of a deal, Gran," Lucy told her.

"Lucy," Gran started but stopped abruptly, a gasp coming from her lips as she moved with her right arm to grab ahold of her opposite arm as though she

was suddenly experiencing a sharp pain radiating up to her chest.

"Gran?!" Lucy exclaimed, alarmed. She looked in her direction, noticing her gran was now unconscious. "GRAN!" Lucy turned back to the road. "SHIT!" she exclaimed.

Out of nowhere, a figure appeared in the middle of the road. As though suddenly, not in control of the steering wheel, Lucy felt a pull, and abruptly the truck swerved toward the guardrail, head on toward the river. It all happened so quickly. The slam into the guardrail, the truck taking flight over the bridge and into the water…

Shaking her head, Lucy tried to clear her mind, finding herself back in the present and not a prisoner of her mind, trapped in the horrific memory. It was bad enough she'd dreamt of that accident every damn night, haunting her dreams.

With a shaky breath, she aimed her camera at her targeted spot and aligned so the lighting was just right. She took another shaky breath before looking back to the camera to see the result. Lucy gasped in surprise and her eyes grew wide as she looked down at the photo. Her eyes were playing a trick on her. She shut them quickly, shaking her head in disbelief. In the photo, at the edge of the broken barrier, stood her gran smiling back at her. Which, of course, simply was not possible.

Opening her eyes, she looked down at the photo again. Her gran was gone. Of course, her mind was playing tricks on her. She knew it was too soon for her to come back here. She should've stayed away.

"Just beautiful Lucy," she heard beside her. Lucy turned her head sharply to the side, lost for words. There standing before her, was her gran. "Happy birthday, sweetheart."

"Gran?" Lucy whispered, in disbelief. "What? How? But you're…"

"Dead?" Her gran looked at her. "Oh sweetie, I thought I'd have time to explain…"

"Explain?" Lucy started.

"About your gift, sweetheart." Her gran smiled softly.

"My…what?" Lucy's mind was racing. Still trying to wrap her mind around the fact that her dead grandmother was now standing beside her, talking to her, she was unable to process what was meant by *"gift."*

"It's part of our family lineage, dear," her gran continued.

"Lineage…" Lucy repeated in a mere whisper. "I don't understand…"

"Oh sweetheart…everything you think you've known about the world is about to change. I thought there was time to teach you…to help you."

"Help me what, Gran?" Lucy asked.

"Navigate the supernatural." Surely Lucy didn't hear her correctly.

"Gran, I don't understand what you're trying to tell me. The supernatural?" Lucy asked in disbelief.

"I know it's very hard to believe, but it's very real, Lucy. Things that go bump in the night, very real," her gran told her, her face growing serious. "But knowledge of that world is just a small blip of the incredible things you're capable of."

"What am I capable of?" Lucy asked, both intrigued and confused.

"Well, for starters…the ability to communicate with the other side…"

CHAPTER 1

LUCY, TEN YEARS LATER

The sound of the bell signals someone has entered the studio. Smiling, I come out of the dark room to greet the customer. Ten o'clock sharp.

Beaufort, South Carolina, has been home for as long as I can remember. Everyone knows everyone and everything. You can't do anything without someone knowing your business within a ten-minute time span. Sometimes, this was intrusive. But in other moments, the familiarity and nostalgia were a welcome distraction from what's become a fairly mundane routine.

Wake up. Get to the studio. Complete sessions. Develop photos. Maybe communicate with someone's loved one somewhere in between. Yes, that's correct. Communicating with the other side…as my gran had told me, after she'd died, of course. I can't forget that detail. My dead grandmother coming back to visit to finally tell me what she'd tried to muster up the courage to on that dreadful day. This ability I'd inherited from my family is a small fraction of the realization that the world as I'd come to know it was flip turned on its axis. The world was not as straightforward as I'd come to know. The supernatural was real. Spirits, demons, more specifically…very real. Dark forces with capabilities of influencing people in the world to act maliciously without an easy way to ward them off back to whatever dark hole they crawled out of. But a demon hunter, I am not.

My family and their abilities to communicate with the other side went back generations in Beaufort. Even more astounding to me was the realization that the townsfolk seemed to be very much aware of this family gift before I even was. And this ability was well received and coveted by those in town. It was a way, when possible, to help bring peace and closure for those seeking a message from their passed loved ones. It almost seemed the town was waiting for the day that I'd not only learn of my abilities, but they were waiting for the moment they no longer lay dormant. My eighteenth birthday, to be more precise. I'd learned, however, that there was one changing variable for each Adams to possess this gift. That variable was the way in which spirits chose to make their intent to communicate known.

The townsfolk seemed especially disappointed when they realized my link to the other side came with restrictions. It wasn't as straightforward as it had been with my gran. My gran could see, hear, and communicate with spirits anywhere she went. How she was able to differentiate the living from spirits was beyond me. It worked very differently for me. But the trick…the message…how I knew a spirit was ready to make themselves known to pass along a message or simply pop in… it was through my photos.

If a spirit wanted to make themselves known and communicate with a loved one with my help, they appeared in a photo as I took it. Now, this doesn't mean I can't see spirits anywhere and everywhere I go. They're quite literally all around me. But we're not in sync with each other. We're not communicating on the same wavelength. As a result, it's overwhelming to stay in a crowded place for too long. Sometimes it would be hard for me to differentiate between spirits and the living. I learned to appreciate my gift for what it was: my innate ability to help others get closure—if they sought me out for it. But exploiting others by publicizing what I could do? Not for me.

While I did see this as a gift, it did come with other disadvantages in many aspects of my life. People in this town needed me. Any plans I'd had to become a world-famous photographer went out the window. I couldn't abandon the people of this town. I'd continued with my intended studies to become a professional photographer…and the picture I'd been chasing after that day 10 years ago did win me the scholarship, I thought was the end all, be all. So, I completed my studies and then opened my own studio in town.

People in town quickly jumped at the advantages photos by *the* Lucy Adams brought to them. It almost became an expectation. And just as this gift began to make existing relationships with the townsfolk questionable, my love life also suffered. Either they believed in my abilities and tried—albeit unsuccessfully—to exploit what I could do, or they didn't believe in me at all and tried to make a mockery of me. It'd always put a damper on my love life. So the solution was simple. Not to have one.

The interesting thing about it all though, is that I'd seen things I could never explain my entire life. But I chalked it up to my imagination or a trick of the mind. My gran had almost dismissed the things I'd tell her so as I got older I believed what most believe in as we grow up. Monsters weren't real. Spirits weren't real. Supernatural world…wasn't supposed to be real. But oh, how wrong I was.

And Gran was right. Communicating with spirits was just the start for me. Over time, I'd started to realize some implications of precognitive abilities while in a dreamlike state. It was still something I was figuring out. But often I'd go to sleep at night and feel a strong pull before the dreamscape starts to feel as real to me as my surroundings when I'm awake. I could sometimes navigate and manipulate my surroundings and then wake up just as suddenly, questioning what exactly it was that occurred. It still didn't make sense to me. But Gran hadn't come through and communicated with me since that day at the bridge 10 years ago. I'd assumed she moved on. While that thought did make me sad, it did bring me a sense of peace knowing she was in a better place watching over me.

"Hi, Cheryl." I smile and start to get the equipment ready for some new headshots.

"Lucy, how are you?" Cheryl asks. Cheryl is pleasant.

"I'm doing well, thank you." I turn on the lights, illuminating the space. "Are we ready?"

"We?" Cheryl looks hopeful. She immediately assumes someone's coming through today.

"Figure of speech, Cheryl." I sigh. "I'm sorry, it doesn't work that way." I know what she's hoping for. And I'm not optimistic for her preferred outcome as she's here alone. No accompanying visitors.

"Right, right." She smiles, shaking her head. "I knew that."

"Let's see what happens, shall we?" I ask. "You look incredible!" She beams and gets into position by the backdrop.

I spent 30 minutes taking photos, each with different positions, different poses, backdrops. I want to give her a variety to choose from. But I refrain from looking at them until they end.

"And that should do it," I tell her. "I got a pretty good variety here. I can go through and make sure you have them within the week."

"I have no doubts, Lucy." She smiles at me. "Your photos are truly amazing."

"Thank you, Cheryl, truly." I smile, then take a breath. I know she's trying her hardest not to ask. But she wants to. And I can't answer until I finally look. And so, taking a deep breath, I look back over the photos, searching. But as I go through them all, there's nothing. I look up at her and she can tell. She sees my hesitance in not wanting to give her the news she prayed would not be the case. I could sometimes sense the desperation, the longing to connect from the living to their loved ones. I wanted the same for them if it meant giving them closure.

"Nothing?" she asks. She doesn't hide her disappointment well.

"I'm sorry, Cheryl, no one came through," I tell her. I sensed when she came in this would be the case. A spirit didn't initially come in with her. I would've seen them at least. "That's not always a bad thing, I hope you know that." That's what I always tell myself. Not seeing or connecting with loved ones gives me the hope that they've passed on to someplace better. Somewhere where they're not stuck in an in-between limbo. Where they haven't been able to move on. I hadn't seen Gran since that day 10 years ago. It had to mean something.

"It's not?" she asks, interested.

"No." I smile. "I like to believe it means our loved ones have moved on to a better place. That when they passed on, they didn't leave anything incomplete and were at peace."

"You really believe that?" She smiled. I could tell my words offered her comfort. Her shoulders visibly relaxed.

"I'm sure there is much we don't know about spirits, even me." I laugh. "But I do believe that."

"And you'd tell me, right? If someone was with me? Even if they didn't fully come through?" she asks.

"Always." I look her in the eye, conveying the truth and how serious I am about this. "I would never, never lie to you or anyone about this."

"Right, no, of course." She sighs. "I'll wait for the photos, yeah?"

"Yeah…by the end of the week," I remind her.

"Great, thank you, Lucy!" She gathers her things and heads out. And I need a break. I have an hour before my next session and could use something to eat.

I lock up after placing the "back in fifteen" sign up on the door and make my way across the courtyard to Betty's Baked Goods. On the short walk, I see one of the storefronts is being actively worked on. I guess someone finally rented the space, a new neighbor. I smile.

I walk into the bakery and look around. It's crowded but at the same time, it's not. Spirits are scattered throughout, existing and sharing the space with the living, chattering, and adding volume. They see me, acknowledge me, but we don't connect. I'd hoped to stay here a while, but I'm already feeling a headache coming on from the overload. The chatter is just too much for me.

I walk up to the register to order.

"Lucy!" Betty exclaims, happy to see me. The feeling is mutual. She's owned the bakery for over 30 years. She knew my gran well. "The usual?" she asks. Looking around, I think maybe today I might need something bolder.

"Actually Betty, I think today I'll take a large hot black coffee and a blueberry muffin," I tell her. She gives me a knowing look.

"One of those days?" she asks, looking around the bakery.

"One of those days." I smile and offer her cash to cover my order. She refuses to take it. Every time she does this, and every time I argue. But there is never a compromise so into the tip jar my money goes, and she cannot argue anymore.

"You're too much Lucy." She laughs, moving to get my order together.

"And you love me just the same." I smile at her and move to the side. I'm trying to focus on what's in front of me and not the chatter that only I am privy to.

"Lucy, the muffins should be out of the oven in about 10 minutes, dear," Betty tells me, pulling me out of my thoughts. "I have a fresh batch for ya."

"No problem." I smile. But I'm dreading the wait inside. I stay to the side, waiting, when the bell rings. More sound, I cringe. Betty gives me a sympathetic look. She knows all too well what I am experiencing.

"Hi there!" A short woman steps up to the register. She is bubbly, this is evident, and bears a pixie-like hair style. I had never seen her before.

"Well, hello to you." Betty smiles. "I'm Betty!"

"Of Betty's Baked Goods?" the pixie asks. *Is it normal to be this hyper?* I think to myself.

"The one and only." Betty smiles. "I know just about everyone in town, but I don't recognize you. Are you new?"

"Guilty." The pixie laughs. "I'm Dawn. Dawn Foster! I'm opening the clothing shop right next door!"

"Oh, new neighbor, huh!" Betty is intrigued, glancing over at me briefly.

"Any way I can get five hot medium coffees, cream and sugar to go?" Dawn asks. "My brother and my husband's crew, they're helping get the shop renovated and ready for the grand opening. They need to refuel."

"Of course! I have some fresh muffins coming out of the oven," Betty tells her. "Best take some of those as well!"

"Oh yes, that's a perfect idea! I can't believe I didn't think of that!" Dawn agrees and pays for the order. "Hey, Betty…"

"Yes, dear?" Betty looks over, moving on to the fourth coffee of the order.

"Being new in town and all…any chance you might know of a photographer who can take some photos to help market the grand opening?" Dawn asks, looking hopeful.

"A photographer?" Betty smiles, beaming. I'm internally groaning. "Why, yes I do."

"Really?" Dawn asks, beaming at her luck.

"Mhmm," Betty tells her, giving her the coffee carefully placed in the carrier. "Lucy here is our professional photographer in town. Everyone goes to her for what they need." She nods her head in my direction. Dawn turns to look at me, beaming. I smile in return.

"Betty exaggerates sometimes." I laugh.

"Nonsense," she rebuts, going over to the oven to remove the muffins and get them ready for myself and Dawn.

"Hi there, I'm Lucy. Lucy Adams." I extend my hand to shake.

"I'm Dawn." She smiles at me. "How lucky am I! What are the chances we'd both be here at the same time! Please, tell me you might have some openings to take photos of the store as we get it ready for the opening?"

"Here you go dears," Betty chimes in, handing us our orders.

"Thank you, Betty." I smile. "A pleasure, as always. "Dawn, let's step out and chat. Why don't I grab those muffins for you?" I take them before she can protest. Selfishly, I want out of the bakery. Outside isn't nearly as crowded as the bakery, and a clear head would make me more efficient for this discussion. I lead the way out, not really giving Dawn a chance to say no.

"So, when's the opening?" I ask, coming to a stop outside her store.

"Construction's slated to be done within two weeks. So ideally, photos would be taken in three weeks and sent to marketing to spread the word," she tells me.

"Okay if I check it out? See what I'm working with?" I offer. She nods enthusiastically and leads the way. Inside there are several men standing around, chatting.

"Coffee and muffins!" Dawn shouts, capturing their attention. I'm looking around, appreciating the inside. I'd been here before when it was a toy store. She'd already changed much in a short time. She certainly had an eye. The men made their way over, eager for the coffee break.

"That wasn't all you brought back." The tall burly one laughs. I glare at him.

"Don't mind Ethan." Dawn shakes her head. "Lucy, this is my husband, Miles. This is Ethan and Josh." The other three seem less intimidating as they approach.

"Hi there." I smile at them.

"Where's Vincent?" Dawn asks. "My brother," she leans in to whisper to me.

"He's setting up some rabbit ears to try to get something on the TV playing while we work," Miles tells her. "It's gets too quiet when the tools are off." I can't help the chuckle that escapes me. Quiet. Must be nice. For me it's never truly quiet. Though surprisingly, there's no one *else* here. They look at me questioningly.

"Sorry," I say but do not explain. Dawn is giving me a look as though she's trying to figure me out but is smiling.

"Lucy's a photographer," Dawn tells them. "I've asked if she can take photos of the place to help promote the grand opening." They nod in understanding.

"My studio is actually right next door," I tell them. Dawn looks at me, surprised. "Sorry, I forgot to mention that."

"We're neighbors!" Dawn exclaims, happily. "Oh, this is so great! I can tell we're going to get along well!"

We dive into casual conversation about the plans for the upcoming opening. I'm avoiding glances in the direction of Ethan and Josh. They stare, and it's obvious and uncomfortable. Miles, I'd already learned, was Dawn's husband. He and her brother Vincent ran a construction company in the next town over and were expanding in Beaufort, which explained their relocation. Ethan and Josh made it very clear of their solo status. And I'm further disgusted and not interested.

The sound of television catches our attention.

"Finally," a man exclaims. "It's not much, but I got something coming through." The man turns to all of us, and I am taken back by this man. He's tall, muscular, and handsome. He's not like others I've come across and avoided. Yes, he's gorgeous. But his eyes. His captivating blue eyes bear into my own, telling a story of loss and pain. I'm intrigued by him. Damn.

"That's Vincent," Dawn whispers to me.

"Whatchya got?" Ethan asks, walking over to click through channels to find something that could help fill their void.

Interested in communicating with the other side? Do not hesitate to call the number below to speak to the Amazing Wanda.

An infomercial plays, advertising someone's claim to be able to connect to the other side. Internally, I'm aggravated. In truth, the reality that there are others out there who, in some way, shape, or form, can reach the other side does exist. But not many. I've proven this. I've explored this over the last 10 years of learning my own gift. A gift I did not go around openly exploiting. And this person, "Amazing Wanda," was a fraud.

"Oh! Cool!" Dawn exclaimed. "Get me a pen! I didn't realize Beaufort had people like this! How amazing!"

"Dawn, come on." Miles laughed.

"This is a joke," Vincent told her, no humor whatsoever. "You know this."

"Not all of it," Dawn disagreed. "I'm sure there are people out there who are truly capable of communicating with the other side."

"No, they can't," Vincent disagreed. "Don't be naïve, Dawn. Anyone who tells you differently is taking advantage of you. You're smarter than that. It's all a joke."

"You don't think it's possible that someone out there may actually be genuine?" I chime in. For the first time, his attention falls on me, and he falters. It's as if he's seeing me for the first time. Again, his eyes are boring into mine, only this time, I can practically feel the energy charge around us. That's new. It's almost as though I must remind myself to catch my breath. I'd never experienced this before. After a moment, he recovers and remembers his argument.

"No." He crosses his arms. "I know for a fact it's all bullshit. People should be ashamed of the lengths they'll go to exploit the pain and suffering of others."

"You know for a fact." I crossed my arms, mirroring his position and stepping a hair closer.

"Yes, I do," he states, jaw clenching. I'm staring in his eyes, searching. And I understand. I can practically sense it.

"So because you've encountered a fraud, all mediums are frauds?" I ask. He falters a moment, looking at Dawn as though she shared something she was not meant to. "Don't look at her, look at me." He looks at me surprised. "You're too easy to read, Vincent."

"To answer your question, yes," Vincent bounces back. "They're all frauds. There is no such thing as the afterlife or spirits. You shouldn't be so naïve to fall into their schemes." I look at him and frown. He genuinely believes this. Shaking my head, feeling sorry for him and whatever he experienced to make him this way, I step away to grab my coffee.

"Don't believe him Lucy," Dawn tells me. "He's a skeptic. *Some* of us are more open-minded." He huffs in the background. A sound to show his disagreement. "Here, I wrote the number down if you're interested."

"Oh thank you, but no," I tell her. "Amazing Wanda isn't truly Amazing Wanda." Dawn looks shocked as the guys laugh in the background. Except Vincent. He remains a dark cloud in his spot.

"She's a fake?" Dawn asks, surprised.

"She is," I tell her with confidence.

"See?" Vincent chimes in with a matter-of-fact attitude about him. "She scammed you, didn't she?"

"No," I tell them. "I've never called those hotlines. But unfortunately, in her case you are right, and you shouldn't waste your money, Dawn."

"How do you know?" Dawn asks, curious. I shrug my shoulder and move on. I'm not entirely comfortable revealing exactly how I know. We'd just met, and given Mr. Skeptic in the corner, I didn't feel comfortable sharing my abilities with them. Or him, that is.

I'd encountered many over the years who were skeptical. Even exes I'd dated in the past had been skeptical. And while dating is safer to not engage into…being with someone who didn't believe in me, that was a hard stop in my book. I couldn't do it.

"Dawn, I actually have to get back to the studio, but if you want to come by later in the week, we can go over different style options for your marketing and get something in the books," I offered. I walked over to where I'd placed my coffee and muffin.

Movement in the corner by Vincent had caught my attention as I picked up the bag with the muffin. I turned back toward him to see what it had been, dropping the bag in shock.

Next to Vincent, with arms crossed and a grin forming on her face, was Gran. She gave me a knowing look before she vanished. It was like the world stopped in that same moment. I couldn't believe my eyes.

"Lucy, are you okay?" Dawn asked, picking up the bag I'd dropped.

And I wasn't okay. I wasn't okay at all.

"I'm…I'm fine," I said, shaking my head, trying to get myself back together. Vincent was looking at me, confused. He was trying to gauge what had prompted my sudden demeanor.

"You sure?" she asked. "You look like you've seen a ghost." She laughed. Vincent rolled his eyes.

"Yeah." I gathered my thoughts. I wished I had my camera suddenly. "Thank you for picking that up for me," I told her. "I've got to run." I rushed out of her shop and made my way to the studio.

I didn't wait for them all to say bye. I felt bad rushing out of there but holy hell.

I hadn't seen Gran in 10 years. I'd assumed she'd moved on. And yet here she was, appearing suddenly out of nowhere, here, of all places by Vincent?!

Just what in the hell was *that* supposed to mean…

CHAPTER 2

LUCY

I don't know what to make of what just happened. Seeing Gran has shaken me to my core. It shouldn't, really, given that I see spirits all the time. But this was Gran. GRAN!! It'd been 10 years since the accident. It had brought me some form of comfort, believing that if she wasn't around then she must have moved on. But I was wrong. She hadn't moved on. She was still earthbound, and something was keeping her tethered to this world.

Suddenly, the memories flooding in from seeing her again are enough to make me feel like I'm drowning. It's as though I can hear it all again…her sharp, sudden gasp as she grabbed her arm in pain, the sound of the tires as I feel the steering wheel being pulled off the road and into the guardrail, the crash into the guardrail itself, the rushing water as the truck was pulled under…

I'm quick to unlock the studio and slam the door behind me, resting my back against the door trying to catch my breath. I recognize this feeling. These panic attacks when the memories would resurface were very common when the accident first happened. I'd learned to cope and work through them but still, unforeseen circumstances were out of my personal control.

Breathe Lucy...I whisper to myself.

I take deep breaths in, slow to exhale, working to help regulate my breathing.

I look around the studio. I'm alone. No one is here. I feel relief but sadness at the same time. Why did she wait all this time to reappear? Why did she not come to me? Why in Dawn's shop of all places? Why next to *him* of all people?!

I look at the clock on the wall...20 more minutes and another client is due to be in. Twenty minutes to pull myself together and be present for my client and what they need.

And I do just that. Compartmentalize, I tell myself.

The scheduled sessions continue uneventfully. Between more head shots, family portraits, a maternity shoot, and an engagement session, no spirits come through. Though with the afternoon crew, you can feel their main priority and goal is exactly what they are in for: a photography session. Not a photography session with a hint of mild curiosity and hope someone will come through for them. I enjoy it when the expectations are clear. And I enjoy it more when it's about the session itself.

I spend time in the dark room developing photos. Some are digital. Some I shoot old school and develop them for those clients who elect in this unique, classic style. I get lost in these. So much so I don't notice it's almost nine-thirty in the evening and realize I should be heading home.

I lock up and start my walk to my cottage. I walk now. I have for the past 10 years.

Under no circumstances do I get behind the wheel of a car. No one ever questions me. They believe it's because I blame myself for the accident. And to an extent, I do. Despite how often the coroner would tell me my gran had a heart attack and was gone before the car was fully submerged in the water...I still do carry that guilt. I had seen something in the road. Some sort of figure materialized in that road. And yet, there was no one there, according to the reports.

But now I don't trust what I see when I drive. And that's not a risk I will take.

Walking is soothing, allows me to clear my mind and just enjoy. Sometimes on peaceful nights, I'll have my camera on me to snap photos when I'm feeling inspired. But tonight, I long for peace and quiet. Spirits fill the streets as I pass by. They do not engage. They know by now if they were to try, I wouldn't make out clearly what they were saying. The barrier is too thick, and this is why the camera. The photos open that line of communication.

I'm so lost in thought I don't notice a truck has pulled up beside me, rolling the window down until they briefly lay on the horn to capture my attention.

I sigh in frustration when I realize *who* it is that's stopped. Mr. Skeptic. He irks me. Never has a human being affected me so strongly.

He's stopped. I've stopped. And we just stare at each other. It's a silent game with each of us silently challenging the other to be the first to speak.

I cross my arms, waiting for whatever it is he intends to say. After all, he had made it a point to stop rather than just keep driving along, minding his own business.

"What are you doing?" he finally asks, his voice bordering on irritation. I look around, as though it's obvious what I am doing. This gets to him. My being a smart ass annoyed him. Noted. "I mean, what are you doing walking alone in the dark by yourself?"

"As opposed to walking with a buddy?" I raise an eyebrow. I'm not technically alone. I am, and I am not.

"You know what I mean," he rebuts. "Have you no sense of self-preservation? Walking alone isn't safe."

I want to laugh. But I remind myself he's new in town. He doesn't know how uneventful this town really is. Nothing bad has happened in Beaufort. Ever. The townspeople are kindhearted.

"It's never been a problem before." I shrug. This irritates him further, and admittedly, I'm amused I could annoy him so much so quickly.

"Where's your car?" he asks.

"I don't have one," I tell him. His eyes widen.

"How do you not have one?" he asks, flabbergasted.

"What is confusing?" I ask him. "I don't have one. I walk." He looks at me as though I've grown two heads.

"Get in the truck," he finally says. It's not a request.

"It's not good to accept rides from strangers," I protest.

"Get in Lucy," he tells me, rolling his eyes. I really don't want to. And it has nothing to do with him. But I can sense how anxious the idea of my walking alone at night is unsettling to him, and I feel the urge to put him at ease, no matter how much he frustrates me.

"Fine," I cave, and finally get in the truck and quickly get my seat belt on. "It's not like I live far."

"Just the same, I'm not letting you walk alone in the middle of the night," he says and starts the truck. "Where to?"

"Follow down to the second stop sign and make a left," I tell him.

"And then?" he presses.

"And then that's it," I say simply.

"That's it?" He looks at me.

"I told you, I don't live far." I roll my eyes and turn to look out the window. I avoid looking ahead. I will not look ahead. Who knows what might materialize and confuse me again. I feel the truck take off and tense in my seat. I silently cursed him for making me get into a truck.

"If you're cold, I can turn the heat on for you," he offers, oblivious to my discomfort.

"I'm fine," I tell him. And I am. I'm not cold.

"Are you usually this stubborn?" he asks.

"Not particularly," I tell him, hiding a smile.

"I find that very doubtful," he disagrees.

"Sorry to disappoint." I laugh. The truck comes to a halt, indicating he's already made the turn. I'm waiting for his outburst.

"You're kidding, right?" He looks around the area. Woods. All woods. Lit up with lighting, of course, but woods nonetheless.

"Nope, this is me!" I make a move to open the truck door, but the lock suddenly goes down. "This isn't funny, open the door."

"You're having me drop you off in the middle of nowhere. How is that any better than walking alone at night?" He looks at me. He's waiting for an answer.

"You're not dropping me off in the middle of nowhere," I disagree. "You brought me home."

"You live in the woods." He looks at me in disbelief.

"Oh yes." I roll my eyes. "And during the full moon, I light up a fire and run around singing naked. Especially on Halloween. It gets really crazy then." I look him in the eyes. His eyes go wide. He thinks I'm serious. "I'm not actually serious, Vincent. Get a grip."

"Where do you actually live?" he presses as he rolls his eyes at me.

"Through this lit up pathway," I tell him. "I live in a cottage in the woods. I'm having you drop me off here because there isn't a straight up driveway to get through without going into a tree." He eyes me warily, unsure if I'm being honest. "Do you need to walk with me as proof?"

"Actually," he turns the truck off, "yes." I roll my eyes and get out of the truck and head to the lit up walkway, not bothering to wait for him. I'm faster than he anticipated as I hear him rushing over to my side. "Slow down, will you?"

"Why?" I ask, not breaking my pace. "You realize I don't even know you and you're following me home. That's creepy."

"It's creepy to want to make sure you get home safely?" he asks. "Most women would be flattered at the chivalrous gesture."

"I'm not most women." I shrug.

"I see that," he answers, finally caught up. Less than two minutes and we've reached the opening to my cottage. I have it illuminated at night with lighting so I can find my way. It's rather charming. Like out of a fairy tale with the overgrown vines that take on their own artistic pathway around the home itself.

"Well, this is me," I tell him. I turned to say goodbye and finally looked him in the eyes. They're striking, even in this lighting.

"You weren't kidding," he tells me, looking around, impressed.

"One thing about me you should know, Vincent," I start. "Since I have a feeling this isn't the last we'll cross paths. I don't lie. Ever."

His eyes are staring at me, intently. I hope the sincerity of my words is clear. He nods his head, appearing to truly hear what I am saying to him.

"Do you walk every night?" he asked suddenly.

"You know what my answer will be," I tell him. "But no. Not every night."

"Given I'll be around Dawn's for a while, perhaps I can offer you a ride when you find yourself walking to the woods in the middle of the night?" he offers.

"I really would rather walk," I answer. It's not about him. It is, but it isn't. I don't want to be in the car.

"Is my company so horrible?" he asks. You can tell he's joking. But on some level, he's anxious about my response.

"Did you consider it may have nothing to do with you in the slightest?" I tell him sincerely. "I've been walking and getting by where I need for a decade now. Maybe I'm a creature of habit, but I don't intend to change that any time soon."

He looks as though he wants to push the matter but stops himself, nodding his head in agreement.

"Well," he starts. "Sweet dreams, Lucy."

"Good night, Vincent," I tell him. "Thank you for the ride." I turn to head inside quickly. I don't turn around though I want to. I could feel his gaze on me. As though not ready to call it a night. But I am. I close the door behind me, not turning on the lights. I wait until he leaves. But it's several moments before he finally turns around and walks back down the path.

Breathing a sigh of relief, I make my way through the hallway leading to my bedroom. A little shut eye couldn't hurt.

Several days pass and I'd managed to avoid Vincent. I'd seen and conversed with Dawn in passing while she continues to get her shop ready for photos. We scheduled a time for me to come set everything up. I got to know the others a bit more as well.

Further sightings of Gran have not happened. Admittedly, I'm disappointed.

"Lucy, you'll come to the grand opening, right?" Dawn asks one day as we waited for our coffee order at Betty's.

"Oh, Lucy doesn't do social events," Betty chimes in, handing us our order. On the one hand I'm thankful for her, but on the other, I wish she hadn't said that. I'd rather enjoy no one else knowing the why behind my social awkwardness. Sure, friends in town understood. But Dawn wouldn't.

"None at all?" Dawn looks at me, surprised.

"None at all," I repeat her words. I don't offer more of an explanation. But you can see she wants to know more, ask more.

"Not even if it's to take some photos of the opening?" she asks, looking hopeful. "Not that I don't want you there just to attend. I don't mean it that way…"

"It's okay Dawn, I'm not offended." I smile at her. "Strictly for work, I can do it." I look over at Betty who is looking at me sympathetically. There's a high chance spirits will overcrowd the place. And with it buzzing so much like Betty's, it's always an overload for me. I almost always get a headache and end up needing to leave. That's why I avoid, avoid, avoid.

"So you'll come?" Dawn asks, hopeful.

"For pictures, sure thing," I tell her. "I can be there for about an hour and a half." There's no way I would be able to last longer than that.

"That's it?" she asks, disappointed. I don't tell her that's about as much as I could handle in a space like that.

"I'll get good shots for you, no worries." I smile, reassuring.

"I'm not worried about that," she admits, as we make our way back out to the courtyard. "I figure you'd stay and hang out as well. Keep us company."

"I think you'll be a bit busy hosting." I chuckle. "Networking and all. Plus, you'll have Miles and Vincent. He's coming, right?"

"Right," she confirms. "But you could keep Vincent company." She's hinting. And I'm not buying.

"I think I'm good," I tell her.

"Oh, come on, I know he took you home the other night." She smirks.

"He played Uber driver to my unrequested ride service," I told her.

"He was being friendly." She laughs.

"That's nice," I tell her, rolling my eyes. We stopped outside her shop.

"Will you come in?" she asks. "Vincent is here…"

"And that would be my cue to head back to the studio," I tell her, starting on my way.

"Oh, come on," she presses. "I found some cool things from the previous owners. Come check it out."

I look at my watch. I have an hour before my next session. "Fifteen minutes, Dawn. I have a session soon."

She beams at me, leading the way. We head around the counter where the register will be. She has gorgeous white built-in shelving framing the wall behind the counter.

"Beautiful, right?" Dawn asks, noticing I'm admiring the craftsmanship.

"It is," I agree.

"Vincent built it," she tells me. I look at her in surprise. As annoying as he is, he's very talented.

"It's incredible," I tell her.

"Thanks," I hear Vincent behind me. I turn to see Miles and him carrying in a box of some sort.

"Check this out, though," Dawn chimes in, suddenly excited. She crouches down and pulls out an old box from one of the shelves behind the counter. Instantly, I cringe.

"Isn't it awesome?" Dawn exclaims. I'm looking at the box in her hands. It's a Ouija board.

"Where did you find that?" Vincent asks, looking at the box with disgust.

"The old owners must have left it behind." She shrugs. "We should try it out!" I want to scream. Firstly, there are no spirits in this shop. Not right now anyway. But secondly, dabbling in things like this is not advised. Messing with realms you don't know enough about can be dangerous. And ever since I'd learned the supernatural world was real…I didn't take these things and my gran's warnings growing up lightly.

"You should throw it out," Vincent tells her. "Don't waste your time on that crap."

"Oh, come on, we used to bring this thing out all the time as kids," Dawn pouts. "You used to love this thing."

"And I grew up. I know better," Vincent tells her. "It's not real when you're the one pushing the pointer."

"I never pushed the pointer!" she disagrees. "Come on, let's try it."

"Dawn, I agree with Vincent about throwing it out," I tell her. She pouts. "You shouldn't mess with things like this anyway. You don't know what or who you're even contacting. It can be dangerous."

"There isn't anything you contact," Vincent rebuts. "It's all crap. Just like believing there are spirits or whatever waiting to talk to you."

"I wouldn't go as far as to say that," I reply, taken aback by his hostility. "But messing with things you don't truly understand isn't safe. I'd really consider getting rid of it."

"Please don't tell me you're naïve enough to buy into this crap." He looks at me as if I were crazy. It hurt. Normally I didn't care what people thought. I was fortunate people in this town knew the truth without me needing to tell them. Sure, I'd encountered skeptics before. But their opinions on the matter didn't seem to bother me as much as hearing these words from Vincent directly.

"Into this—" I point to the box, "—no. But believing that we may not be alone…what's so wrong with that?"

"Because it's all a hoax," he tells me, determined in his preconceived notions. "Whoever told you otherwise clearly did a number on you if you really think spirits are real and there's an afterlife."

"Say it wasn't real," I push. "Is it so wrong to at least believe in something so much it gives you hope?"

"I believe in what's real and what isn't," he states. "And spirits, Ouija boards, it's all bullshit. You think it's real—it's not."

"I don't need to think about anything," I tell him. "This isn't about what I do or don't believe in. It's about others and the hope believing gives them and the peace of knowing their loved ones are happy on the other side and have moved on. Closure—doesn't that mean something?"

"It would if there were any truth to it," he pushes. "But it isn't real. And people can't truly move on and grieve if they're holding on to some false hope of what will never happen."

I stare at him in silence. He doesn't know how offensive this is to me. Why should he care even if he did? His skeptic roots go so far, I doubt if the evidence were presented so clearly to him that it would make a difference. He's grieving. I can see it. And I suddenly feel bad for him. He makes more sense to me now.

He's taken back in surprise as I place my hand on his forearm in comfort. I try to ignore the spark I feel with my hand touching him. He looks down at my hand, then into my eyes.

"I'm sorry, Vincent," I tell him, softly. "I'm sorry for whoever you lost that you feel this way."

He doesn't say anything. He's stunned. He's confused. Unsure how I know, undoubtedly thinking Dawn may have said something. But she didn't. She didn't need to. I don't know who he lost or when or how. But he's grieving and in pain. And perhaps desperately tried making a connection to the spirit realm but was left disappointed one too many times.

"I'll see you all later." I remove my hand and start to walk away.

I stop and glance into the window as I head to my studio to see an uproar of commotion between Dawn and Vincent. And there, next to him once more is Gran. She looks toward me in the window with a sad look to her before she vanishes again.

Her disappearing act is getting old.

CHAPTER 3

LUCY

"Alright, let's see those pearly whites," I joke, squatting down to capture another picture for my latest client. She laughs, allowing me to capture a great candid before formally going back into a pose.

"I appreciate this on such short notice Lucy, really," Susan, my client, tells me. Susan's lived in town for the last 15 years. Her kids are fully grown and most recently, her youngest has gone away to college. I can tell, as I've passed her in town, that she's lonely. I believe her husband passed not long ago. I can sense there's more to wanting a last-minute session. Simple interest for general photos doesn't happen quite often. Usually there's more planning, more purpose in what look my clients try to capture. But Susan came in today, frazzled and upset.

"Do you want to keep going or do you want me to take a look…" I know she's truly hoping by my taking her photo, someone she's been missing will come through. Perhaps her husband. She smiles tentatively at me. Her silent admission to the true goal.

I smile at her, understanding what she needed.

I start sifting through the photos until I land on one where she's looking off in the distance. A look of longing on her face and there, beside her, I see the gentleman.

In less than a second, he was gone from the photo as quickly as he had appeared. I see him as if he's taken his place beside her. She cannot see him. He can see her. He can see me. I can see him. And now, I can hear him.

"Oh, how I miss you, Susan," he tells her.

"I'm Henry." He looks at me in introduction. I understand.

"Henry misses you Susan," I tell her gently. You never know how someone will take this. Her hand covers her mouth, covering her sudden gasp. She's looking around, trying her hardest to see him.

"Oh, he's here?" she asks me, tears filling her eyes. "He's really here?"

"He's standing beside you," I let her know. "To your left."

"Henry, I miss you so much." She turns, speaking to air.

"I miss you too, sweetheart," he tells her, but she can't hear him. "She's been so lonely since I've been gone. So alone. The kids all left." he tells me. "I don't want my being gone to hold her back, Lucy. Please tell her. Tell her I'm okay, and that I don't want her to be alone. There's so much more out there."

"Susan." I look at her, taking her hands in mine. "I know with Henry gone and the kids all moved away it's been lonely. I know you love and miss him terribly. But Susan, Henry doesn't want that for you. There's so much more out there. He wants you to live your life."

She's crying more openly now.

"I just don't know how to be without you, Henry," she says aloud.

"We hid a list of places we wanted to see…we wanted to travel the world together. My passing was sudden," he tells me. "Tell her to go to our tree in our garden, where we carved our initials? We buried the list under those initials. Tell her to go. See the world. I'll be with her every step of the way, always."

"The tree in your garden, where you two carved your initials?" I tell her. Her eyes grew wide. "You two buried a list of places you were planning on seeing. He wants you to take that list and go see the world. He wants that for you so much Susan."

"But without him?" She shakes her head. "It was supposed to be the two of us."

"He'll never not be with you," I assure her. "Our memories of our loved ones help to keep them alive in our hearts." She pulls me into a tight embrace. I glance at him, smiling at us in appreciation.

"Thank you," he tells me before leaving Susan and myself alone in the studio.

"I can't thank you enough Lucy," Susan tells me as she pulls away. "Is he still here?"

"No," I admit.

"I feel I really needed this today," she admits.

"Our loved ones have a sense of when we need them sometimes, I think," I tell her. "Are you going to go dig up that list?"

"I think I will!" She smiles, wiping away her rogue tears.

"I'm happy to hear it," I tell her.

"I should get going." Susan composes herself and starts gathering her things.

"I'll get the photos to you by the end of the week, Susan," I assure her.

"I didn't really want photos," she admits, looking down.

"I know." I smile. She looked up, surprised. "But believe me, you'll want the memories."

I walked her out to the door. Before leaving, she turns to me, embracing me in a hug once more.

"I cannot thank you enough," she whispers.

"Of course." I hug her back. "Take lots of pictures of the places you visit, Susan. I can't wait to see them!"

"Absolutely!" She walks off. You can tell she's much lighter than when she initially arrived. I feel drained but seeing the much-needed shift in Susan is why having this gift is completely worth it.

Later that day my head was pounding. I could use some caffeine. I normally limit it to one cup but today…today, more is essential.

"Hi, Betty," I greet her as I walk in.

"Food or hot beverage, Lucy?" she asks. She can already tell I'm worn down.

"Beverage, Betty," I tell her. "A very large hot beverage."

She doesn't take long to pour me a hot cup of coffee. I take it from her in appreciation, placing the money in the tip jar. She'd argue, I'd argue. The result would be the same.

"Another one today?" she asks.

"You always seem to know." I smile at her. She reminds me so much of my gran.

"You're an open book, sweetie." She laughs.

"Eh, maybe because you've known me so long." I shrug.

"Come sit." Claire, the barista helping Betty with the crowd today, takes over incoming orders as Betty comes around the counter and joins me at a nearby table. "How've you been doing?"

"I've been okay. Business is booming," I tell her.

"Business or…*business*." She laughs.

"Both," I admit.

"Light crowd here today?" she asks. I look around.

"Thankfully," I say. "The chatter is always so distorted when so many of them are around, it gets disorienting."

"Why is that? I don't think I've ever asked," Betty inquires.

"Your guess would be as good as mine, Betty. It's been 10 years but there's always something new to learn," I tell her. "I think it's so distorted because technically…we don't exist on the same plane. So, the signal doesn't come through well enough. But if they want to truly come through and communicate, they gravitate my way once the camera is aimed and ready."

"I wish your gran could see how much you've grown, Lucy." Betty sighs. "She'd be so proud."

"I've seen her," I finally say after a moment of silence. It's the first time admitting it out loud. Her eyes widen at my admission.

"What?" she asks, intrigued. "She's communicated with you?"

"No," I admit, sighing in frustration. "You know Dawn's brother?"

"The tall brooding one?" Betty asks, eyebrows wagging suggestively.

"You're ridiculous." I laugh. "Vincent."

"That would be him." She smirks. "He's not married. I noticed." She winks at me.

"Yes, the unmarried one who is also a skeptic," I tell her. Her smile disappears. Betty, admittedly, can be protective of me, especially when it comes to those who criticize what I'm able to do.

"Skeptic, you say." 'She's in thought.

"You know," I tell her. "I've come across people skeptical of spirits and the belief they exist over the years. It's not something I haven't heard before. But it's different with him."

"Oh?" 'She's intrigued. But I won't elaborate.

"Well anyway," I move on. "I've seen her briefly appear with him. Twice."

"Did she know him?" Betty asks, confused.

"I don't believe so." I shrug. "Dawn says they've all recently moved to town. I don't know if they've ever crossed paths. But it was the first time since a month after the accident I've seen her. I wish she'd come through and talk to me."

"Have you taken photos? See if she'll come through?" she asks.

"Of him? No," I tell her. "But I've taken photos in passing of the store to gauge where the best lighting is for the scheduled photoshoot at the end of the week. There's nothing."

"You'll figure it out, Lucy." She takes my hand, offering assurance. "I know you will."

"Your confidence in me is flattering." I smile. I look around the room and pause, smile instantly leaving my face. Mr. Skeptic was grabbing his order, and turned around and caught my eye. "Oh, come on." I sigh. Betty, taking notice, turns to look.

"Vincent, dear," Betty greets him. Hesitantly he comes over to say hello. So much for avoiding him.

"Betty, good to see you." He smiles at her. "Lucy."

"Vincent." My tone matches his. "How's the progress on the store?"

"Almost done, actually," he answers, looking surprised by my sudden interest.

"That's great," Betty chimes in. "What will you be doing once it's all done?"

"We have several projects lined up between here and Savannah," Vincent tells her. Savannah?

"Savannah?" Betty asks, almost as though she read my mind.

"The construction business is based out there," he explains. "So, we'll be going back on forth depending on what's needed and when." I cringe at the thought of being in a car for any extended period. He noticed.

"Ever been to Savannah, Lucy?" Vincent asks.

"Oh heavens, Lucy doesn't get into cars," Betty answers for me. "Not since the accident." Vincent looks surprised and curious.

31

"She did the other night," Vincent tells her. His eyes are not leaving mine. He has no idea what accident Betty is referencing. How could he?

"He gave me no choice," I add. "Won't be happening again, right, Vincent?"

"I'm sure I can persuade Lucy here to get in a moving vehicle again." Vincent smirks.

"Highly unlikely," I respond, standing up. Betty looks amused at watching our back-and-forth exchange. She's wearing a similar smirk I saw on my gran when I first saw her with Vincent. "I have to get going. Thank you again for the coffee, Betty."

"Anytime, dear." Betty smiles. I give a curt nod to Vincent, acknowledging him before I grab my cup and head out. I needed air. I needed to be alone. My headache hadn't improved much...so I set out walking to clear my thoughts and in truth, escape a bit from those I passed in town—spirit and living.

Without realizing, my feet took me to the bridge. *The* bridge where the accident happened 10 years ago. I rarely, if ever, come back here. The memory is too painful. They'd repaired the guardrail since then. It looks sturdier. No longer falling apart.

I take out my camera, hopeful that maybe like the time 10 years ago, maybe Gran will come to me. Talk to me. Explain what it is she's doing...why after all these years she's been around and hadn't moved on.

I took several photos—of the bridge, the water.

But as I sort through each shot, there's nothing. Absolutely nothing. And yet, a feeling comes over me as though I'm forgetting something equally important. I just can't place what it is.

The night of the grand opening had finally arrived. The photos taken to market the event turned out great. Uneventful though. And here we were, introducing Dawn Foster, the newest designer in Beaufort on her opening night.

Admittedly, I was dreading being there tonight. Usually with large crowds came other visitors that couldn't be avoided. There was always the possibility of a spirit trying to come through. I place an AirPod in my right ear. Just in case I found myself conversing with someone otherworldly, it would be easier to make people think I was on a call as opposed to talking to myself. More so to make sure Dawn and her family believed it than others.

Taking a deep breath, I step inside. The turnout to support Dawn is incredible. It's crowded. In every sense of the word. And I worry being around so many spirits chattering about will disorient me sooner than normal. It was sensory overload.

I don't waste any time starting to snap photos of anything and everything. The more I could take, the more I could produce for Dawn of the event and possibly bow out sooner. I knew I had some great candid shots of Dawn as she worked the crowd.

"Lucy!" Dawn wanders over, pulling me into an embrace. "Thank you so much for coming!"

"I wouldn't miss it," I assure her, though I'm looking around the room nervously.

"But you're not staying the whole night," she pouts. She'd been trying to convince me to stay and keep Vincent company each day leading up to the opening. But I couldn't.

"We've been over this, Dawn," I tell her.

"Are you sure I can't convince you?" she presses.

"No." I smile. "Now get back in there, lady. It's your night!"

"Fine." Dawn sighs and disappears into the crowd. I see her run over to Ethan and Miles, hugging them. I take a picture, smiling but make the mistake of looking down at the photo. Because there, standing next to Dawn is a woman, a gorgeous woman. Just as quick, she's gone and now standing next to me. Her face is passive. I can't quite read her. But she's beautiful with blonde hair pulled up in a tight ponytail, dressed casually, as though she had been out for a jog in her last moments. I see an infinity tattoo on the inside of her left wrist.

"You can see me," she surmises.

"I can," I tell her, adjusting the AirPod in my ear.

"I didn't think anyone could actually see us," she tells me, a small smile forming on her lips.

"Have you tried communicating through other mediums?" I ask her, surprised.

"Too many," she tells me. "He's tried so hard to communicate with me. Almost three years he was searching for someone who genuinely could communicate with us. But they couldn't see me…hear me. He gave up."

"Who?" I look between Ethan and Miles, wondering which of them she was referring to and how they were connected.

"Vincent," she says.

"You knew him?" I ask, surprised. I look around the room but can't see him. I'm not even sure if he'd arrived yet.

"Oh, yes," she tells me.

"Do you want me to help pass along a message?" I ask her. I assume she would. And I also dread if she says she does. Because I've seen firsthand how cynical and skeptical he is. It would be disastrous.

"No, no," she rushes. "I want so much for him, but for him to know I'm still around isn't one of them. He can't know that."

"Why not?" I ask, curious.

"Because then he'll never move on," she admits. "I want him to live his life and be happy. Not be stuck in this limbo of his anger and grief."

"Not that I'm not happy you connected with me but…if you didn't want me to pass along a message, why did you make yourself known?" I ask, interested.

"Something about you." She smiles.

"Well," I chuckle, "I am the first in—it seems three years—who can actually communicate with you."

"No, it's not that." She laughs. "It's something more. Something that tells me you're just what Vincent needs to move on." I'm no longer laughing.

"You want him to move on," I state.

"I think he's afraid it would mean he's forgetting me," she tells me. "He's stubborn that way."

"He's certainly something," I mumble. She laughs. "I'm Lucy," I tell her.

"Charlette." She smiles. "Charlie—he always called me Charlie."

I smile in return. Charlie. Before I could ask her more, she vanishes. And I stumble, exhausted from the overwhelming chatter of the room and from the interaction with Charlie.

"Woah there." Miles appears out of nowhere, catching me and helping me regain my balance. "You alright Lucy?"

"Yeah, just a little lightheaded," I tell him. He looks at me, concerned.

"You know, Dawn's parents are in town for the opening," he starts. "Neal's a doctor. He could look at you if you need."

"I'll be okay." I smile. "Thank you though."

"You sure?" He looks wary.

"Positive," I tell him. "I should probably get back to it before I head out, yeah?" He nods but isn't convinced I'm okay. Especially since I wobble a bit as I try to make my way through the crowd. I do my best to pull myself together as much as is expected of me to get Dawn the best pictures of tonight. I don't want to let her down. For the most part, I'm successful. I've grown accustomed to putting on a show, trying to show those around me that I was okay, that I wasn't falling apart or affected negatively when surrounded or interacting with spirits. My alarm going off alerts me that an hour and a half is up, and I'm packing my equipment.

"Heading out already?" Dawn made her way back over when she saw me packing up.

"Yeah, I'll have these over to you as soon as I can though." I smile, assumingly.

"I'm not worried, Lucy." She smiles in return. "Your work is amazing. I know the pictures are going to be out of this world."

"Well, thank you," I reply. "That means a lot."

"Miles said you weren't feeling well," she continues. "Do you need a ride home?"

"I'm okay, really," I tell her. "I'll make it back without problems."

"Did you park far?" she asks. I shake my head no. I don't bother explaining to her that I choose to not own a car. I chose to walk. In the short time I've known Dawn, I don't foresee her taking that bit of information very well.

"I'm going to head out," I tell her, giving her a hug. "Hey, Dawn…" I start but hesitate, not sure how best to ask.

"Yeah?" She looks at me, curious and unsuspecting of what my question will be.

"Who…who's Charlie?" I ask. Her eyes widen, jaw drops slightly.

"Did Vincent tell you about her?" Dawn steps closer, lowering her voice. I shake my head no. "How do you know that name?"

"Why? Who is she?" I ask. Dawn looks around, making sure no one is listening. I assume she's making sure Vincent isn't around.

"She was his wife," she tells me quietly. "She died three years ago."

It all starts to make sense. Why he acts the way he does. The seeds that were planted with each failed communication attempt to the other side. I knew he lost someone close—I could sense it. But I didn't think how deep the pain went for him. And I suddenly felt terrible for him and angry because I wanted nothing more but to give him peace of mind.

I don't ask how she died. I don't need those details. I know what she wore when it happened, and it seems she was taken from him tragically and suddenly. My heart aches for him. I look around, still not seeing him, but I do spot Charlie hanging back with other spirits; her focus is on me. She knows at this point I cannot hear her if she were to try to communicate. But she's watching me, her eyes pleading with me in an unknown message she hopes I'll understand. Don't tell Vincent—that's what she had wanted to make sure I *didn't* do. But how do I explain myself to Dawn without telling her?

"That's...that's horrible," I finally say.

"How do you know that name?" she asks again. She's not angry. She's curious and if I'm not misreading her expression, hopeful of something.

"Dawn, come on!" Ethan shows up, pulling her away from me, and I'm thankful for the interruption. "Time to give your hostess speech."

"But..." she starts but it's useless to struggle against him. Ethan's bigger, stronger, and determined as hell. You could tell. I use this opportunity to sneak away, hoping to go unnoticed as I made my way home.

For the first time, I wished Vincent and his annoying truck were around because I wasn't sure how easily I would make it home tonight. Betty's place is closed so I debate. Chance it and make my way home to my cottage, or walk the few steps to my studio and crash there for the night. I always kept spare attire... just in case.

It doesn't take long for my body to decide for me. My body decides for me, and I stumble on the short walk to the studio.

CHAPTER 4

LUCY

Friday night and the lights are low
Looking out for a place to go
Where they play the right music
Getting in the Swing

"Dancing Queen" is playing in the background. Gran is already starting a jam session, and the song has yet to truly build. But she loves it. She's all about ABBA. I indulge her. You can't help but sing along with the lyrics.

Everything is fine
You're in the mood for a dance
And when you get the chance

"Not loud enough yet, Lucy." Gran laughs. I roll my eyes. We're plenty loud. Any louder and we'll wake up without our voices. Unless that's her intention.

There's a slight fog on the road ahead. The way it always formed in Beaufort after a heavy rainstorm. The sun is beginning to set, and I'm focused on getting us back home and calling our impromptu photo session to an end. There would always be tomorrow.

Gran wants to chat. I can tell it's something serious, but I can't help but joke with her to lighten the mood.

You are the dancing queen
Young and sweet
Only seventeen

It all happens so quickly. Gran is gasping in pain. I can't focus. She needs me. But she's already lost consciousness. The car is swerving, as though some sort of force is pulling the steering wheel in the direction of the water.

The water is rushing in and I'm panicking. I'm trying to unfasten the seatbelt to get to Gran. Maybe I could save her…get her out somehow. But the water is too fast and I'm stuck. I'm submerged. I can't breathe. I'm trying to fight it. I'm trying to catch my breath but the more I try, the more I feel the water fill my lungs. It's burning. It hurts…I'm focused on Gran and only Gran until it all goes black…

I startle awake. I awake in darkness. In panic, thinking I'm still stuck in my recurring nightmare, I scream and struggle to move from my position. I land on the floor. It's enough to startle me and realize I am, in fact, still here. I am, in fact, finally awake. I crawl over to a table lamp, turning it on and looking around, catching my breath. I'm in my studio.

"It wasn't real, it wasn't real," I repeat to myself.

I look at the clock. It's almost six in the morning. The sun should be rising soon. But I am in no way prepared or ready to greet the new day.

I grab a change of clothes and go clean myself up. Fortunately, I had enough sense to keep today's sessions blocked, unsure how being in a crowded event would play out. It wiped me out more than I had expected. Last night…well, it went as expected and slightly not as expected.

I know what's likely in store for me when I find myself in crowds. Hence, I avoid them. But this was for Dawn, and I truly wanted to make sure her night was a success. But I didn't anticipate the Charlie discovery.

I wanted so much to encourage Charlie to pass along her message to Vincent. Almost three years he had spent desperately trying to connect with her spirit. Each time, clearly taken advantage of. I wanted to argue with her that closure might be what he needs to move on as she wanted. But she knew him. She witnessed his heartache each time he realized he'd been tricked. I couldn't even begin to imagine his pain.

A frantic knock from the front door catches my attention. What the hell? It's nearly seven in the morning now, and I know there are no sessions scheduled. I cautiously look in the peephole to see who could be here of all places.

Oh. I unlock the door and open it, to have a frantic Vincent help himself inside, brushing past me. He looks at me, bewildered. I look at him, unable to make sense of his disheveled state. There are no words exchanged but the silent expectation for one of us to finally speak.

"Is Dawn okay?" I finally ask. Why else would he be showing up in disarray?

"Dawn? She's fine, why wouldn't she be?" he answers. There's a slight hint of anger behind him, and I can't help but wonder if Dawn told him I asked about Charlie.

"You tell me." I put my hands on my hips. "It's nearly seven in the morning and you barge in here. What is wrong with you?"

"You weren't home," he says. As if I'm supposed to understand his point.

"I gathered that," I say, making him angrier. "I know where I am, thank you very much."

"But no one else did." He begins pacing. "Dawn has been trying to get ahold of you all night, trying to make sure you were okay. Miles said you could barely walk straight when you left. They were worried you drove yourself off the road only to find out from me you don't own a car…no, you insist on walking!"

"Would you stop pacing!" I demand. "You're giving me a headache!"

"Do you realize how worried everyone's been?" he presses.

"I told Dawn and Miles I was fine, and I was," I tell him honestly. "There was nothing wrong with me when I left. And there's nothing wrong with me now. I didn't realize they'd be so worried."

"Why wouldn't everyone worry?" He looks at me like I'm crazy. "Everyone has come to care a great deal about you in the short time they've known you." I pick up on his use of "everyone." Not specific to Dawn, as I had intentionally done.

"I didn't mean for them to worry," I tell him, softening my voice.

"If you'd just answered one message…they've been trying to reach you since you left the party," he continues and once more begins to pace.

"Again, with the pacing." I shake my head, roll my eyes, and go over to my bag to check my phone. Battery dead. "My phone's dead. I don't keep a charger here. I didn't know."

"If you'd planned on crashing here, why not have your charger?" he asks, stopping to look at me.

"Because I hadn't planned on staying here," I tell him. "I intended to go home."

"Alone, again. In the dark," he adds. He's shaking his head like the idea of my walking in the dark offends him. I can't help but wonder if there's more to it than he's letting on.

"Yes, but I was tired so I came here," I tell him.

"So you weren't fine," he accuses.

"I was fine," I press. "I was fine but tired. What is your problem? What is with your third degree?"

"Everyone was worried," he says after a moment of silence. "*I* was worried." I stare at him, unsure of what to say. What's the right thing to say?

"I didn't mean to worry anyone," I tell him. I take a tentative step closer, placing my hand on his forearm. Much like I had done the other day.

"Just, don't do that," he says quietly.

"I can't promise it won't happen again." He starts to protest but I continue. "You have to understand, it's just me. For 10 years, it's been just me. I told you, I'm a creature of habit."

He's thoughtful, processing what I'm saying.

"Your parents?"

"Never knew my dad," I tell him. "And Mom skipped town when I was young. Small towns suffocated her."

"What about your husband or boyfriend, or whatever?" I roll my eyes.

"Is that your clever way of trying to determine if I'm otherwise attached?" I smirk. He looks away, embarrassed.

"It's just me, Vincent," I tell him. I remove my hand and back away.

"Lucy," he starts.

"I'll call Dawn and apologize for making everyone worry," I assure him. "I'll stop at the shop on my way back home."

"No sessions today?" he asks.

"No," I tell him. "Day off for me today."

"Do you have any plans?" he asks, suddenly. "Would you be open to...I don't know...grabbing some breakfast or something?"

I look at him. He's looking anywhere but at me.

"Are you asking me on a date, Vincent?" I look at him, surprised. He looks troubled. At war with himself.

"Maybe?" He seems unsure. He takes a step closer. "Try as I might, I can't seem to stay away from you anymore. I can't seem to get you off my mind. I'd like to at least get to know you."

"I'm not sure whether I should be creeped out, flattered, or insulted." I laugh.

"Be serious, please." I stop laughing. "I'm trying," he adds.

"You're right, I'm sorry," I apologize.

"So...breakfast?" he asks. "Or something?"

I hesitate. I don't date. I'm not single by chance. It's a choice. The "I see spirits and sometimes have casual conversations with them" thing always impacts the relationship I'm in. It's never just about us as a couple. It's will she or won't she be weird today? Is she or isn't she serious? And then the worst kind is those who are skeptical to begin with. And being with someone who can't believe in me is something I simply won't do.

"I'm not really dating right now, Vincent," I tell him, avoiding eye contact.

"Lucy, if you're not interested you can say that," he tells me. "I won't be offended."

"Remember I told you...I don't lie," I remind him. "So, when I say I'm not dating, there's no smoke and mirrors."

"Does not dating mean you're not eating anymore?" He smirks. I glare at him. "Breakfast among friends?"

"We're friends now?" I ask. I'm genuinely surprised by his admission of his trouble being around me versus wanting to suddenly get to know me. I'd spent the weeks leading up to the opening avoiding him.

"Well, maybe the past few weeks were rocky," he admits. "But friendship is a good starting point."

"Friends," I repeat, trying to wrap my mind about being *friends* with Vincent Henry. "Okay, yeah. But can we raincheck on the breakfast or something?"

"Yeah." He smiles. "I'll go check in and let everyone know you're okay."

"I'd appreciate it," I tell him. He looks like he wants to say more but second guesses himself. With a brief nod, he walks to the door to leave.

"I'll see you soon, Lucy," he says.

"See you soon, Vincent." I watch as he leaves and makes his way through the courtyard. I see Charlie seated on the bench not far from my studio, watching with a smile on her face. I don't reach for my camera to try to gauge an interaction. I need to regain some energy before I do that. I realize it's not so much my interaction with a spirit causing this but how strong of a spirit Charlie is. And I'm not sure what to make of that. So much powerful energy emitted from her. It was very new for me. In times like these, I wished Gran was around to help guide me.

With a sigh, I gently close the door and lock it up once more.

A week later, I have Dawn's photos developed and a flash drive of everything ready to go. I wait until closing time to head over and provide her with everything.

"Dawn?" I go into the shop.

"In the back!" I hear her shout. I do as instructed and see she's going through inventory.

"How's it been since the opening?" I ask.

"Well," she smiles, "I'm pleasantly surprised it's taken off as well in such a short time."

"I'm happy to hear it!" I tell her. "I actually brought your photos." I hand her the portfolio, the flash drive securely situated on the inside flap. She takes the portfolio from me, all other tasks forgotten as she excitedly opens the flap to look through everything.

"Lucy," she says in awe. She seems pleasantly surprised. "These are incredible."

I smile.

"No, I'm serious," she tells me. "I'm sure you've heard it all before but Lucy, what are you doing in a small town with a talent like yours?"

"It's home," I tell her.

"You can build a home anywhere," she disagrees.

"Perhaps, but it's the people who help make the place you're in feel like home," I tell her. "I don't have family of my own here anymore but the people of this town. They're as close to family as you get when you're alone."

Beyond

"Family supports family," Dawn tells me. "If they know you, they'll want you to put yourself out there and let the world know your talent."

"Dawn, they need me here." She doesn't understand. "And I'm happy here."

"But are you?" she presses.

"I don't think I understand," I tell her, genuinely confused.

"Are you happy in this town when most of the time you keep to yourself?" she asks. She's nervous to speak so directly, unsure how I'll react.

"You mean because I choose not to go to gatherings?" I ask.

"Partially, yes," she tells me. "I hope you're not offended, Lucy. But you're young and talented. You should be living your life, not hiding away."

"I just don't do well in crowds," I tell her.

"I understand opening night," she starts. "But I rarely see you hang around Betty's. You're always so quick to run back out the door, and it's not that crowded at the times we've both been there."

"I can't explain it, Dawn." I shake my head. I can't explain without telling her the truth.

"Why not?" she asks, taking my hand. She's offering me comfort.

"Because I won't lie to you," I tell her. "I refuse to lie but I can't tell you why." She watches my face carefully, thinking.

"Do you not trust me?" she asks, saddened at the thought.

"It isn't a matter of trust or distrust," I explain. "There are just some things about me that are my own information to keep. And I like that those aren't things you readily know. It's refreshing."

She's thinking, processing.

"Does it have to do with why you asked about Charlie?" she suddenly asks. I look at her in surprise.

"Dawn," I start.

"No wait, listen," she interrupts. "No one, *no one*, but Vincent called her Charlie. She was always Charlette. And out of nowhere, right before you all but rush to leave, you're asking about her? Not Charlette, but *Charlie?*"

"What do you want me to say?" I sigh.

"I've paid attention, Lucy," she tells me. "Each time you've been in the shop... how you reacted to that Ouija board. How offended you were when Vincent went on his rant about mediums being frauds and ghosts not being real…how it literally looked like you *saw* a ghost that first day we met…"

Now I'm pacing.

"Lucy," she says, getting my attention. I look at her. "Can you communicate with spirits?"

We stared at each other for a long time. I will not lie to her.

"Yes," I say, simply. Several emotions process on her face so quickly. Her eyes go wide. A smile starts to form on her face and she's practically bouncing up and down in her seat in what looks to be excitement.

"How long have you been able to communicate with them?" she asks.

"My gran would've said I was able to communicate in some way since I was a child," I tell her. "But it really kicked when I turned 18."

"This is unbelievable!" she exclaims. So she doesn't believe me. "It's absolutely incredible! And you must have encountered Charlette…how else would you know to call her Charlie." It isn't a question. She's making a statement of fact. And because she's not asking, I'm not confirming. "We should tell Vincent, oh-my-god!"

"No," I state.

"What? Why not?" she asks, confused. "He's been trying to find someone who could communicate with her for years!"

"I know," I tell her.

"He told you?" she questions.

"No," I answer. "Vincent has yet to directly tell me he's been married before, let alone that he lost his wife."

"Then how—" she stops, realizing how it is that I know.

"I don't want him to know what I can do," I tell her.

"You don't think he'll believe you," she states.

"I know he won't," I say.

"But if a spirit is nearby…you could prove it to him, right?" she asks.

"I don't have to prove anything to anyone," I state, crossing my arms. "But it's not that simple. I can see spirits everywhere I go, sure. And whenever they're around, I can hear distorted chatter when they're trying to either reach out to me or trying to get their loved ones to hear them. But it's not clear. And it's disorienting."

"That's why you avoid crowds." She makes the connection. I nod. "How then do you communicate if you can't hear them clearly?"

"My pictures," I share. "If a spirit wants to come through and connect—whether it's with me or to have me help pass along a message—they'll appear briefly in a photo I've taken."

"How's that work?" she asks, confused.

"From what I've learned, the photos help thin the veil between the spirit realm and ours. It helps make their messages clearer but it's only for a short time."

"I've never heard of it working like that before," she muses out loud. "Not that I presume to know the first thing about it."

"It doesn't," I tell her. "Everyone's gift presents differently. Betty says my gran didn't need photos to be able to communicate with them."

"Betty knows?!" she all but screams.

"Most of the town does." I laugh. "My family's been known for their supernatural abilities for a long, long time. It's like our legacy. The town relies on us and this part of what we can do…we can help bring them peace. Offer closure."

"Is that part of why you won't leave?" she asks.

"Part of it." I smile. "It's not the reason keeping me here. But it's part of it." She nods in understanding. "You're taking this awfully well…"

"I told you I'm more open minded." She laughs.

"I see that." I smile.

"Listen," she starts after several minutes pass, "I know you don't do crowds… but would you want to come to dinner tomorrow night? My parents are still in town, and we're all gathering. I even promise to make sure Vincent is on his best behavior." I laugh.

"Sure." I smile. "Dinner sounds nice. Just send me the address and I'll be there."

CHAPTER 5

LUCY

I'd agreed to go to Dawn's place for dinner with her family. Why did I agree? I was still asking myself as I left my cottage to head over there the next day. It would be a far walk—it's farther than I've had to go given usually those who live in town aren't too spread out. But I enjoy the possible sights I'll see. They're on the outskirts of Beaufort...close to town but far enough where they have their own privacy if they wanted. Normally, I'd be inclined to bring my gear with me. But something told me it would be better to not.

I pass areas I'm not too familiar with which I make a note to correct. How had I lived here all my life and yet not seen everything? I'd thought we'd seen all there was to Beaufort...which admittedly is already not too much.

I double checked my phone for the address as I finally came across a large home. Once I'm in the right place, I walk up the driveway, appreciating the property. The land itself is abundant. But the modern architecture of the home is exquisite. Perfect lines connecting the various levels. There's a sense of familiarity as I take it all in. As though at one point, I'd been here.

Taking a deep breath, I ring the bell. I don't wait long before the door swings open and an excited Dawn is greeting me, pulling me into the house and into a tight embrace.

"I'm so happy you made it!" she exclaims.

"Thank you for inviting me." I smile.

"Of course!" She pulls away, looking me over. I hope I'm not underdressed in my tight black pants and green cascading top. "You look great! Come this way!" She's pulling me through a hallway and into the kitchen where I can see many have gathered. "Look who's here everyone!"

"Hi." I awkwardly wave. I recognize Miles immediately. There's another man with them and the blonde bombshell next to him I recognize from the Dawn's grand opening, but we weren't formally introduced thus far.

"Lucy, this is Sarah, my cousin, and her husband, Kyle," Dawn introduces us.

"Hi there." She smiles and comes over to shake my hand. "I've heard a lot about you. Dawn has become one of your biggest fans." I look at Dawn, hoping not all that she shared involved talk of spirits.

"Well, I must admit I've become a fan of her work as well," I say, truthfully. "What is it you do, Sarah?"

"I restore old vintage cars." She laughs when I look at her in surprise. "I know, surprising. Everyone has the same look on their face as you just did."

"Her work's amazing," Kyle says, gushing as he enters the room. "Hey Lucy, good to meet you." I smile at him in greeting.

"It's actually why you haven't seen me around all that much," she tells me. "My shop is based out of Savannah, and I often travel."

"If you're mainly out of Savannah, why Beaufort?" I ask.

"It's home," Kyle says. Now I'm confused. Beaufort is home?

"You look confused." Sarah laughs.

"Admittedly, I am," I tell her. "You've lived here before?"

"Our family did, yeah," Kyle tells me. "This house has been in the family for generations. My aunt Samantha's updated it through the years, of course."

"How long since you've all been here?" I ask.

"We moved away before Vincent was even born," Dawn says. "And he's nearly 33 now."

"Yeah, Dad had an opportunity Mom wouldn't let him pass up running the hospital in Savannah, so we all moved," Dawn explains.

I'm genuinely surprised by this bit of information. And the realization that if their family was from Beaufort, then maybe they knew my family as well. And if they knew my family…there's a possibility they knew what my family could do. And that was dreadful to me.

"And everyone's back for the foreseeable future?" I ask, slightly nervous.

"I think Mom and Dad are getting everything in order for Dad to cut back at the hospital, which would make a commute more manageable for him," Dawn says, looking at Miles who is nodding in agreement.

"The plan was always to come back." He shrugs.

"Besides, when we envision starting our own families Savannah isn't the place," Sarah adds. "We like the idea that everyone knows everyone in a small town." They laugh.

"You'll definitely get that from Beaufort," I agree. "Can I help get anything ready?"

"I was about to set the table if you want to help me with that?" Sarah offers. I nod and make my way over, grabbing the plates. I realize there's seven rather than eight plates, which confuses me.

"Shouldn't there be eight settings?" I ask, looking around the group.

"We're not sure if Vincent going to make it," Dawn tells me.

"A job in Savannah ran into a bit of a hiccup, and he's held up." Miles explains. "He said he'd try but that usually means he isn't coming."

"If you'd let me tell him Lucy would be here, I'm sure he'd be here in a heartbeat." Dawn laughs. Miles rolls his eyes while Kyle nods in agreement. I can't help but blush.

"Oh, what'd I miss?" Sarah asks.

"Nothing," I tell her, counting the silverware to make sure there's enough for the plates.

"Vincent is into Lucy." Dawn shrugs. "He'll ask her out eventually. You know how he is."

"Eventually?" Kyle laughs. "I thought he already did." Everyone turns to look at me expectantly. Rather give them what they're looking for, I turn my attention to setting the table.

"I'll just be in the dining room, setting up." I don't linger. I make my way out of the room. But that doesn't deter the group as I can hear they're hot on my heels for some answers.

"Did Vincent ask you out?" Dawn asks. I shrug my shoulders, setting the table. "Oh my god, he did! He totally did!" I look up at Dawn, rolling my eyes. Sarah looks surprised but not horrified at the idea of Vincent and I going out.

"It's not a big deal." I brush it off.

"Eh, on our end it kinda is," Sarah says. "It's great though."

"When are you guys going out?" Dawn asks. "I can help you get ready!"

"We're not going out," I tell her.

"But he asked you out…" Dawn says, confused.

"Dawn, sweetie," Miles says, placing his arms on her shoulders in a calming gesture. "I think that Vincent asking her out doesn't mean Lucy said yes."

"Of course, she said yes," Dawn says, then turns to look at me. I avoid all eye contact.

"I don't think she did," Sarah adds.

"It's not a big deal," I tell them. The guys are looking at each other, as if they know what's next to come. They're slowly backing out of the room leaving me alone with Dawn and Sarah.

"It is so a big deal!" Dawn says, hands on her hips. "What the hell, Lucy?!"

"Why is this bothering you so much?" I ask.

"I mean, if she's not interested in Vincent then you can't attack her for saying no, Dawn," Sarah adds in my defense.

"Anyone with two eyes can see that isn't the case, Sarah," Dawn denies.

"We've agreed to be friends," I say nonchalantly.

"That's cute," Dawn says sarcastically.

"So are you or are you not into Vincent?" Sarah asks, confused.

"I haven't thought about it," I tell her honestly. On the other hand, after he asked me out I've certainly started thinking about it. And the conclusion is the same. "It doesn't matter anyway. I'm not dating."

"Right now or at all?" Sarah asks, confused.

"At all," I answer. Their eyes bug out.

"When was the last time you were in any relationship with a guy?" Sarah asks in disbelief. I must think. I truly can't recall.

"If you can't remember it's been too long," Dawn says. "Lucy, that's crazy. You're a woman. You have needs. What are you thinking?!" I roll my eyes.

"I have my reasons for not getting involved with anyone," I tell her, giving her a pointed stare.

"What reasons are they?" Sarah asks, not noticing my silent exchange with Dawn.

"My own," I simply say. Sarah doesn't seem too put out that I won't divulge more than I've offered.

"Lucy, you can't hide forever," Dawn tells me.

"I'm not hiding," I tell her, trying my best not to feel offended.

"You are," Dawn tells me. "You've hid away for so long you can't even see it."

"Dawn, this really isn't the time," I say, heading to the kitchen to grab more essentials to set the table. Kyle and Miles are suddenly trying to appear occupied but are failing miserably. I can tell they were eavesdropping.

"You two aren't convincing." I laugh. "What needs to go to the table?" Kyle hands me a bowl of roasted vegetables.

"Did he really ask you out?" Kyle asks quietly.

"He did," I tell him truthfully.

"Good for him." He smiles.

"That's it?" I ask, surprised.

"I'm not going to give you the third degree." Kyle laughs. "You'll never hear the end of it from Dawn now that she knows he's asked, and you turned him down." I groan. It's not about that.

"It's just a big deal on our end to know he's put himself out there," Miles says, a shy smile forming. "I know you don't know or understand why, but it's a big deal." Except I do know. And I do understand. And I feel terrible about it.

"Lucy," Dawn says, coming into the kitchen.

"Dawn, I thought tonight is a family dinner. Not give Lucy the third degree about the decisions she makes for her life," I tell her.

"I just want to help you," Dawn pouts.

"It's not helping me," I say.

"But—" She's disrupted when two new faces enter the room. I surmise it's their parents.

"Hello, hello!" the woman greets everyone cheerfully. She's making her rounds across the room, hugging everyone. She seems friendly. Genuine.

"Sorry we're late," the man—Dr. Henry—adds as he greets the group.

"You're right on time," Sarah says. "Everything's just about ready."

"Oh good!" Mrs. Henry smiles.

"Mom, Dad, meet Lucy," Dawn says, bringing the attention back to me. "Lucy, these are our parents."

"Hello." I smile and move to shake their hands, only to be pulled into a hug by their mother. "It's so nice to meet you, Dr. Henry, Mrs. Henry. Thank you for having me tonight."

"Oh, please call us Neal and Samantha." Samantha moves out of our hug. "We don't do formalities, not in this house." She smiles.

"I'll try." I smile. It's weird to me to be less formal.

"Oh, you're just as beautiful as described," Samantha gushes. "Neal, just look at her."

"I'm sure Dawn exaggerated." I laugh.

"Oh, not Dawn dear." Samantha takes my hand. "Vincent." And once more, I'm blushing. "Let's all have a seat, shall we?"

We all start to make our way to the dining room and take our seats. It's awkward silence at first until Neal speaks up.

"Vincent's not coming?" he asks.

"Held up at a job site in Savannah," Kyle tells him.

"Or he's avoiding Lucy here," Sarah teases.

"He didn't know she'd be here, Sarah," Dawn defends.

"Why would he be avoiding Lucy?" Samantha asks, confused.

"Poor girl turned him down," Kyle says.

"That isn't what happened." I roll my eyes. "Can we please move on from this?"

"For now," Dawn says. And I know she means it.

"So Lucy," Neal chimes in. "What is it you do?"

"I'm a photographer," I tell him.

"That's wonderful!" Samantha says. "What do you photograph?"

"A variety, really," I tell them. "It depends on what's needed. I'll schedule sessions for headshots, newborn photos, engagement shoots, things like that."

"Do you do major events?" she asks. "I saw what you created from Dawn's opening night. Your photos are exquisite. You've got quite the eye."

"Thank you." I smile. I'm flattered. "I don't tend to do big events."

"How come?" Sarah chimes in.

"I don't particularly favor that type of environment," I tell them.

"Crowds or the celebrations?" Sarah asks.

"Crowds," I answer but don't offer more.

"Are you claustrophobic?" Kyle looks at me, surprised.

"I can't say that I am, no," I tell him. He shrugs.

"I figure, why else would someone avoid crowds." He laughed. I look at Dawn, hoping my silent gaze is enough to portray what I'm curious about. If she told them all. She subtly shakes her head no. And I feel I can relax again.

"Have you lived in Beaufort long?" Neal asks.

"My whole life," I tell him. "My family goes back generations. Can't seem to get away from it," I say jokingly. They laugh.

"Generations, you say?" Neal adds. I can see what he's thinking. I nod.

"Oh! What's the last name?" Samantha asks. "Our family goes back as well, but we moved away so long ago."

"Adams," I tell them hesitantly.

"Adams…Adams…" Neal is thinking. And suddenly, his eyes grew wide. "Any relation to Agatha?" Shit.

"Yes," I tell him. I'm wary. "My gran was Agatha." Both Samantha and Neal's eyes are wide in surprise and excitement.

"You knew her gran?" Dawn asks.

"Oh, very well," Samantha says. "The entire town knows the Adams family well. They are very well known."

"Did you guys build the town or something?" Kyle teases.

"No." I laugh.

"How is Agatha these days?" Neal asks.

"She passed away 10 years ago," I tell them. There's silence around the table.

"I'm so sorry, dear," Samantha says. "How did it happen?"

"Car accident," I say. "Though, officially a heart attack just before the accident."

"Oh goodness," Samantha exclaims and then realizes something. "Neal, didn't we read about an accident in the paper years back? The truck that went over the bridge and into the river?"

"Yes, I recall that," Neal answers. He's thinking. And I'm wishing this dinner would end. "But there were two passengers…" They all look at me.

"Who was the other passenger?" Kyle asks, missing what seemed to be obvious to everyone else at the table.

"Really, Kyle?" Dawn rolls her eyes.

"Me," I tell him.

"Is that why you don't drive, Lucy?" Dawn suddenly asks. All eyes fall to me in surprise.

"Not entirely, no," I share.

"How the hell did you get here then?" Kyle asks.

"I walked." Everyone is staring at me like I have two heads.

"You walked?" Sarah asks. "From town?"

"Yes," I answer.

"That's insane." She looks beside herself.

"On the contrary, it's good for you." I laugh and am desperate for a change in topic. I have no interest in going into what I cannot explain. How I managed to get out of that truck when I was submerged with it. I still had no clue.

"So you're moving back?" I ask Samantha and Neal.

"Yes, we've missed this place." Samantha smiles, understanding the need to discuss something less tragic.

"And it's a good time for me to cut back at the hospital," Neal adds.

"I told her that." Kyle rolls his eyes.

The rest of the dinner isn't as eventful. But I can sense there's more questions they want to ask me, but they respect my privacy. I'm helping Samantha with the dishes when she finally speaks, circling back to earlier topics of the night.

"I still cannot get over that Agatha was your grandmother." Samantha smiles. "She was such a wonderful woman."

"She really was." I smile.

"Very *talented* too." Samantha emphasizes "talented," and I pause. I look at her and she's giving me a pointed look.

"Not that I was aware of at the time," I tell her. She nods in understanding.

"It took a very strong, compassionate person to do the things she could do," Samantha continues. "So genuine and selfless."

"She was the best person I knew." I smiled.

"It's okay that you want to keep that side of your life to yourself," Samantha says. I look at her, surprised she's so intuitive. "It's takes a lot for a person to take that leap of faith and believe the unknown."

"It seems you took a leap and believed?" I answer.

"Yes." She smiles. "But I've seen firsthand what your grandmother could do. She really helped me gain closure when I lost someone dear to me."

"Hearing that…it means a lot to me, Samantha." I smile. "Thank you." She gives me a hug.

"Of course." She smiles back. "I'm so happy our paths have crossed again, Lucy. I do hope we'll see more of you around here."

"Me too," I admit.

"Shall we get dessert ready?" Samantha asks. I nod and help get everything situated for the dessert. We've all just taken our seats once more when we hear the front door open and close.

"Hello? Mom? Dad?" I hear Vincent call out. Well, crap. Dawn is sitting across from me, suddenly excited. He's searching for where everyone has gathered and finally makes the discovery, only to stop short when he sees me sitting at the table. He's surprised at first. Then a smirk covers his features.

"Vincent, you made it!" Samantha stands up to greet him, pulling him into a tight embrace.

"I'll go grab another plate." I stand up and head back over to the kitchen. Someone's followed me in, and I'm trying to fight the nerves that are suddenly overcoming me. Plate in hand, I turn around and stop short. He's right there. Literally, invading my personal space and catching me by surprise.

"Lucy," he greets. "I knew we'd be getting together soon for breakfast or something, but if you'd just wanted to skip straight to meeting my family you could've just told me."

"You're funny." I roll my eyes. "Your sister invited me. It would be rude to say no."

"If I knew you'd be here, I'd have tried to get away sooner to be here," he admits. Playful demeanor is pushed aside, and I can sense he's now hesitant.

"Kyle said that actually," I tease.

"Oh god, what else did he say?" Vincent groans.

55

"Not much more than that," I tell him. "I'm good at changing the subject." He laughs.

"I do wish I'd come sooner," he admits. His hand hesitantly reaches up to help secure a rogue strand of hair behind my ear. I feel electricity surging around us. A force is pulling us together, and it's harder to fight it. I could see him looking back and forth between my eyes and my lips. I can't help it; I lick my bottom lip, and he's drawn to the movement. I can see him lean in…there's already little space separating us.

"Hey guys, what's taking so long?" Dawn suddenly barges in, and the trance is broken. Vincent groans, frustrated by the interruption. Her eyes widen at what she just possibly interrupted. "I'm so sorry!" she's apologizing profusely. "Carry on!" She squeals and bolts out of the kitchen.

"Saved by the Dawn," I laugh nervously.

"Were we, though?" He looks at me.

"I don't even know, to be honest," I admit. "But it is getting late. I should start to head out."

"If you're heading out, I'm driving you," he tells me. "You'll argue. I'll argue. You'll get in the car."

"Why are you so sure that I'll get in?" I challenge him.

"Because no one would enjoy the walk that waits for them this late at night in an area that's new…unless you come up this way all the time?" He quirks an eyebrow.

"I really don't like driving in cars," I whisper. He steps even closer, taking my hands in his. He's gentle, and his touch brings me a comfort I'm not accustomed to.

"I get it," he assures me. "I may not understand why, but I get it makes you uncomfortable. I'll go slow, okay? Please humor me and let me do this?"

I stared at him, unsure. But he's right. It's not a close walk. I'm not familiar with the area, and that's probably worse than getting into his car when he safely knows his way around.

"Alright, let's go," I say. It doesn't go unnoticed that he still has not let go of my hands. I could let go, but I don't want to. I let him lead me back to the dining room to say goodbye to the others.

CHAPTER 6

LUCY

Samantha insisted I take dessert home with me, given I had decided to call it a night. There was resistance and insistence that the dessert could stay put where it was. But she won in the end.

The ride back was awkward initially. We're riding in silence. I'm mainly staring out my window, avoiding looking ahead just as before. There's a silence and a tangible tension in the air between us. I'm admittedly nervous around him and this revelation alone unnerves me. It makes it difficult for me to stand firm on my "no dating" stance.

"Did you have a good time tonight?" Vincent finally asks.

"I did." I smile.

"Hopefully they didn't give you too hard of a time." He laughs. I laugh as well, thinking back on the awkwardness of it all.

"It wasn't too bad," I admit.

"Not too bad?" Vincent repeats. There's a nervous undertone to his voice. He's unsure. I can't blame him.

"Your family cares a great deal for you," I tell him, turning to look at him.

"They're just protective," he tells me. "But they can be extreme."

"I think they just want to see you as happy as they are," I say. "You're lucky to have them, Vincent."

He glances in my direction, giving me a smile.

"I didn't realize it was just you in town…" he says sadly. "That your mom left when you were younger."

"I don't remember her all that much," I admit. "Here and there post cards used to pop up, but I think they were intended for Gran. It's been 10 years since I got anything, though. Gran raised me."

"Where's your Gran?" he asks.

"She passed away 10 years ago," I tell him. It's the second time tonight I'm discussing Gran.

"Oh, I'm sorry!" He reaches to take my hand in his, giving me a gentle squeeze. It's not lost on me that he hasn't let go. And I feel he won't unless I do. But I don't want to.

"It was a long time ago," I say.

"I feel no matter how much time passes, it doesn't get easier," he tells me, eyes back on the road.

"You're right, it doesn't," I agree. I didn't realize we've come to a stop outside the walk path to my cottage. The truck is turned off. Neither of us make a move to get out. He still has a hold of my hand.

"What happened to her?" he asks.

"Car accident," I tell him. "Though official reports confirm she had a heart attack before the accident."

"I'm so sorry, Lucy," he tells me. "Was she driving?"

"No," I tell him. Taking a breath, I look at him. His eyes are full of sorrow. "I was behind the wheel. We'd gone out driving, exploring different places for me to take photos of. It was a thing we did. She'd suddenly called out in pain or shock, I don't know…and lost consciousness. I'd seen something on the road. It all happened so fast. The car swerved—almost like something was pulling the steering wheel forcefully off the road, and the truck went through the guardrail and into the river." I look at him when I hear his gasp.

"But you made it out," he says.

"Somehow, I made it out," I tell him.

"You don't know how?" he asks, surprised.

"I really don't," I tell him.

"Maybe someone got to you? Before you were fully submerged?" he muses.

"I was fully submerged." I look away. "I remember being stuck. I remember the water completely entering the truck before it all went dark. Then I was laying partially in the river, partially on the grass, no one was there."

"You remember it?" he asks.

"Vividly," I say.

"This is why you won't drive?" he asks me.

"Partially," I admit.

"And the other reason?" he asks. I take a breath and look at him.

"Truthfully I don't trust myself behind the wheel," I tell him. "I thought I saw something on the road. A figure that I couldn't quite make out. But they claim no one was there." There's silence. Neither of us say anything. Possibly unsure what to say with how serious of a turn our conversation went.

You are the dancing queen
Young and sweet
Only seventeen

We both jump, taken back by the fact that not only is music suddenly blaring through the truck, but that there's anything at all considering Vincent turned the engine off as soon as we pulled up. I'm too focused on the fact that, of all things to be blaring, it's ABBA. And the exact song which was playing the day of the accident. It takes me just a moment to recover. I'm used to things like this. I'm used to spirits occasionally manipulating the energy around them—if strong enough—to make it known they're around. I'm glaring at the radio because it annoys me. She avoids contact with me directly but followed Vincent around and now this?

"What the hell?" Vincent asks, trying to push at the buttons to turn it off. It seems to be lost on him that the truck is turned off. I'm carefully looking around, looking for any visuals of Gran to make her stop. I look straight ahead, out the windshield to see her standing, facing us right outside. And I want my gear. Why now? Why manipulate the radio now, with Vincent of all skeptical people? To get me to tell him? To send me a message?

I'm suddenly out of the truck, undoubtably confusing Vincent.

"Lucy, hey." He rushes out. "Wait." I can hear the song blaring from his truck.

"I need to get home," I tell him, not turning around. I want my camera.

"Wait." He catches up and lightly catches my arm. I'm looking at him, waiting. "Look, I know that was weird, but we don't have to end the night." He looks sheepish.

"You mean your truck doesn't usually start playing random music when it's turned off?" I make a joke. He laughs nervously.

"I wanted to grab my camera," I admit.

"And do what?" He laughs.

"What most people do with cameras..." I state, as if it's the most obvious thing in the world.

"Far be it from me to disrupt creative processes," he jokes. "But do you need to do this now? Look, Mom sent dessert, do you want to have some before we call it a night?"

"Raincheck?" I ask.

"How about tomorrow night I come by, and we hang out?" he offers. He's figured out raincheck is indefinite.

"You seem intent on getting into my house, Henry." I cross my arms.

"We can go anywhere, Lucy," he tells me. "I just want to spend time with you. Get to know you."

"As friends," I clarify.

"It is a good starting point." He smirks.

"Okay, fine," I agree. And at that moment, the music stops. We both glance over at the truck.

"So weird," he says, shaking his head.

"Right." I shrug. "Weird."

I'd gone back out after Vincent had left that night to try to snap some pictures in hopes Gran would come through. I wasn't successful. But it did successfully frustrate me all over again.

I didn't cancel on Vincent the next night. He came by with a variety of movies to choose from and a damn picnic basket. A picnic basket. He pulled out all the stops on his determination of being my friend. But I wasn't stupid or naïve; I know he doesn't want just that. In fact, he'd made sure to ensure we spent any free time he and I had together in some way. It'd gone on this way for almost two months.

And while I wouldn't admit it to him, he was growing on me. I missed him when he wasn't around. He was sweet, thoughtful, and compassionate. It was hard to see how someone as amazing as him could be so cynical. We never spoke of the radio incident.

A couple weeks ago, he shared his story with me. About Charlie. And I finally, finally understood his aversion to my walking alone. More specifically at night.

~~~~~ TWO WEEKS AGO~~~~~~~~

"You're really bothered by my walking home at night, aren't you," I muse, as he'd insisted on driving me home from the studio late tonight. I didn't even know he was back from Savannah. There were more days in the week he was away on a project. But he always made it a point to message me or call me to check in. Something I'd tried casually reminding him that he didn't have to do. To me, we were friends. Becoming best friends at this point. To him, we were dating.

There's a long pause before he speaks. I worry initially I've offended him. But he's remained in silence, I learn, to muster the courage to share something very personal with me.

"I was married…"he says, softly.

"You were?" I emphasize the word "were."

"I was," he repeats. I don't push him to elaborate. It's his story. His pace in which he sets to share it with me. "She died three years go." I stay silent. Of course, I know this. But he doesn't know I know this.

"I'm so sorry, Vincent," I tell him, reaching out to hold his hand. "You don't have to tell me what happened…"

"No, I want to," he assures me. "On one hand I think it'll explain why I get anxious to know you're walking around town…but on the other, I really care about you, Lucy. I can't explain what's pulled me to you…I never thought I'd feel this way again. Not since my wife."

I don't know how to react to his admission to the extent of his feelings. I feel so much for him as well, but I don't know if I can go down that path. If he knew the truth of my abilities…he would not believe me. Believe in me.

"Charlie was an avid runner," he tells me. "Always training for the next marathon. And sometimes when she was so focused on making sure she could beat her

61

previous time, she'd be out late running. The night she died, she was out running. Someone lost control of their car. It was so surreal and happened so quickly. They think the driver blacked out; they didn't understand what had happened to lose control of the car in that way. She didn't make it."

"Oh Vincent." I sigh. Charlie's outfit made more sense now.

"I don't want you to pity me," he says abruptly.

"I don't..." I assure him.

"I just want you to understand." He looks at me, eyes pleading. "I know to you we're in this 'friends' situation no matter how many times we debate the reality—that we're dating—but when I think of you out there walking, alone and at night...my mind goes there, Lucy. I don't want anything to happen to you."

And he was right in what telling me would imply. I understood more where he was coming from, as someone who was clear in their intentions with me, when he insisted on driving me. It was his way of knowing with certainty that I was safe. And that knowledge did weird things to my heart. For the longest time, it was just me. My wellbeing, what I was up to...I never had to remember to make sure someone other than myself were aware of what I was or wasn't up to. I wasn't used to this.

Today I have a session with an old friend in town. She'd lost a boyfriend three months ago, and I could tell she was curious if he had a message for her.

I'd locked the door to the studio when she arrived. I did this sometimes just in case a spirit came through. I wanted to make sure everyone had their right to privacy with their loved ones, especially when the true purpose behind the session was evident.

"Okay, Emma," I start. "You ready?"

"As I'll ever be," she says.

"You just want to know if someone will come through?" I confirmed. "Not looking for something specific."

"I just need to know," she tells me. "Is that okay?"

"Of course," I assure her.

"I just have had the feeling someone's been with me," she admits.

"If someone has been, let's see if they'll come through." I smile.

I start taking some shots at different angles. I know Emma doesn't care for the overall finished product, but I want to produce something special for her, in case someone comes through. You usually see something lingering behind, and the memory is there.

After 10 minutes of taking pictures, I start looking through all the photos until finally, there he is. He's young with black hair gelled back. As quickly as I see him in the photo, he's gone and standing next to Emma, arms crossed. He doesn't seem friendly at all. So, it'll be *that* kind of visit.

"Any chance you know someone who gels their black hair back?" Emma looks surprised.

"It's Johnny," he says. Annoyance comes off him in waves. I can feel his energy.

"Okay. Johnny, then," I correct.

"He's here?" she asks.

"He is," I tell her. "Standing beside you."

"Is he the one who's been following me around?" Emma asks. I look at him expectantly.

"And so what if I am," he challenged.

"Well, you're a peach," I tell him, voice full of sarcasm. "You intentionally made yourself known. Clearly you have a reason."

"Yeah. Emma's out on dates," he said, full of anger.

"And?" I press.

"What's he saying?" Emma asks. "Is he mad?"

"He says you've been out on dates?" I ask, and she recoils slightly.

"Just a few," she admits.

"A few too many," he says. "How can she do this to me? Doesn't she understand how much that hurts me?" Some lights in the studio start to flicker. Emma's looking around, nervous.

"Right, I see," I say. "Johnny…do you know that you're dead?"

"Yeah, I figured that one out," he says. "What's your point?"

"Emma's going to have to move on with her life eventually," I tell him. "I know you don't like it. No one does. I'm sure it's making you feel like she's forgetting you by moving on."

"Damn right it does," he says. He looks at her. "You said you loved me."

"Emma, I think Johnny's feeling you're moving on and forgetting about him," I tell her.

"Oh goodness, no," she says. "It's the opposite." She starts to cry.

"What do you mean?" he asks her, the edge and anger simmering down. Lights return to normal.

"He wants to know what you mean," I told her.

"With him gone, I feel like I've been losing my mind. Before I started feeling like he was with me," she starts. "I miss him so much. Some days I can't get out of bed. It feels like I'm drowning. I thought, maybe if I met some new people that would help distract me from this feeling."

"Has this feeling gotten worse at all since you felt Johnny was with you?" I ask.

"Yeah," she admits. "I don't understand where some of what I'm feeling comes from. It's like this overload of anger, an overload of sadness. I've been seeing a therapist to help me with the grief."

"I had no idea," Johnny whispers. He tries to reach out for her, but he can't touch her, can't offer her comfort.

"Sometimes," I start, hoping Johnny really hears me. "Spirits who pass suddenly can become very angry. And when they stay behind and linger, their energy grows so strong that it can influence others around them." He looks at me, surprised.

"Are you saying she's been feeling like she's drowning because of me?" he asks. "Because she could feel me? I was making it worse?"

"Not intentionally, but it can happen." I look at him sadly.

"At first I just wanted to check in on her," he explains. "Just make sure she was okay…"

"I know," I assure him.

"But then I saw she was going out on dates, and I got so mad." He looks down, ashamed.

"Emma, he didn't realize that by being around, his energy was affecting you to the extent that it was," I explain to her. "He just wanted to know that you were okay and misunderstood when he saw you going out on dates."

"Oh, Johnny, never ever will I forget you," she says. "You were my everything and no one will ever change what you mean to me. No matter how much time passes."

"But what do I do now?" he says, unsure.

"When spirits don't move on into the light, they have unfinished business," I explain. "But something tells me you heard what you needed to help you cross over."

"Cross over to what?" he asks.

"I'm not sure," I tell him. "Do you see a light anywhere?" He looks around until a look of astonishment and peace crosses his face.

"You'll watch over Emma? Yeah?" he asks. "Make sure she's okay? I do want her happy…"

"She's got the entire town and myself watching out for her, Johnny." I smile at him.

"I love you, Johnny, so so much," she says.

"I love you, too." He looks at her. After a moment, he starts walking toward whatever he and he alone is seeing until eventually he is gone. I sigh in relief, both relief the toxicity is gone from the environment but also in relief that this visit resulted in a spirit crossing over.

"He's gone," I assure her.

"Gone gone?" she asks.

"He's crossed over," I tell her. "He won't be lingering around. And while I know that won't help the pain or the grief you feel for your loss, I hope this will help you move toward healing. His energy wasn't helping you be able to move forward," I told her. "And maybe, don't stop seeing your therapist?" I suggest. "If you're feeling depressed, there is help for you, you know that, right?"

"I do, Lucy." She smiles. "Thank you so much. I don't have the words."

"It's why I'm here." I laugh. I lead her over to the door and unlock it. As I open it, I see Vincent lingering outside.

"Thank you again, Lucy," she gushes. "They say you're incredible but to witness it firsthand? Wow."

"I'll see you, Emma," I tell her. She nods and takes off. Vincent walks over, smiling at me and leans down to kiss my cheek. I've yet to allow him to do more than that. I'm insane, I know.

"Do you usually lock your door during sessions?" he asks.

"Every time," I answer. "I like to respect their privacy." He nods in understanding and follows me in.

"Did you want to grab dinner tonight? Dawn has been pestering me for a possible double date," he asks me.

"There's that word again," I say, rolling my eyes.

"What other way would you describe what we're doing?" He laughs. "Never mind, I know how you would."

"You're not happy with me," I gather.

"It's not that, Lucy," he assures. "I guess I just don't understand what it is that holds you back. It's been an amazing couple of months. What's so different if there were real labels and exclusivity attached to it?"

I sigh. I don't have an answer for him. I'm thinking, looking around, but stop short when I see Charlie in the doorway, quirking her eyebrow at me.

"I don't have a good dating history, Vincent," I tell him. "I couldn't rely on those I've dated in the past."

"I don't think you need me to tell you that I'm not them, Lucy." He comes over and gives me a hug. "You set the pace for this, always. Hell, I'm easing into this as well for my own reasons, you know that. But I don't want to hide how I feel or what my intentions are." I tighten my hold on him, trying to show him that I'm hearing his words. "Hey, how about a photoshoot?" he suggests suddenly. I back out of the hug, surprised he'd want the photoshoot, and glance at Charlie who seems to like the suggestion.

Well, shit. I feel like she wants to come through. And I can't say no simply for her benefit.

"Alright, hot shot," I say. "Take a seat." I change the backdrop, trying to put up with this false pretense of this genuinely being a photo session.

"You know, one of these days we should set something up for new head shots for me and the guys. New marketing for the construction business couldn't hurt," he says.

"Whatever you want," I tell him. "Just let me know when, and we'll make a plan." I start taking some shots. I let some time pass before I indicate we're good.

"Let's see…" he comes over, leaning over me. He's so close. I don't want to look. I want to get rid of him and then look. But he wants to, and I can't say no. I don't have a legit reason why to wait. And so, we do. All it takes is one photo and she's there. But I'd only showed him one…so I must keep cycling through.

"Just what are you doing, Lucy," she says, amused. I'm trying to ignore her.

"Aww, don't ignore me," she pouts. I give her a side glare.

"You okay, Lucy?" I stiffen.

"I'm great," I assure him and keep cycling through.

"You're not," Charlie says, amused. "You're stubborn as all hell. What are you doing?"

"Here, keep pressing this button here." I show him. And walk over to "reorganize" or make it appear as though I'm cleaning and reorganizing. He takes over, not questioning me. He's oblivious to the sudden shift my in demeanor and for that, I'm grateful.

"What do you mean?" I whisper.

"I mean, why are you being so dense when it comes to Vincent?" Charlie says, throwing her hands up in the air.

"Lucy, these are incredible." I turn to look at him. He's smiling at me.

"So incredible, Lucy." Charlie is up close next to me, whispering and mocking in my ear.

"Hey, Vincent," I say. "Would you mind grabbing me a coffee from Betty's?"

"Sure thing," he tells me, carefully placing the camera down. "Anything specific?"

"She knows my usual." I smile, and he nods. I wait until he's out and the door is closed to turn around and glare at Charlie.

"What am *I* doing?" I ask. "What are *you* doing?"

"I'm just having a little fun," she admits.

"Charlie, you said you don't want Vincent knowing you're still earthbound," I tell her, looking at her like she has two heads. "This? Appearing and trying to have me have a conversation with you literally goes against that."

"He doesn't have to know it's me?" she shyly suggests.

"He doesn't know I can see and communicate with spirits," I tell her.

"I know, and I don't get it," she says. "He cares so much for you, Lucy. It's so wonderful to see him opening himself up again, and you're being so stubborn. What is the issue? Have you always been this stubborn?"

"Why? Do I need to remind you how he feels about this subject?" I ask her.

"Okay, point, Lucy," she admits.

"You actually *want* me to be with him?' I asked, surprised.

"I told you that night of the opening." She smiles. "There's just something different about you. And it has nothing to do with this ability of yours. You're good for him."

"Charlie, if he finds out what I can do and that you've been around and I didn't tell him, how do you think that'll go over?" She looks down, unsure. "The longer this goes on, the worse it'll be."

"But if you tell him now, he still might not manage it well," she speaks.

"No, he'll think I've taken advantage of his pain and am exploiting him. I'd rather lose him now than later. I know how this goes," I tell her.

"How what goes?" My back is to the door, so I did not see or hear him come back. I quickly grab my AirPod and stick it in my ear hoping he does not notice it's an after-the-fact-type insertion. I turn around to look at him, giving a slight glance at Charlie who smirks at me then vanishes. So she likes to joke around. I make a mental note.

"Got to go," I say to no one and take the AirPod out of my ear. "Just a movie."

"Got your coffee." He smiles, handing it to me. I step closer to take it, giving him a kiss on the cheek in appreciation. I took him by surprise.

"Betty asked if it was one of those days." He laughed. "I wasn't sure what she meant but said maybe."

"It's one of those days," I confirm.

"Want to talk about it?" he offers. I shake my head no. "How about that date?"

"Why not?" I give in. We were going on a double "date" tonight. And Charlie, I'm sure, was somewhere laughing at my inability to be decisive on all things Vincent.

CHAPTER 7

LUCY

I'd started regretting agreeing to the double date as soon as Vincent casually mentioned the location of our dinner was going to be a surprise. Admittedly, it worries me because I had no way of preparing myself for the type of environment I would find myself in. He told me to dress formally—I assumed cocktail dress would equate to his definition of formal. And if I was wrong, then I would be overdressed at whatever venue he secretly was taking me to. It was a difficult situation.

Vincent arrives at the exact time he'd promised.

"You look beautiful," he says, leaning in to give me a kiss on the cheek. Safe territory.

"Not overdressed?" I ask.

"Not overdressed," he confirms. "You're perfect."

"And you still won't tell me where we're going?" I try again.

"Nope." He smirks and takes my hand to lead the way to the short walk to his truck. I'm nervous. Both for the overall dinner but also for the unknown. Charlie is nowhere in sight. Gran has yet to make a reappearance.

"I don't think I've ever been on a date where I had no clue where it would actually be," I tell him.

"So you're admitting it's a date." He laughs. I roll my eyes.

"Don't dwell on it, Henry," I tell him.

He opens the passenger door for me when we finally reach the truck. I fasten my seatbelt and take a quick look around and out the windshield before taking a breath and putting my focus on either him or looking out my own window.

"Short ride?" I ask, hopeful.

"It's just outside of town, Lucy," he tells me. "I think you'll like it."

"Hmph," I grunt. I know I will not mind the company—the living company. The ride is calm. We enjoy the silence and I enjoy the scenery.

"You know," Vincent says, finally. "I think I've just realized you won't look straight ahead."

I look at him in surprise.

"Just now?" I ask.

"Yeah," he admits. "Is it connected to your past accident?"

"I told you," I start. "I don't trust what I see when looking out a car window."

"Because you saw something or someone on the road that night," he remembers.

"Right," I tell him. "Can you imagine if that happened again, even as a passenger and I caused another accident by freaking out?"

"But Lucy," he says with caution. "They told you there was no one on the road that night."

"That they could see," I mumble. He glances at me for a moment.

"You don't think you saw…a…spirit or whatever, do you?" he asks. I stare at him, unsure how to best answer. The truth is I have no idea. But what if I had? What if a spirit of a woman suddenly appeared in the middle of the road and me—who had no idea of my gift at the time—mistook that ghost for a real person?

"Or whatever?" I ask.

"You know what I mean," he answers. We are stopped at a red light. He uses the brief stop to look over at me.

"I don't know what I think about that night, Vincent," I tell him truthfully. "Could it have been? Maybe. Could I have imagined it? They like to think so. I don't know to say one way or the other what it truly could have been."

"Lucy, you have to know that stuff isn't real," he tells me softly. The sound of a horn behind us startles him, bringing his attention to the now green light. He starts on our path again. I do not respond. "Right?"

"I don't want to talk about this right now, Vincent," I tell him, looking away. I do not want him to see I'm hurt.

"I'm sorry," he says. But I keep looking out the window. Silence would be favorable. I can hear him sigh. A few moments later, he's parking the truck, and I turn to see the sign to an Italian restaurant beautifully hanging at the entrance of the restaurant. A very, very crowded restaurant. I know by reputation. "I hope you like Italian food." He smiles. I try to smile, to convey the appreciation at the thought of bringing me here.

"I love Italian," I tell him.

"It was Dawn's idea," he admits. "I thought we could do something together at home, in town. I know you prefer that. But she seemed to insist."

"Interesting and thoughtful of her," I simply say. "Shall we?"

Vincent comes around to the passenger door to help me out. I say a quick thank you and let him lead me to the entrance where Miles and Dawn were already waiting.

"We're so glad you two could join us!" Dawn exclaims.

"Dawn, Miles," I greet. "Good to see you." I am looking at the restaurant behind them trying to calm my nerves.

"Shall we?" Miles offers. And I'm being shaken out of my reverie and led inside. Dawn has already given our information to the hostess, and the moment we're led to the area of our reserved table, I want to turn around and run out. The entire restaurant is overflowing with both the living and the dead. They're everywhere. So much chatter. So many spirits filling the space it makes my head spin, and I wobble a bit, only to be caught by Vincent.

"Are you okay?" he asks, worriedly. I nod my head, trying to focus on taking slow calming breaths. We're at our table, sitting with a full-on view of all the others in the restaurant. There is no escaping it. It's in moments like this I wonder how Gran did it. Unlike me, she didn't need a camera to help thin the veil to communicate. I, however, do. And the new spirits I'm seeing realize soon that I can in fact see them. Which made the situation I had found myself in much worse. They want to be heard. And in realizing I could see them, they assume I could be that gateway for them, and they bombard me. I'm suddenly surrounded. But they grow frustrated when they realize I can't hear them. There are so many of them.

"You can see us, can't you?"

"You can hear us?"

"Oh, please say you can hear us, I need to get a message to my son. Can you talk to him, he's just across the way."

"I need my wife to know I'm still here, please."

But all I hear as they circle me at our table is warped speech. I don't hear them clearly. I don't know what they're saying. But their frustration grows, and I'm overwhelmed. It feels like my head is spinning.

"Hello and welcome. I'm Hailey, and I'll be your waitress this evening," our waitress says. "Can I start anyone off with drinks?"

Dawn, Miles, and Vincent order, and now everyone's looking at me expectantly. But I'm so confused.

"I'm sorry, what was that?" I ask.

"Anything to drink?" Hailey asks, looking at me as though I'd lost my mind. She's glancing between me and Vincent with slight disdain.

"Water, please," I say. I want her to leave. She writes it down and lets us know she'll be back shortly with our drinks. Everyone's looking over the dinner menu but me. I don't even know if I could stomach anything with how nauseated I'm starting to feel. I feel a kick under the table. Not hard enough to hurt but enough to capture my attention. I look at Dawn, the culprit of it all. The kick. The reason we're here to begin with.

You okay? she mouths to me, concerned. Miles and Vincent are focused on the menus, debating their options versus recommended specials. I shake my head no and it's like a lightbulb has gone off. I can see the moment she realizes what is wrong and the error in choosing this venue.

I really don't know if I'll last through the dinner, but I'm determined. I'm purposely choosing to focus on one person at a time.

I pick something random from the menu as Hailey comes back to serve the drinks and take our orders. And after several moments, I excuse myself to escape to the restroom.

I rush to the sink to splash water on my face. It's quiet here. And I wonder, for a split moment, how long I could get away with staying here. I hear the door open and a worried Dawn comes rushing in.

"Oh god, Lucy," Dawn cries. "I didn't even think when I picked this place."

"It's not exactly something you should have to worry about, Dawn," I assure her. "It's my problem, no one else's."

"But you said you avoided crowds," she disagrees. "I should've respected that. I didn't imagine how bad it could be for you."

"Just depends on the type of place," I tell her, focusing on slow and steady breaths. "It's so crowded tonight."

"Should we go?" Dawn offers.

"No, no," I tell her. "I can do it. I may not be the best conversationalist."

"Are you sure?" Dawn doesn't look convinced. "Because really, we can leave."

"I'm sure," I tell her. I grab a power towel and dry off my face. "Ready to head back out?"

"Are *you*?" she asks. I nod and take a deep breath to brace myself.

Some spirits continue to try to bridge the communication gap, albeit unsuccessfully. Eventually, they disperse and stop overcrowding me. But they're still present and energized.

"So, any plans for Thanksgiving, Lucy?" Dawn asks.

"I usually stay in," I tell her. I'm staring at the food on my plate to keep a focal point.

"Oh, say you'll join us this year?" Dawn pleads. Thanksgiving is an entire month away.

"Don't feel like you have to, Lucy," Vincent assures me, reaching out to take my hand in his. He gives me a gentle squeeze. I look in his eyes and see he looks worried. This version of Lucy in front of him is a complete 180 compared to what he's used to. I feel bad.

"Why wouldn't you want your girlfriend over for Thanksgiving?" Dawn asked.

"Lucy isn't my girlfriend," Vincent says, though there's a tone to his statement that isn't lost on me.

"Wait, what?" Dawn asks. "You've been going out practically for months. I figured that distinction was applied."

73

"He just got me to agree to the fact we're dating," I chime in, deciding to throw Vincent a bone here. He laughs. "What's meant to be will be."

"She'll come around eventually." Vincent smirks.

"Lucy, is that you?" I look to the side to see Clara, owner of the florist shop in town.

"Hi, Clara," I greet her.

"How are you, dear?" she asks.

"I'm well and you?" I'm polite but admittedly still anxious. She's here with family...and a spirit as well.

"Oh good, good," she says. She's awkwardly looking around the table and finally introduces herself. Though Dawn already knows Clara.

"You don't have your camera with you," Clara says suddenly. And I'm frustrated. I know why she's asking.

"I'm out to dinner tonight, Clara," I tell her pointedly. I don't want to go into detail about this. Not with Vincent here. "I don't make it a habit of bringing my equipment."

"Of course." She nods in understanding, but I can see she wants to press the matter further.

"If you call the studio, we can set up a time for you to come in." I stare at her, daring her to push it further.

"Come Clara," the gentleman with her urges her. He gets the hint. She does not. "Let's leave everyone to their meal."

"Right." She sighs. "I'll talk to you soon, Lucy." She's urged along and doesn't wait for my reply. I truly don't have one.

"Well, that was odd." Miles laughs. "You really are in high demand, Lucy."

"What can I say?" I laugh nervously.

"Do townsfolk truly think you'll bring your equipment with you when you're off the clock?" Vincent asks, surprised by the incident.

"More often than you'd think," I tell him.

I manage to get through dinner without full on passing out. The guys offered to bring the cars to us so Dawn and I were waiting once more outside—thankfully—by the entrance.

"Did she really think you'd carry around your equipment anywhere you go?" Dawn asked in disbelief.

"She did," I tell her, taking in a deep breath.

"What would she have done if you had your equipment?" Dawn asked.

"She'd expect me to snap a photo and see if someone came through," I answer.

"A little presumptuous," Dawn says, put out.

"People of the town expect it, to some degree," I tell her. "What I've learned is this was the norm with previous generations. We've always been there to help those who need us. To help them find peace. So how could I not?"

"Lucy, boundaries are also important," she tells me. "It drains you sometimes…communicating with them, being surrounded by them. You must remember your well-being is important. You're still in the land of the living, you know?"

"I know." I smile at her. The guys have pulled up, and we say our goodbyes.

Once more, we're on the route and I finally feel like I can breathe. Such a heavy weight has been lifted the more distance is put between me and that restaurant.

"You doing okay, Lucy?" Vincent asks. "You seemed really out of it throughout dinner."

"I know, I'm sorry," I apologize. "I really don't do well in crowds."

"You weren't kidding." He laughs. "But you're okay now?"

"Much." I smile. And we sit in comfortable silence until we make it back to the pathway to my cottage. I don't have to ask if he plans on walking with me. At this point, it's a given. We walk hand in hand together on the lit pathway to my door. "I'd invite you in, but I do feel I should rest after tonight's exciting events."

"You'll be okay on your own?" he double checks. I appreciate his concern more than I can express. I'm overwhelmed, even, until finally I throw caution to the wind and suddenly pull Vincent down to me and kiss him.

He's surprised at first but then responds immediately. I feel like my entire body is alight with an electric current. I feel Vincent's tongue cautiously seeking entrance, and I grant it to him without hesitation. A fire erupts and we're closer together than I thought possible. I can feel his hand snaking around my waist, pulling me closer while his other moved up to my hair. My arms are snaked around his neck. We move together with perfect synchrony. I wonder how in the world I avoided kissing him this entire time.

Eventually, I pulled away.

"Well, shit," I say, gasping for breath.

"Not very lady like, Adams," he teases me. "Not that I'm complaining but what brought that on?"

"I just want to show you how much you mean to me," I tell him. "And how much it means to me how you've been there for me, being patient with me."

"Always, Lucy." He leans in to kiss me softly on the lips. "You should get inside, get some rest."

"Good idea," I say quietly. Though I don't want to leave. I want to keep kissing him. And I realize more in that moment that I very well could fall in love with this man. And as this realization hits me, I know we can never get to that point until he knows everything about me. And accepts me.

Reluctantly, I pull away and open the door to step inside.

"Goodnight, Lucy," he says and starts to walk back the lit pathway to his truck. I'm watching him as he walks, occasionally looking back at me and smiling. It's then I see her, for just a moment.

Gran's turning to walk with him. But not before glancing at me and nodding. The first acknowledgement she's truly given me since I first saw her again.

I step inside and lock the door behind me, leaning against it, closing my eyes. *I'm so screwed,* I think to myself. I open my eyes to see Charlie before me, nodding to my camera equipment. I don't need more than that to get the hint.

I snapped a photo of the space before me, look at the photo and she's beside me.

"It's about time, Lucy." She smiles.

"That's what you wanted to say? It's about time?" I ask her.

"No," she admits. "It's been so long since I've seen him happy. It's a wonderful sight to see."

"Do you want him to know you're around?" I ask her. I knew originally she had said no. But the thought there was the slightest chance she had changed her mind and have me step in made me anxious. I didn't want him to know. Not yet. She shakes her head no.

"If I ever tell him what I can do and he asks me about you, you know I won't lie to him, right?" I ask.

"I don't expect you to lie to him," she confirms. "But I won't be the reason you finally stop hiding all of yourself from that man. You should tell him. But on your terms. When you think it's right."

"I guess I'm confused, Charlie," I tell her. "Usually, spirits are earthbound when they have unfinished business. Vincent, to some extent is yours, isn't he?"

"I'm not sure," she tells me. "But I certainly don't see myself stepping into any lights any time soon. I feel like I need to make sure all are okay. Safe. Happy."

"All?" I ask, not sure who she means. All the Henry's? She smirks at me just before she disappears again. *Well, thank you, Charlie for adding more confusion into the pot,* I think to myself.

CHAPTER 8

LUCY

I'm standing in the middle of a winding road. It's chilly. How I ended up in the middle of the road is beyond me. There is no one in sight. No cars. Just the ever-growing fog which usually arises after a heavy rainstorm. I couldn't tell at first where I am. All the roads and no landmarks make for a confusing sight. How I got here, I had no clue.

I start walking, instinct pulling me in the northbound direction. It is after a few minutes I see what is ahead, and I stop in my tracks. It's the bridge. THE bridge. I can see the broken-down guardrail. It's still old and rusted, like it had been the night of the accident. Not new like it was now. What is happening?

Like a twist of fate, I can suddenly hear ABBA's "Dancing Queen" blaring in the distance. And I realize, I'm back at that night. Only this time, not as the driver. I'm a bystander in my own dreamscape, and I desperately want out, I want to wake up but nothing I do makes it happen. I pinch myself. I pull my hair. Nothing. I'm still here.

The truck blows past me, headed in the direction of the bridge.

"Gran?!" I hear my frantic scream as the truck nears. I want to look away, but I don't. And I want to move away from my spot in the middle of the road, but I can't. Something's keeping me here. I'm struggling against some invisible force that won't release me from my immobile position.

I'm in front of the truck, and I see myself behind the wheel frantically trying to gain control of the truck which has suddenly launched itself in the direction of the guardrail. I watch as my efforts to regain control fail, the truck crashes, loudly, through the guardrail, flying into the river. "NO!" I scream. And I'm suddenly running toward the truck. Whatever force held me in place releases me enough to move and act. I can't help it. I'm staring down and watching the truck quickly, quickly be pulled under.

"Someone help!" I'm shouting. But there's no use. "Please! Someone save them! Help!" This feels too real to be a dream, I realize quickly.

"Hurry dear," Gran's voice comes beside me. I look at her, bewildered. She'd never appeared in any of my dreams. They say when spirits appear in your dreams, it means they're visiting you in their own way. But never, never in the 10 years she'd been gone had Gran come to me.

"Gran?" I ask, surprised. I'm staring at her and back down into the river. The truck is no longer visible. There's no one around. "Gran, what do I do?"

"You need to hurry, Lucy," she tells me.

"I don't understand," I cry.

"HURRY!" she urges, and next I feel something push me into the water, submerging and being pulled under, under, under until I'm reaching the door. I'm fighting against the need to breathe and the urgency to act.

I startle awake, gasping. It felt like I was there, in the water. Pushed, that is, into the water and pulled under until I reached the door. I'm trying to catch my breath. Trying so hard. But I can't help but wonder what the hell that dream was truly about.

In all the dreams I'd had of the accident, never was I a third-party visitor witnessing events that had happened. It was always me, embodying my past self and experiencing everything all over again. And yet, something changed. This was different. And it was as if I was truly there that night. As if I were in the middle of the road suddenly appearing. But that made no sense. Who was I embodying this time?

My head was throbbing trying to process my dream. I couldn't think. I couldn't focus. My head was in such a haze. I wished today was a day I could just call it and lock myself away from everyone and everything. But it wasn't possible. I had several errands to run through the day and some sessions lined up so staying in bed wasn't quite the option. I couldn't let anyone down.

I checked my messages, something I was trying to get better about now that I knew, in some way, there were now people out there who cared about my well-being. It took some getting used to, but it felt good.

I'd decided to get an early start and so here I was, waiting for Betty's largest hot coffee and a muffin.

"You look terrible, dear," Betty tells me as she hands me my order.

"Always with compliments, Betty." I smile.

"Have a seat, dear," she offers.

"I don't know, Betty, I have errands to run," I tell her. I'm looking around and am surprised at the business of the bakery this early in the morning. I can't take the chatter when I'm still recouping last night's debacle. It's like the hangover that never ends.

"Errands can wait," she tells me. "Have a seat. Recharge a bit."

I do as I'm told and sit and wait until she finally sits to join me. She has questions, I can tell. Betty's always curious.

"Have you been sleeping, Lucy?" she asks as she takes a seat, my coffee and muffin appearing before me. I lean into the steam of the coffee, taking an appreciative breath.

"No more than the usual amount." I smile sadly at her.

"Still having the nightmares?" She looks at me with concern.

"They've never truly gone away," I share. "This was different, though."

"How so?" she asks.

"Well, for starters, I've never dreamt that I was a third-party visitor with a full access pass to watching the events transpire." I shrug. "And Gran was there."

"She was there?" she asks, intrigued. "There as in, you were watching the accident and she was in the truck like that night, or there as in, she appeared to you?"

"She was in the truck..." I started. "But then, I was too. But she appeared to me."

"You've said in the past she's never done that," Betty recalls, deep in thought. "That she's never visited you and communicated with you."

"That's correct," I tell her. "And yet, there we were, watching the truck submerge together from the bridge, and she was telling me to hurry."

"To hurry?" she asks.

"Yep." I take a sip of coffee. "And I have no clue what she was talking about."

"What happened next?" Betty is curious.

"Something pushed me into the water, pulling me toward the truck," I remember. "And then I woke up."

"Oh my," Betty exclaims. "What do you think it all means?"

"I really wish I had a clue, Betty." I sigh. "It took me a long time to figure out how my gift worked. How to make the connection by taking pictures. But dreams? I don't entirely understand that yet."

"Have you ever thought about trying to find someone who can offer guidance?" she suggests. I chuckle.

"Most mediums I've come across in the past are frauds," I tell her. "And it's a shame."

"What about your mother?" she suddenly says.

"My mother?" I ask, taken back.

"Well, yes," she presses.

"My mother left town when I was a little girl, Betty, you know that," I tell her.

"I know, Lucy." She nodded in understanding. "And I don't condone what she did at all. But sweetie, didn't this gift pass along to her as well?"

I sit back in my seat, thinking seriously about what she is saying. I'd made it a purposeful point to not think about my mother. Gran had always said the best thing my mom had done was leave. That she would've taken me down a dark path with her had she stayed in a town that suffocated her.

I never thought much more into the implications of what Gran had said about the small-town life suffocating her. But now, knowing what I know and doing what I can do, I couldn't help but wonder if what suffocated her was her having the ability to communicate with spirits in some way as well. Or was it the pressures of the expectations the townsfolk placed on our family?

People in town knowing was sometimes a blessing and a curse. A blessing, because I never had to walk around looking like the crazy person if I suddenly snapped a picture of a spirit and suddenly was up and communicating with what looked like air to others. People just knew. They accepted it. But it was a curse *because* they knew and accepted it. They couldn't help wondering if someone had a message for me to pass along to them. Much like Clara the other night.

"You knew my mother, right, Betty?" I ask.

"Well yes, dear," she says. "The entire town did."

"So could she communicate with spirits as well?" In not thinking about my mother, I didn't bother with the realization of her possessing similar gifts. Betty is looking at me thoughtfully.

"She could," she finally says. "And I don't know the first thing about it. But I feel she might've been able to do more than just communicate, like your gran."

"Gran could do more?" I asked, surprised.

"She had a sense about things sometimes," Betty tells me.

"Are you telling me Gran had premonitions?" I ask, partially in disbelief. I knew there was more to what we could do. But without Gran's guidance, I was stuck figuring things out at a snail's pace. I felt there was so much more to my world than I knew or was prepared for and that thought made me angry. Angry that Gran never talked to me about it. Never taught me what to expect. Angry that time had taken her away from me before being able to learn it all.

"I'm not sure, sweetie," she admits. "I really don't know the first thing about it. I certainly don't presume to understand it."

"I wish she talked to me about this before the accident." I'm rubbing my temples, trying to rid myself of this headache which is only growing stronger. I'm looking around, wondering if there's a spirit in the bakery now. I don't see anyone but have the sense I'm being carefully watched.

"I'm sure she thought she had more time, Lucy," Betty offers in comfort. I'm thinking...thinking back to how Gran was before everything happened in that truck. The way she was talking to me. Almost like she knew she wouldn't have many more moments.

"Can I tell you something that's probably crazy?" I ask. She nods.

"I feel like she knew something was coming," I tell her. Tears fill my eyes at the mention and thought of it.

"You think she knew?" Betty asks. "How?"

"How do we do any of what we do?" I chuckle.

We sit in comfortable silence, taking in every possibility and revelation discussed. And I can't help but think of my mom. I never wanted to connect with her. But I couldn't help but wonder if maybe I should go down that path and connect. A one-time thing. For answers. I'm so lost in thought I don't hear the bell sound with the door opening.

"Oh Lucy, you're here," I hear Clara come up. I look at her and see she's carrying a bouquet of red and pink tulips. I'm confused. "I have these for you." She doesn't make to hand them over. But I'm further confused as to why she's here rather than wherever these were intended to be delivered.

"Oh, what lovely tulips," Betty acknowledges.

"Yes, very lovely," Clara agrees.

"Where were they meant to be delivered?" I ask. I'm suspicious. Not of the gesture of the flowers but of the person doing the delivery.

"To your studio." She shrugs.

"Which this is not," I point out.

"Well, you weren't there," she claims.

"No, I understand that," I acknowledge. "But deliveries typically mean you can leave them behind. No one has to sign for these."

"I figured I'd find you and make sure I delivered them to you in person," she presses. She's looking me over. "You don't have your camera. Again." And I didn't. I had what I needed in the studio for the scheduled sessions in the afternoon.

"Why on earth would Lucy carry around her camera everywhere she went?" Betty stands up, hands on her hips. Protective Betty is coming out. She knows just as much as I do where this is leading.

"Why would she not?" Clara presses, placing the flowers on the table.

"Because she's not at our beck and call, Clara," Betty exclaims. "You should be ashamed of yourself. You should know better."

"What is so wrong with wanting to try to make a connection?" Clara asks, looking back and forth between myself and Betty. "There's no one else who can do what she can in town. She's our only connection to our loved ones. It's selfish not to offer her ability at any moment's notice."

"I've never taken away a chance to help offer peace and closure for the people of this town," I tell her, offended. I stand up.

"There's a difference between Lucy offering her help and putting herself into that position and expecting it at the snap of a finger, Clara," Betty says.

"What position? What's the big deal?" Clara asks.

"If you don't see how communicating with spirits negatively affects her, then you are not the woman I've come to know." Betty turns to look at me.

"Well, when then?" Clara asks, frustrated. "When can we finally do this? I have about 20 minutes before I need to be back at the shop to put together a new order."

"Clara." I take a breath. "If spirits come through, it can sometimes take more than that. You can never put a time limit on connecting with your loved one. And with that attitude, I doubt someone would want to come through. When you're truly ready, call. I'll come to you and take some photos of your floral arrangements for your website."

"But—" Clara starts to argue but the look Betty's giving her stops her cold. "Fine." She throws her hands up. "Here's the card that came with the tulips. I'll call you, Lucy." She hands me the card and leaves. Betty and I exchange a look.

"You are under no obligation to take photos for that woman," Betty tells me.

"I know," I say.

"No, hear me Lucy." She takes my hand. "You owe them nothing. If people can't respect you and your boundaries, then they're not deserving of you sharing your gift with them. Do you understand?" I smile at her.

"What would I do without you, Betty?" I smile.

"You're smart." She laughs. "You'll figure it out. Who are the flowers from?" I look at the card. I smile.

Just a little note to let you know I'm thinking of you…
-Vincent

"Who's got *the* Lucy Adams blushing like that?" Betty's reaching for the card. I manage to keep the card out of her hands.

"A little privacy. Jeez." I laugh.

"Oh, please." She laughs. "There is no privacy. That's not in my vocabulary, so show or tell."

"They're from Vincent," I tell her. Her eyes grew wide. "Happy?"

"Vincent Henry sweeping our Lucy off her feet. I'm very happy." She laughs. "When did you two become an item?"

"We're not an item," I deny.

"Right...no, of course not." She nods her head.

"I'm going to go." I laugh.

"But it was just getting good." She laughs but I roll my eyes.

"Bye Betty!" I take the tulips with me as I head over to my studio. I won't let her see, but I can't help smiling from this kind gesture.

When I get to the studio, I get my phone out to send Vincent a message.

-Tulips are lovely. Thank you! –Lucy

-Of course. Are you feeling better after last night? -Vincent

-A bit. The morning is taking a pleasant turn. -Lucy

-Can I see you tonight? -Vincent

-My place at 7? –Lucy

-If I say I'll pick you up, will you let me drive you? -Vincent

-Not a chance Henry. -Lucy

-I'll see you at 7. -Vincent

I now am anxious to get today's events taken care of as quickly as possible to get home and spend time with Vincent. It was mind boggling. Months ago, I was avoiding putting the words "dating" and "Vincent" in the same sentence. But now here I was, with him constantly on my mind, turning to mush at thoughtful gestures like sending flowers. What was wrong with me?

I had several photos to develop for different clients. I spent the morning in the dark room developing the non-digitals. I always lost track of time when I worked on these. Even so, it was my favorite thing to do.

The afternoon sessions were fortunately uneventful. I lock up, bringing my gear with me and head back to my cottage to get ready. There was no concrete plan. But he had left different movies over in case we ever found ourselves just spending time indoors. Once inside, I start worrying over what I should or shouldn't wear. I was on my fifth outfit change when I realized, it's Vincent. I could wear just about anything, and he'd still think I looked good. And I took comfort in knowing that. I settled for something very simple, casual. My leggings and blue button down. I was comfortable.

A knock at the door told me he was here. And I was suddenly very nervous.

I'd been alone with him before. So what did I have to be nervous about? It's just Vincent. Taking a breath, I open the door. He's smiling widely at me, happy to see me. And he's got a box of what looks like graham crackers under his arm, packs of chocolate in one hand, and marshmallows in the other. I laugh.

"Planning on setting fires?" I ask.

"Hello to you, too." He steps inside. "I figured we'd put that fireplace of yours to good use."

"Smores are one of my all-time favorites," I tell him. And he smiles wider, as if that were even possible.

"Good plan?" he asks, hopeful.

"Very good plan." I smile. I'm helping him place everything down on the coffee table. We both move it closer to the fireplace, so everything is in reach. "Do you want something to drink?"

"I'm okay for now." He steps closer to me, wrapping his arms around me. "Have I said hello?" I snake my arms around his neck.

"Not properly," I pout. He laughs but wastes no time leaning in to kiss me. It doesn't take long before we lose ourselves in this kiss. But one of us needs to be sensible. I pull away reluctantly. "Smores?"

"Smores." He nods. He's getting the fireplace lit, and I have the skewers for the marshmallows. Once ready, we've taken our place by the fire.

"Did you have a good day?" I ask him.

"No injuries today," he tells me. "So, yeah, I'd say it was a good day."

"Does it happen often?" I ask, chuckling.

"Anything can happen on a construction site." He shrugs. "But we do what we can. I was thinking about you today."

"Got to be careful not to think too much," I tease.

"Ha ha Adams." He rolls his eyes. He wants to say more, I can tell, but he doesn't.

"Are you okay?" I ask him. He looks at me, uncertain but smiles.

"I'm perfect," he tells me. I can tell there's truth in his words. "Do you want another smore?"

"I'm okay for now." I smile and reach out, taking his hand in mind. There it is again. Every time I touch him, it's as though there's an electric shock moving through my body. I feel the energy charging around us, and a tension is clearly building. I look up at his eyes which are dark with desire.

I lean in, placing a chaste kiss on his lips. But it doesn't satisfy the current that's itching to build. Words don't need to be exchanged. There's an unspoken communication of what we want because a moment later, I'm leaning in once more and his hand is weaving in my hair, bringing me closer. He holds me securely as we're giving in to our desire. His tongue asks for entrance, moving cautiously across my lower lip. I hear him groan as I grant him entrance.

I'm not thinking for once. I need to be closer to him. I straddle his waist, taking his face in both my hands as I kiss him with everything I have. I try to convey everything I feel in this moment. His arms wind tightly around me, and I'm airborne. Vincent's stood us up, holding me securely. I lock my legs around him, and he lays me down gently on the couch.

He's leaving some space between us as he looks into my eyes, searching for any sign that what we're doing is not okay with me. I'm too lost in this energy and need that I start unbuttoning his shirt and pull it down on his shoulders. He throws it somewhere in the room behind him, and his lips are back on mine. I pull him down, not wanting any separation and then I feel him. I grind against him, and he groans. He pushes against me, testing for my reaction and it feels amazing. I want him to keep going. He takes my reaction as encouragement to be more consistent and determined in his movements and the feeling building within me is incredible. I moan as he hits the right spot through his grinding, and I throw my head back in pleasure. He's trailing kisses down my neck, sucking gently. The sensation is wonderful paired with his movements. I open my eyes, wanting to turn to look at him but stop short.

It's like an ice bucket was thrown on me. I yelp in surprise and push Vincent off me suddenly. He falls to the floor, taken by surprise. But then so am I as I see Charlie sitting by the fireplace, watching in amusement. I can't make out what she's saying. If I had to guess it's as though she's bummed I've stopped her show. I glare at her and redirect my focus on Vincent.

"I'm so sorry, are you okay?" I help him up.

"Yeah." He groans as he stands up. He's trying to subtly readjust himself, and I feel terrible. And I want to glare at Charlie all over again but can't with Vincent's attention on me. "I'm sorry."

"*You're* sorry?" I look at him, shocked.

"If I did something that you weren't comfortable with…" He's reaching for his shirt. I want to stop him, but the mood is ruined.

"You didn't." I step closer to him, leaning up to kiss him. I really could get lost kissing him. But I remember we had an audience, and now I can't do it. "I promise you didn't do anything I didn't want to do. I'm so sorry."

"Lucy, you don't have to apologize," he assures me. "There isn't a rush on anything." He kisses me. "Though I think it'll be safer if we call it a night?" He laughs.

"Probably a good idea," I tell him. I walk him to the door. He leans down to kiss me. "Please let me know when you've made it back safely?" He nods his head, smiling. I watch as he makes his way down the pathway, and I finally close the door, locking it securely.

I turn around. Charlie's still there, amused as hell. And I'm angry.

"You know I can't hear you right now, right?" I ask her. She nods. "Well, newsflash. I can see you. And that, that wasn't okay! Ever hear of privacy?" She looks sheepish. Shaking my head, I clean up our mess and start going to bed.

I looked over and she was still there.

"Do I need my camera?" I ask. She shakes her head. "If there's a next time, I would hope you can respect my privacy and not sit there watching. Jesus. All that was missing was popcorn. That shit's weird, Charlie."

I don't wait for her reaction. I slam the bedroom door shut, knowing full well if she wanted, she'd help herself into my room. I can't help that if I'd just tell Vincent about what I could do, then I'd be able to handle that situation right then and there instead of having him leave. But could I do it? Could I really trust him with that information, knowing where he stands on the subject?

I wasn't sure I could.

CHAPTER 9

LUCY

It was nearly impossible to fall asleep last night. Between what almost happened with Vincent and the discovery of Charlie watching us, I was too wound up to sleep. I feel a big violation of my privacy with Charlie sitting there, watching. It was horrifying. All she needed was a bowl of popcorn and she'd be all set.

Spirits made it a point to avoid entering my home if they could control it. So last night? I'm stumped at what part of her thought it was remotely close to being a good idea to watch us. Was she there the entire night and I'd been so focused on Vincent to even notice? Or had she just appeared at the worst possible moment? I mean, really. What the actual hell?! But despite all that, if I was being honest, I'm partially relieved that her "voyeurism" stopped us last night. Because the two of us were so lost in our passion and desires, we weren't thinking clearly. Neither of us were intent on stopping. I sure as hell wasn't going to. So, on one hand, I'm glad something did.

There's no denying Vincent and I are getting closer. I couldn't quite put into words what I was beginning to feel for Vincent. I'd avoided being with someone for the longest time. I'd always questioned if it was real — if they were with me because they genuinely cared for me or if, in some twisted way, they wanted to exploit what I could do. In some ways, people already did that. I'm not blind to it. Clara was a perfect example.

But with Vincent?

For one, he didn't know about my ability. Further, he didn't believe in spirits to begin with.

Secondly, he was so incredibly thoughtful and compassionate that it made me realize just how long it had been to have someone truly care for me. I felt seen with him. Cared for. Cherished even. I was beginning to wake up most mornings with Vincent being the first on my mind. The first one I wanted to see and talk with as I started my day. I wanted to share new things with him as I discovered them. I wanted to share with him the amazing feeling I would have when I'd help someone cross over.

And I couldn't.

Realizing I couldn't snaps me back to reality. I couldn't be with him truly if he didn't know. And if he did know, I couldn't be with him if he didn't believe in me. I just couldn't do it. And I prayed he trusted me enough to have faith in the possibility. I desperately hoped for the outcome I had no confidence in. Because maybe…maybe I may be in love with Vincent Henry.

I'm out of bed, dressed and so not ready for the day. I'm exhausted. Charlie is nowhere in sight as I move through my home.

"Yeah, you better not be here," I grumble under my breath.

I don't bother brewing my own cup of coffee. I fully intend on stopping at Betty's before paying Dawn a visit. And I fully intend to visit Dawn.

I'm caught by surprise when I open the door. Vincent is here. He's standing before me with a sheepish look on his face, holding two cups of coffee from Betty's. He seems unsure if I'm happy to see him here unannounced. But I am. I can't help it.

"Coffee?" he offers, a nervous smile on his face. I stepped forward, ignoring the cup, and offer him a kiss. It's tasteful. Nothing over the top.

"You're a mind reader." I smiled at him. "You have to be."

"Heading over to Betty's, were you?" he asks, smiling at me.

"Don't I always?" I laugh, taking the cup he's offering me.

"Lately, I'd say you have been if I really think about it," he thinks. "Did you sleep okay? You look exhausted."

"I am exhausted," I admit. He takes my hand in his, and we start heading down the path away from my home. "Did you drive this morning?"

"Actually, no," he tells me. I looked at him, surprised. "You enjoy walking. I figured we could walk into town together."

"That's really thoughtful, Vincent." I smiled at him. "Thank you."

"But also, I know you say last night didn't offend you," he starts, "but I just have to make sure."

I stop walking and look at him. He looks nervous.

"Would I lie?" I ask him. He smiles, sheepish.

"No," he answers. "You've been pretty adamant that lying is one thing you won't do."

"I enjoyed last night," I tell him, blushing. "And while I mean it wholeheartedly, I'm admittedly not sure if I'm ready to revisit that again…"

"Hey," he starts, taking a step closer to me. His non-coffee clad hand cups my cheek. "I meant what I said. There isn't a rush on anything." I leaned into his touch. It's bringing me comfort. I don't have the right words to convey how much I appreciate him. Well. I do. I have the words. But I will not allow them to surface.

"Anyone ever tell you how incredible you are?" I smile at him.

"You're not so bad yourself," he teases and leans down to kiss me.

We enjoy the walk into town together. My mind wanders, thinking over our conversation and about honesty. I'm feeling like a jerk. I pride myself for being honest. But he doesn't know the biggest part of me. As much as I want to reason with the idea that we're in the getting to know each other stage and with that, information is learned over time. But it's a big omission. And I feel like a big fat liar.

Vincent's the one person I don't want to hurt. But inadvertently, I am doing just that. The more lost in thought I am, the more I realize just how much he'll likely hate me once I tell him about what I can do. How much he'll hate me if I do manage to tell him I've seen and communicated with Charlie. Now Charlie doesn't want me to. But I won't lie to him.

"I have a project to finish up in Savannah that might take a couple days before I can be back," he tells me. "Can I see you before I leave town later?

"Definitely." I smile. "What time?"

"Is 5:00 okay? Do you have any sessions?" he asks.

"No, I should be wrapping up for the day around four," I say.

"Then it's a plan." He smiles. We're passing through town, seeing the different mom-and-pop shops starting to open. Those who see us greet us as we pass by. And then there's Clara. Glaring at me from her window. Her glare makes me feel uneasy.

"What's with Clara?" he whispers in my ear as we pass her shop. I'm doing my best to ignore her.

"What do you mean?" I ask.

"If looks could kill…" He chuckles.

"Ooh, the death glare she's sporting?" I clarify. "She doesn't always look that way?" He shakes his head, laughing.

"She and I had a disagreement over my availability for photo sessions," I tell him. I omit the reason behind the urge for the pictures. But on the surface, this is exactly what her issue was.

"Well, hopefully you two will figure it out," he assures me.

"I get the feeling things won't settle with her," I tell him truthfully.

"I'm sorry, Lucy," he says sadly.

"It's okay." I smile. We stop in the courtyard, in between my studio and Dawn's shop. "Well, thank you, for the coffee."

"Thank you for the walk." He smiles. Neither of us move in our intended directions. I might as well tell him Dawn is my current destination.

"I'm actually stopping in to meet with Dawn." I nod my head in the direction of her shop.

"Ah." He nods in understanding. "I'll leave you to it."

"I'll see you later," I tell him. He leans in for another kiss, which I happily return. I wait until I'm sure he's gone before I turn on my heels and march my way over into Dawn's shop.

The door's unlocked. She's already open but fortunately no one is in yet. I look around and when I realize she's not up front, I assume she's in the back like before.

"Your sister-in-law is a real piece of work Dawn." I march back there, stupidly and without a filter.

"Lucy?!' Dawn says in surprise. "What a surprise!"

"Charlie's insane Dawn," I keep going, putting my things down and taking off my coat. I've yet to look up to her. "Wait until I tell you what she did last night."

"Charlie?" It's not Dawn's voice I hear. And at that moment, I look up, surprised as all hell to see Sarah with Dawn. Dawn is shaking her head.

"Oh, hey Sarah." I give a fake smile. "How's it going?"

"Don't 'how's it going' me." She stands up, hands on her hips. "What in the hell are you talking about? *Charlie?*"

"We can explain." Dawn stands up, walking over to me. I can see her mind turning, wanting to come up with some explanation. But there's no need.

"It's simple, really," I tell her. Dawn is looking at me nervously. "I can see spirits. With the right equipment, I can communicate with them." Sarah is looking at me like I've lost my mind.

"Right." She rolls her eyes.

"It's true, Sarah," Dawn tells her.

"Oh Dawn, not you, too." Sarah shakes her head. "After everything Vincent's been through, you're not going to believe this are you? I thought I liked you, Lucy."

"Like me or don't like me, Sarah, I won't lose sleep over it," I tell her. "But the reality is I can't hide the fact that I can, in fact, communicate with spirits. It's a gift passed down through my family for generations."

"And do you have meetings with the Easter Bunny and Santa Claus as well?" she feigns excitement.

"I get how it sounds, Sarah," I tell her.

"Oh, you do?" Her voice is still filled with sarcasm.

"Sure." I shrug. "You are not the first person I've encountered who thinks I'm weaving some tale, trying to play at heart strings to make a buck. You won't be the last. But I don't go advertising this. I don't seek people out. And at times, spirits lurking around can be a buzz kill."

"Sarah, she's telling the truth," Dawn urges. "Lucy doesn't lie. And she's seen Charlette." Sarah pauses a moment, processing, but is angry again. She's focused on Dawn.

"You've seen Vincent get his hopes up for years trying to find a way to communicate with her, only to be taken advantage of," Sarah says. "You've seen his heart breaking each time all over again. How could you be foolish to believe that of all people, the one he's finally opening himself up to is the same one we've befriended who might be able to successfully communicate with her?"

"I know for a fact she can," Dawn pushes. "The night of the opening, before Lucy left, she asked me who Charlie was. Not Charlette. *Charlie*. None of us referred to her by that name. You know that, Sarah."

"She must have heard about it from Vincent," Sarah brushes off.

"Actually, he only told me about being previously married and losing his wife a couple weeks ago," I tell her. "The opening was months ago."

"Then how did you know that name?" Sarah asked, hands on her hips.

"Because she introduced herself as Charlette but told me Vincent called her Charlie," I explain.

"I can't believe this." Sarah shakes her head in denial. "You could've looked all this up on the internet. Her obituary. Anything."

"Sure, online would tell me she was beautiful with blonde hair. But the night she passed she was wearing dark gray leggings with a matching top. Her hair was pulled up tight in a high ponytail. She also had an infinity tattoo on the inside of her left wrist."

Sarah's eyes grow large, and she sits down.

"Charlette wasn't on social media," Dawn reminds Sarah. "There would never be a picture circulating about that tattoo."

"But how?" Sarah asks, her coldness melting away.

"I don't fully understand it myself, Sarah," I tell her. "But when I turned 18, it kicked into high gear, and eventually I learned photos were spirit's way of coming through to communicate clearly with me."

"And Dawn has known about this?" Sarah clarifies.

"Most people in this town know—my family's been helping townsfolk for years. Dawn does and interestingly, your mom knows," I tell them.

"My mom?" Dawn is surprised.

"She's not so subtle." I laugh. "But I guess when she lived in Beaufort years ago, your parents knew my gran. She helped your mom communicate with someone who had passed."

"I can't believe she didn't say anything." Dawn is surprised.

"I think she was respecting my privacy." I shrug.

"But Vincent doesn't know," Sarah states.

"Did you hear yourself about him just moments ago?" I ask. "He's understandably the biggest skeptic."

"But if you've seen his wife, why wouldn't you tell him?" Sarah asks, curious.

"Because she doesn't want me to tell him," I explain. "She wants him to be able to move on and worries if he knows she's still here then he'll hold on to that and never move on. I don't agree with her logic. I think he needs closure."

"But you plan on telling him?" Dawn asks.

"I have to tell him about what I can do." I sat down. "After last night, I don't see a way around it. So yes, in telling him what I can do it will probably circle back to the fact that Charlie is around."

"What happened last night?" Dawn presses. She's intrigued.

"Yeah, you barged in here saying she was a real piece of work," Sarah recalls.

"Vincent and I spent some time together last night," I tell them. They both look surprised. "Nothing happened...we did fool around a bit."

"But?" Dawn presses once more.

"But I ended it abruptly when I realized Charlie had a front row seat," I tell them.

"She was watching you guys?" Dawn asks, shocked. I nod.

"Was she angry?" Sarah asks.

"No, she looked pleased with herself," I tell them truthfully.

"She's not angry that you and Vincent have been getting close?" Sarah is curious.

"Opposite," I tell them. "She thinks I'm good for him. But she won't go into any lights to cross over until she's made sure *all* are safe and happy."

"Who's all?" Dawn asks.

"I have no clue." I shrug. "She's cryptic. Do you think any of you guys need closure surrounding her death—besides Vincent?"

"I mean, as tragic as it was what happened to her, we're doing okay," Dawn says. "Not that we don't care or miss her, but we don't feel a void needs filling."

"Then who the hell does she mean when she says all?" I'm frustrated. And getting a headache. I take a sip of coffee.

"You went to Betty's without me?" Dawn whines.

"Oh, uh. No," I tell her. "Vincent showed up at my door this morning with coffee."

"He did, did he?" Dawn smirks.

"How close did you guys get last night?" Now Sarah is smirking.

"Does it matter?" I ask them. They're looking at me like I have two heads. "However close we got, it was cut short on account of Charlie and her peeping ways."

"Buzz kill," Dawn pouts.

"It's for the best," I say.

"What do you mean?" Sarah asks.

"I mean, I can't get close to Vincent in that way without him knowing what I could do. And he won't believe me," I tell them. "So basically, as soon as he knows that's the end of this thing we have."

"I wouldn't be so sure," Dawn tries to assure me. "He may surprise you."

"We'll see, I guess." I sigh. "Either way, I'm trying to mentally prepare myself for the end."

"You shouldn't think that way." Sarah takes my hand, trying to offer comfort. "He might surprise you."

"Maybe," I agree. "In my world it isn't always a happy ending." My alarm goes off, reminding me I must get back as I have a morning full of sessions.

"Do you have to go?" Dawn asks.

"Busy morning," I tell her.

"Oh, engagement shoots or family photos?" Dawn asks.

"Um—" I think a moment. "It's mostly random headshots."

"Headshots?" Sarah asks.

"Yeah." I shrug. "Interestingly no one on the schedule today really needs headshots. There's no new business that warrants marking promotions. But here we are."

"Wait, you said with your photos spirits come through and you can communicate with them?" Sarah stops me.

"Yeah." I'm not sure of her point.

"Do spirits come through during your sessions?" Sarah asks.

"Sometimes," I tell her. She's got a look on her face I can't quite decipher.

"So people in town know what you can do…and they know you might be able to make contact during a session…" Sarah deduces.

"I think I know where you're going with this, Sarah," I tell her. "But I don't accept money for using my gift to help people in this town."

"Oh, no," Sarah backtracks. "I don't think you're exploiting this town. But I sense maybe they are exploiting you."

I look her in the eyes. I don't have a good answer for her. Especially since the Clara incident comes to mind as soon as Sarah says it. I don't have words.

"They need me," is all I can say. And I look back and forth between the two of them before I grab my coat and coffee and head out to the studio.

CHAPTER 10

VINCENT, THEN

"If you just close your eyes and take a breath," she says. "Place your hands on the table, palms up."

I do as I'm told.

I'm here at the recommendation of my sister. She's into all this otherworldly spiritual connectivity. Serena, the would-be psychic, sitting across from me, was supposedly well known. Was supposedly incredible in how she communicates with those who would have "left the earth" as she put it.

On some level, I was desperate for the ability to connect with Charlie. Just once. One time. I wanted to connect with her. Ask her why. Why she had been so intent and insistent on going for that damn jog late at night. Why couldn't it wait?

Charlie was always stubborn. She wouldn't be told. Wouldn't listen to reason. Not when she had her mind set on something.

I thought that maybe if I could connect, I'd have some form of closure. And maybe could start to heal and move on from the endless guilt I felt for not pushing her to just stay home for once.

But I could tell this was pointless. I'd already been to countless people who claimed to be able to connect with the other side. I couldn't shake the feeling someone or something was with me. Especially more recently. And it had been two and a half years. They had all been frauds. And I was growing angry at their audacity to exploit the pain they could clearly read coming off me in waves. I guess I was an easy target.

"Imagine the person you wish to contact," she instructs. "Spirit, we call to you. Spirit, we summon you. Heed our call, spirit. Commune with us."

Internally I'm rolling my eyes.

"Yes. I think I'm getting something," Serena suddenly says. The lights are flickering. This seems so far-fetched, it's almost comical. I'm not trying to be pessimistic. But I've been down this road, and Dawn will believe anything.

"Your loved one is here." She opens her eyes. "Open your eyes." I do as I'm told but remain detached and devoid of all reactions.

"He's really here?" I ask. If she is as genuine as she claims, she will know I'm lying. She'll know it's my wife I'm seeking.

She's staring at me intently. "He says he's sorry. He didn't mean to go so soon." Ah, the standard bullshit.

"Why did you?" I play along. "We could've had more time together as a family."

"He's upset, Vincent," she tells me. "He doesn't know why he went so abruptly. He doesn't understand."

"What does he need from me?" I ask. "How can I help him move on?"

"He's at peace. He's happy. He wants you to know that and let him go," she tells me.

"Can I ask one more thing?" She nods her head.

"The connection is growing weaker. Ask before we miss our window!" she pushes.

"Of course, of course," I rush. "How many people actually buy into your freak show?"

She drops her hands.

"Excuse me?" She's feigning offense.

"You heard me," I tell her, standing up. "How many people do you actually think you are fooling with your bullshit smoke and mirrors? And for what? To make a buck?!" I'm shouting. I'm angry now.

"How dare you insult me! The spirits!" she shouts.

"Because you're a joke!" I tell her.

"I am not. You communicated with your husband. Now you're refusing to pay because what? You didn't get enough time!?" She is reaching and she knows it. I can the small beads of sweat forming on her forehead. Lies. All of it.

"I didn't have a husband. I had a wife," I told her. Her eyes grew wide. "And you're a fraud. Mark my words, I will make sure everyone knows you're a fake!"

"You can't mess with my livelihood!" She looks panicked.

"And yet you think you can mess with everyone's lives!" I barge out, slamming the door behind me. I'm over this. I've had enough.

I've lost count how many times I've been given the false promise of the possibility of communicating with my wife again. And every single time it's the same typical bullshit. Web of lies, exploiting pain. I was done. Clearly, there was no such thing as an afterlife or maybe Charlie would've made herself known to me in some way. But instead, nothing. And yet everything.

Needing a fresh start, my family decided to move back where it all began for us. Beaufort, South Carolina. I'd only been a small handful of times as a kid but never for any extended period. My family moved away around the same time as my aunt and uncle. My cousin Kyle was about three years old so Dad could run a big-shot hospital in Savannah. Savannah was home until now.

My sister, Dawn, was ready to open her own shop and jumped at the idea of doing so in our hometown. As for my brother-in law and myself? We owned Henry-Foster Construction, based out of Savannah. The biggest hurdle would be how to effectively branch out during the highest demand of our time.

Kyle and his wife, Sarah, wanted the small-town life. Me? The fresh start was the appeal. But I couldn't let go of Savannah. As such, I'd be the go-to man running the home base out of Savannah, commuting back and forth. But all main projects got put on hold as soon as Dawn found the perfect shop to open her boutique in. Kyle and I got roped into the major remodel, and she'd given us the pressing timeline of three weeks to an opening.

And for what reason? None. There was no reason for the rushed timeline other than Dawn wanted it. My sister, ladies and gentlemen, was a royal pain in the ass.

We'd been working for hours when Kyle had finally had enough.

"Dawn, I swear, if we don't get some fuel in our systems, you can kiss your timeline goodbye," Kyle says, dropping his hammer and crossing his arms.

"Alright, alright relax," she tells him. "I saw a bakery or something just across the courtyard. I'll go grab some coffee."

"Hey, check this out!" Miles appears from the back carrying some old TV. It looks ancient.

"I guess the previous owners left some things behind," Kyle adds.

"I wonder what else they left behind!" Dawn exclaims. "Was there more stuff in the back, Miles?"

"Yeah, there's a lot back there." He smiles at her. They'd been married five years but have been together since middle school. These two were joined at the hip since day one.

"I'll have to check it out!" Dawn says, excited. "Think that TV will work?"

"I'll see if there's something in the back to test it out," I tell her. "Go get those coffees, please."

"She wants a strike on her hands, that's what this is." Kyle laughs. But she finally gets the hint and grabs her purse to head out. I make my way to the back, looking for whatever else was left behind that'll help try to get some cable. Noise other than our tools would be good to fill the background. After some time, I finally found a set of rabbit ears and figure why not? Let's try to get the old tube working.

"Coffee and muffins!" I hear Dawn but am too focused on getting this to work. I didn't notice that Dawn managed to sucker some townie into coming into the shop with her.

"Finally!" I shout. Victory. How did people manage with these things back in the day? "It's not much, but I got something coming through."

Interested in communicating with the other side? Do not hesitate to call the number below to speak to the Amazing Wanda.

An infomercial plays, advertising someone's claim to be able to connect to the other side. I'm instantly annoyed and aggravated at the mere mention.

"Oh! Cool!" Dawn exclaimed. "Get me a pen!"

"Dawn, come on." Miles laughed.

"This is a joke," I tell her. "You know this."

"Not all of it," Dawn disagreed. "I'm sure there are people out there who are truly capable of communicating to the other side."

"No, they can't," I disagree. "Don't be naïve, Dawn. Anyone who tells you differently is taking advantage of you. You're smarter than that. It's all a joke. "

"You don't think it's possible that someone out there may actually be genuine?" the girl next to Dawn says. For the first time, I finally look at her and for a moment, it was like I forgot to breathe. She's striking. She's petite with long strawberry blonde hair. And her eyes. The depth of her striking green eyes pulls me in. They are soulful. I feel drawn to her, and there's a clear shift in the energy in the air. That's new. After a moment, I shake my head, trying to clear my mind and focus.

"No." I cross my arms. "I know for a fact it's all bullshit. People should be ashamed of the lengths they'll go to exploit the pain and suffering of others."

"You know for a fact." She crosses her arms, mirroring my position and stepping a hair closer.

"Yes, I do," I tell her, jaw clenching. She's staring into my eyes, searching. For what? I have no clue but a moment later, she looks as though she's found her answer.

"So because you've encountered a fraud, all mediums are frauds?" she asks. I'm caught off guard. I'm looking at Dawn. In the short time she's met this stranger, what the hell has she managed to share about me that she should not have.

"Don't look at her, look at me." I snap my attention back to her, surprised at her demand. "You're too easy to read, Vincent."

"To answer your question, yes, "I bounce back. "They're all frauds. There is no such thing as the afterlife or spirits. You shouldn't be so naïve to fall into their schemes." She looks at me, frowning. It's as though I've offended her. Why would this offend her? But she's stepping away, seemingly getting ready to leave.

"Don't believe him, Lucy," Dawn tells her. Lucy. So, her name is Lucy. Crap, focus Henry. "He's a skeptic. *Some* of us are more open-minded. Here, I wrote the number down if you're interested."

"Oh thank you, but no," she tells her. "Amazing Wanda isn't truly Amazing Wanda." Dawn looks shocked as the rest of the guys laugh in the background. Except me, of course.

"She's a fake?" Dawn asks, surprised.

105

"She is," Lucy tells her with confidence. Wait, she'd been scammed before too? Perhaps she understood and is sensible.

"See," I chime in. "She scammed you, didn't she?"

"No," she says. "I've never called those hotlines. But unfortunately, in her case you are right, and you shouldn't waste your money, Dawn."

"How do you know?" Dawn asks, curious.

"Dawn, I actually have to get back to the studio, but if you want to come by later in the week, we can go over different style options for your marketing and get something on the books," she offers. She's moving to grab her coffee and bag from the bakery. But she's suddenly looking my way again, and all too quickly, it looks like all the color drains from her face as she drops her bag. If I believed it, I could've sworn she saw a ghost.

"Lucy, are you okay?" Dawn asks, picking up the bag she had dropped.

She didn't look okay.

"I'm...I'm fine," she says, but I can see that she is not. She's trying to pull herself together and is failing miserably. I didn't quite understand it. But I wanted to. I wanted to understand her. And that was confusing as all hell.

"You sure?" she asked. "You look like you've seen a ghost." She laughed.

"Yeah," she rushes. "Thank you for picking that up for me," she thanks Dawn. "I've got to run." She doesn't wait as she bolts out the door.

"Way to go airhead." Dawn turns to me, arms on her hips. "You and your grouchy attitude probably scared her off."

"I'm not grouchy." I cross my arms.

"You are," she disagrees. "She's sweet. You could've been nice."

"That was nice," I press. "And I won't sugar coat that. You know full well the countless frauds who kept telling me all the wrong things when I was trying to find a way to get closure with Charlie."

"And I'm not downplaying what you've been through nor am I saying they weren't frauds," Dawn tells me. "But there are people out there who do believe in the unknown. And being a little more respectful toward their beliefs won't hurt you." She walks away, shaking her head.

I turn the TV off, suddenly no longer interested in seeing what we could manage to get to work on this piece of crap. We're back to work; the warden is back on her power trip and running the show. I almost wish she'd just leave and let us work. You'd think we didn't know how to do our jobs or run our business.

"The custom bookshelf I told you about would be a nice piece behind this register, Dawn," I call out, examining the space.

"I love that idea!" Dawn gushes.

"You saw the sketches, right?" I'm double checking. Because once I start, there's no way in hell I'll stop.

"Yes, Vincent." She rolls her eyes.

"I'm making sure," I tell her. "I know how you can be, and there's no backtracking once I start."

"I won't change my mind," she promises.

That becomes my focus for the next couple of hours. I don't realize just how late it is. At some point everyone left. They have lives. I simply don't and prefer to just focus on the task at hand. I'm reaching for the hammer in the spot I've always left it only to come up empty. I look over. It's not there, which is odd. I had just used it. Where the hell could it have gone? I'm moving everything every which way, and it's nowhere in sight.

Frustrated, I decide to call it a night. I'm in no mood to rearrange everything over a damn hammer.

I lock it up and head to my truck. The courtyard is empty at this time of night. I'm not far down the road when I see someone walking on the sidewalk straight ahead of me. I squint, unsure if my eyes are playing tricks on me, but I recognize her right away. I don't need to see her face. I know it's *her*. And she's walking alone in the dark. And my mind goes there, I can't help it. I think of Charlie alone that night running in the rain and the asshat who claimed to have lost control of his car while it ran a red light of its own volition. Because unknown dark forces take over automobiles and run down pedestrians. Does this girl—Lucy, was it?—have no sense of self-preservation? She's insane! What is she thinking!

Before I realize what I'm doing, I'm pulling over to the side of the road and roll down my window. She stops. We're staring at each other, neither one of us saying a word. What is she waiting for? An invitation?

"What are you doing?" I finally break the silence and ask. I'm irritated and need to remind myself to keep myself in check. She looks around as if it's the most obvious thing in the world, and I roll my eyes. She's a smart ass. Good to know. "I mean, what are you doing walking alone in the dark by yourself?"

"As opposed to walking with a buddy?" She raises an eyebrow. See? Smart ass.

"You know what I mean." I roll my eyes. "Have you no sense of self-preservation? Walking alone and at night isn't exactly safe."

"It's never been a problem before." She shrugs. Never been a problem? Just how often does she stupidly come out at night and walk alone?

"Where's your car?" I ask. Maybe I can drive her to her car. Then she won't be walking late at night alone.

"I don't have one," she says. She doesn't have one. WHAT?

"How do you not have one?" I ask.

"What is confusing?" she asks me. "I don't have one. I walk." She's lost her mind. She had to have lost her mind.

"Get in the truck," I tell her. She can argue all she wants and insist on walking, but there is no way I'm leaving her here alone. Nope.

"It's not good to accept rides from strangers, "she protests.

"Get in, Lucy," I tell her, rolling my eyes.

"Fine," she caves, and finally gets in the truck and quickly gets her seatbelt on. "It's not like I live far." She looks uneasy being in the truck, and I must wonder if I make her uncomfortable or if it's something else entirely. She won't look straight ahead. She's staring out her window. Again, I think nothing of it. She could be mad that I'm insisting on her getting into the truck when she clearly prefers to walk.

"Just the same, I'm not letting you walk alone in the middle of the night," I tell her and start the truck. "Where to?"

"Follow down to the second stop sign and make a left," she says.

"And then?" I press. Why was it like pulling teeth with her? Was she always so...so...what word was I looking for? Stubborn?

"And then that's it," she tells me.

"That's it?" I look at her.

"I told you, I don't live far." She's rolling her eyes at me.

"If you're cold, I can turn the heat on for you," I offer. She seems truly uncomfortable.

"I'm fine," she says. But I can tell she's not. I just don't understand why she's not. She doesn't really seem cold though.

"Are you usually so stubborn?" I ask her.

"Not particularly," she says. I can see her trying to fight a smile. I doubt her though. She's as stubborn as they come. I can tell.

"I find that very doubtful," I disagree.

"Sorry to disappoint." She laughs. The truck comes to a halt. I'd already made the turn she's instructed and am stopped, looking around, trying to find where it is she lives. There's nothing around us but woods. Has she lost her mind? Just what is she playing at?

"You're kidding, right?"

"Nope, this is me!" She makes a move to open the truck door, but I'm faster. I've locked the door. "This isn't funny, open the door." Yeah, she's mad.

"You're having me drop you off in the middle of nowhere. How is that any better than walking alone at night?" I look at her, waiting for an answer.

"You're not dropping me off in the middle of nowhere," she disagrees. "You brought me home."

"You live in the woods." I look at her like she's crazy. There's no way. "Where do you actually live?" I press.

"Through this lit up pathway," she tells me. "I live in a cottage in the woods. I'm having you drop me off here because there isn't a straight up driveway to get through without going into a tree." Is she being truthful? Is she lying? "Do you need to walk with me as proof?"

"Actually—" I turn the truck off. That's a wonderful idea. "Yes." She rolls her eyes and gets out of the truck, heading to the lit up walkway, not bothering to wait for me. She's a lot faster than I thought she'd be. I'm running to catch up, calling out to her. "Slow down, will you?"

"Why?" she asks, not breaking her pace. "You realize I don't even know you and you're following me home. That's creepy."

"It's creepy to want to make sure you get home safely?" I ask. "Most women would be flattered at the chivalrous gesture."

"I'm not most women." She shrugs. And I believe it. There's something about her I can't quite place. She's intriguing.

"I see that," I say. Less than two minutes and we've reached the opening to a cottage. It's rather charming.

"Well, this is me," she tells me. She turns to look at me and whatever she had intended to say is lost. She's just staring at me. And admittedly, I can't help but stare and feel myself getting lost in her eyes.

"You weren't kidding," I finally say, breaking out of whatever trance she had on me and take in the scenery.

"One thing about me you should know, Vincent," she starts. "Since I have a feeling, this isn't the last we'll cross paths. I don't lie. Ever."

I can see she's sincere with her words. She wants to make sure I know and believe this is her truth. And I do. I bet I'd believe just about anything she told me. Who was this girl?

"Do you walk every night?" I ask.

"You know what my answer will be," she tells me.

"Given I'll be around Dawn's for a while, perhaps I can offer you a ride when you find yourself walking to the woods in the middle of the night?" I offer. At least this way it takes her off the road late at night. She'd be safe.

"I really would rather walk," she tells me.

"Is my company so horrible?" I tease. But I'm curious if it really is me. And if she's not sensing the same vibes between the two of us as I had been. It was all a bit off putting. Since Charlie, I hadn't been interested in exploring new relationships. I wasn't stupid. Eventually, the natural progression would have me going out more. But no one caught my attention. Not until Lucy. And I wasn't sure what to make of the feelings she was suddenly igniting.

"Did you consider it may have nothing to do with you in the slightest?" she asks me. I can see she's being sincere. "I've been walking and getting by where I need for a decade now. Maybe I'm a creature of habit, but I don't intend to change that any time soon."

I don't like the idea of her walking by herself. But I can see no matter what I say or do, it won't change her mind. And right now, who am I to even make such demands?

"Well," I finally start. "Sweet dreams, Lucy."

"Good night, Vincent," she tells me. "Thank you for the ride." I smile and watch her retreat inside.

I release a breath I hadn't realized I was holding and start on the pathway back to my truck. I wasn't sure who Lucy truly was, but I wanted to know her. She's invading every facet of my mind. I make it back to my truck and am about to start the engine to head home when an object on the passenger side catches my eye. My hammer. My hammer is now suddenly positioned in the seat Lucy had been seated in moments ago.

What the hell was going on?

CHAPTER 11

VINCENT, THEN

I'm staring at the hammer lying in the passenger seat, confused as all hell. I know I didn't take it with me. I know the last place I'd seen and used it was Dawn's shop. And then it went M.I.A, which prompted my leaving and calling it for the night.

And yet, here it was, out of the blue. The illogical part of me wonders if Lucy had it? But then I'm calling myself a moron because she was nowhere in sight to have been able to take it to begin with. My mind was playing tricks on me.

I turn the truck on, shaking my head and trying to clear my thoughts. Because this makes no sense, and I don't want to focus any more attention on this hammer.

Friday night and the lights are low
Looking out for a place to go
Where they play the right music
Getting in the Swing

"What the hell?" I say, more to myself than anyone. Of course, there's no one around. I thought the radio was off, but I guess I was wrong. Beaufort must not get good reception if they're playing ABBA on the radio. Is there nothing current?

I turn off the music and start my way home.

I'm exhausted, and clearly, I'm losing my mind.

My sleep is shit. For the first time in what feels like forever I dream of Charlie. And for once, it's not a recurring nightmare of the night she died.

I'm in a field of tulips. Which is odd because Charlie liked lilies…not tulips but there they were. She was off in the distance, smiling at me. I tried getting closer to her but the closer I reached, the further away she would go. It was frustrating. I wanted to talk to her, but I couldn't reach her no matter how hard I tried to.

"Lovely girl," a voice says beside me. I turn to look and am confused. An elderly woman with grayish hair is beside me, looking into the distance at Charlie. I've never seen her before. I have no idea who she is but I feel at ease with her. She has a calming effect.

"Do I know you?" I ask, but she just continues smiling.

She reaches down and picks several tulips from the field, carefully looking at each one.

"Tulips," she says. "Quite beautiful."

I'm confused. She's giving me a knowing look, and it all fades away as quickly as it came.

I woke up more frustrated than when I went to sleep. I'm exhausted. I'm putting all my focus on that damn bookshelf I designed for Dawn in preparation for her opening night.

"You look well rested," Dawn notes, her voice laced with sarcasm.

"I didn't sleep well," I tell her.

"Oh, I'm sorry." She softens her tone. "Do you want some coffee?"

"Only if you're headed over there," I tell her.

"I'm stopping over at Lucy's studio to look over her work and make a plan for what I envision for the photos. I can grab some for you on my way back." She smiles at me. She's walking toward the door, and I remember to ask.

"Hey, Dawn. Any chance you moved my hammer last night and put it in my truck?"

"Your hammer?" She looks confused. "You were using it when we all left. What would it be doing in your truck?"

"No clue." I shrug and get back to work.

It takes a couple days but the shelf is done. Dawn is pleased with it so that's a good sign. I haven't seen Lucy wandering around at night. Admittedly, I'd been hanging back late just in case she got it in her mind to take a nighttime stroll.

I'm walking into the shop with Miles after a quick supply run and see she's here. She's looking at the new shelving unit I built.

"Vincent built it," Dawn tells her. She looks genuinely surprised.

"It's incredible," I hear her say.

"Thanks," I chime in, figuring I might as well make sure she knows I'm around.

"Check this out, though," Dawn chimes in, suddenly excited. She crouches down and pulls out an old box from one of the shelves behind the counter. Instantly, I cringe.

"Isn't it awesome?" Dawn exclaims. We're looking at the box in her hands. It's a Oujia board.

"Where did you find that?" I ask, looking at the box with disgust.

"The old owners must have left it behind." She shrugs. "We should try it out!" I want to scream. She's completely lost her mind to even make such a suggestion. Really though, what is she thinking?

"You should throw it out," I tell her. "Don't waste your time on that crap."

"Oh, come on, we used to bring this thing out all the time as kids," Dawn pouts. "You used to love this thing."

"And I grew up. I know better," I told her. "It's not real when you're the one pushing the pointer."

"I never pushed the pointer!" she disagrees. "Come on, let's try it."

"Dawn, I agree with Vincent about throwing it out," Lucy tells her. She's sensible today, good. Dawn pouts. "You shouldn't mess with things like this anyway. You don't know what or who you're even contacting. It can be dangerous." I take it back. She's not sensible.

Here I thought she also didn't believe in that stuff. But she must believe on some level.

"There isn't anything that you contact," I disagree. "It's all crap. Just like believing there are spirits or whatever waiting to talk to you."

"I wouldn't go as far as to say that," she replies. Perhaps I'm coming off stronger than intended. "But messing with things you don't truly understand isn't safe. I'd consider getting rid of it, Dawn."

"Please don't tell me you're naïve enough to buy into this crap," I look at her. How do I help her see reason? That none of this is real? Looking at her, it looks as though I've offended her, and I'm confused as to why.

"Into this—" she points to the box, "—no. But believing that we may not be alone…what's so wrong with that?"

"Because it's all a hoax," I tell her. "Whoever told you otherwise clearly did a number on you if you really think spirits are real and there's an afterlife."

"Say it wasn't real," she pushes. "Is it so wrong to believe in something so much it gives you hope?"

"I believe in what's real and what isn't," I simply say. "And spirits, Ouija boards, it's all bullshit. You think it's real, it's not."

"I don't need to think anything." She crossed her arms. "This isn't about what I do or don't believe it. It's about others and the hope believing gives them and the peace of knowing their loved ones are happy on the other side and have moved on. Closure—doesn't that mean something?"

"It would if there were any truth to it," I push. "But it isn't real. And people can't truly move on and grieve if they're holding on to some false hope of what will never happen."

She's staring at me like he's seeing through me. Like she can see deep into my soul. She stares for some time until a realization hits her. She almost looks like she suddenly understands something.

She places a hand on my forearm. An electric current sears through me at her simple touch. She's offering me comfort, I can sense it, but I don't understand why she thinks I need to be comforted. I'm trying to ignore the spark I'm feeling. I look from where her hand is placed to her eyes, searching for something. What? I have no clue.

"I'm sorry, Vincent," she tells me softly. What is she sorry for? "I'm sorry for whoever you lost that you feel this way."

I'm taken back. How could she know? She didn't, did she? Did Dawn say something?

"I'll see you all later." She removes her hand and leaves the store. I'm stunned another moment before I snap out of it and zero in on Dawn.

"What did you tell her?" I ask. I'm doing my best not to sound like an ass. But if she told Lucy, then of course I'd be angry. It's my story to tell.

"I didn't say anything." Dawn looks at me, her eyes pleading with me to believe her.

"How could she know I've lost someone?" I press. I'm rubbing at my temple, feeling a headache coming on.

"I really don't know, Vincent," she tells me sincerely. She looks at the door Lucy had just walked out of. Dawn is lost in thought. She's processing something. "But she's quite perceptive."

"Clearly," I agree. I can't quite place what it is about Lucy. Initially, it was her lack of care for self-preservation that irked me to no end. I couldn't wrap my mind around the fact she willingly made a habit of walking around everywhere alone. *Alone*.

"She really gets under your skin, doesn't she?" Miles laughs.

"Why do you say that?" I'm taken back.

"You've been glaring at that door for the last ten minutes." He's laughing.

"It's nothing." I shake my head.

"No, what is it?" He stops laughing, giving me his full attention.

"Nothing, there's just something about her that I can't quite place," I tell him.

"And has nothing to do with the fact that besides maybe believing in spirits, she's actually quite kind and beautiful?" Miles presses.

"I hadn't given it a thought," I deny.

"Oh please." Dawn laughs, carrying a bunch of hangers to place them on the different displays which have been built and set out. "One look at her and you're lost in her eyes." Miles laughs.

"I hardly know her," I say.

"But you want to," Dawn sings, walking passed me.

"Dawn," I warn.

"Don't Dawn me," she says, turning to look at me. "It's a good thing. You're taking notice and it's a good thing."

"It has been three years," Miles says cautiously. "You're bound to meet people who catch your eye."

"That's not what this is," I deny. Deny, deny, deny. But they see through me and if I'm honest, I can't even convince myself. I want to know her.

You are the dancing queen

Young and sweet

Only seventeen

Dancing queen

Feel the beat from the tambourine, oh yeah

You can dance

You can jive

Having the time of your life

Ooh, see that girl

Watch that scene

Digging the dancing queen

That damn song again is suddenly blaring through the studio. We're all looking at each other in surprise as no one turned on any sound systems.

"What is it with this song?!" I say, looking for where the remote is to try to turn off the sound system.

"What do you mean?" Dawn asks.

"It came on in my truck the other night I drove Lucy home," I told her.

"You drove her home?" Dawn asks, ignoring the song entirely.

"Focus, Dawn," I tell her.

"I don't know," she admits. "I've never listened to a lot of ABBA." This is giving me a headache.

"Here's the remote." I throw it to her. "You figure it out. I need caffeine. My head's killing me."

I go over to Betty's and order a cup of coffee from the barista, Claire.

"Vincent, dear," I hear Betty call from the side. I turn to look and pause a moment. She's sitting with Lucy. I'm hesitant. Lucy doesn't look like she wants to see me. That's promising, I think to myself.

"Betty, good to see you." I smile at her. "Lucy."

"Vincent." Her tone matches mine. "How's the progress on the store?"

"Almost done, actually." I figured she'd want to ignore me. But her interest surprises me.

"That's great," Betty chimes in. "What will you be doing once it's all done?"

"We have several projects lined up between here and Savannah," I tell her.

"Savannah?" Betty asks.

"The construction business is based out of Savannah," I explain. "So, we'll be going back on forth depending on what's needed and when." I see Lucy cringe at the mention of the back-and-forth road trips. She really doesn't like cars, does she?

"Ever been to Savannah, Lucy?" I ask.

"Oh heavens, Lucy doesn't get into cars," Betty answers for her. "Not since the accident." Car accident? She was in a car accident? When? What happened?

"She did the other night," I tell Betty, but I'm focused on Lucy.

"He gave me no choice," she adds, almost put out and whining. "Won't be happening again, right, Vincent?"

"I'm sure I can persuade Lucy here to get in a moving vehicle again." I smirk. Maybe if I made light of it, she'd feel more comfortable with the idea of getting in my truck…or…a car. Right.

"Highly unlikely," she responds, standing up and getting ready to leave. Already?

"I have to get going. Thank you again for the coffee, Betty," Lucy says.

"Anytime, dear." Betty smiles. Lucy acknowledges me one last time with a simple nod before heading out.

"What do you think, Betty?" I ask after Lucy's gone. "Think she'll come around?"

"Give her some time, dear." Betty smiles. "She's got a lot going on. It takes her a bit to truly warm up and open up her heart."

"Oh, I didn't mean it in that way." I'm backpedaling. Was that obvious?

"Of course you didn't." She laughs and pats me gently on the cheek before heading back behind the counter to help Claire. The bakery is picking up.

The night of the grand opening, I'm stuck in Savannah. I'm trying as best I can to finish at the job site but a valve burst and there's water everywhere. There's no way we can leave a client's place in this state. We need to get the parts to replace it and then get the drywall up and secure to move on to the next phase of the client's remodel.

It's taking longer than planned to get it handled but when we do, I rush back to my place to get myself dressed. I still have the long drive ahead of me, but I promised I'd be there. And I will be. But I'll be there for the very end at this point. I feel guilty.

My phone's been blasting all afternoon. They're likely looking for me because I'd promised to be there early and it wasn't working out this way.

I don't bother to read the messages; I text Dawn letting her know I'm on my way. I explained there was an emergency on site and hope she will understand.

At a red light, I check the latest message. Dawn is telling me to be careful and not rush, which I appreciate.

I take my time driving to Beaufort. The roads aren't lit well, I'm finding. Which is quite hazardous if anyone were to be wandering around this late at night. And I think of Lucy and grow annoyed.

I find parking easily and head in. I go find Dawn right way. I knew Lucy was handling the event but she's also nowhere in sight. I figured she would be. It isn't lost on me the disappointment that I feel at the realization that she isn't here.

"Dawn," I say. "I'm so sorry I'm so late!" She's hugging me.

"Don't even think it." She shakes her head. "Any chance you saw Lucy? I've been trying to reach her?"

"No, why?" I'm confused.

"Miles said she didn't look okay when she left earlier," she tells me.

"Did she have anything to drink?" I'm trying to contain how worried I'm suddenly feeling.

"She didn't have anything," Miles says, walking up to us. He nods his head as a way of greeting. "She focused on getting pictures in before she called it a night and left. But she wasn't steady on her feet."

"Did she park far?" Dawn asks.

"What do you mean 'parked far?'" I'm taken back. "She doesn't have a car."

"What?" Dawn shrieks. "What do you mean she doesn't have a car! She didn't say anything!"

"She doesn't own a car," I tell them. "She walks."

"Everywhere?" Dawn looks beside herself.

"Yeah," I tell her.

"Why didn't she say anything!" Dawn is pulling her phone out, trying to get ahold of Lucy. "Damn it." She's worried.

"She's not picking up?" I ask.

"No, straight to voicemail," she tells me. "Do you know where she lives?"

"Yeah," I tell her.

"Well, what are you waiting for, please go check on her," Dawn urges me. I nod and run out the door. All possible scenarios are running through my mind. I look at the time, it's nearly one in the morning already. I didn't think parties would go on so late in Beaufort of all places. I don't bother to drive. I know it's close by so I'm running. Running to the second stop sign, make the left and am running up the pathway.

I'm frantically banging on the door. The lights are off. So maybe she's sleeping. But after 10 minutes, there's still nothing. I call Dawn.

"Anything?" she asks as soon as she picks up.

"Nothing," I tell her. "She's not answering the door. Has anyone heard from her? Seen her?"

"No," Dawn says. "I thought I'd check with Betty, but she left two hours ago."

"We'll keep looking," I tell her.

"I'm worried, Vincent," she tells me. "Maybe it's all in my head but I'm imagining the worst ever since you said she might have walked home."

"Don't worry, we'll find her," I tell her. She doesn't need to know I'm panicking too. I'm more worried than I realize. I care more than I realize. And so I wander around town for hours trying to find her. It's almost seven in the morning. I'm walking through town trying to think where else she could be and a light breeze picks up, a paper gets caught on my shoe.

I look down and it's the marketing ad promoting the opening. Lucy really did a good job with the pictures. I was beyond impressed. And then a thought occurs to me. Her studio!

I'm running to the courtyard, making my way to the door.

I frantically knock on the door, hoping she's here.

After a few minutes, I hear the click of locks, telling me the door is being opened and I'm relieved. She's here. I push past her and go inside. What the hell was she thinking? I'm waiting for her to say something, anything.

"Is Dawn okay?" she asks.

"Dawn? She's fine, why wouldn't she be?" We've been going crazy trying to find her and she's thinking about Dawn?

"You tell me." She puts her hands on her hips. "It's nearly seven in the morning and you barge in here. What is wrong with you?"

"You weren't home," I say. She has no clue what I am talking about or what I am referring to.

"I gathered that." She's being a smart ass again. Can't she see this is serious? "I know where I am, thank you very much."

"But no one else did." I start pacing. "Dawn has been trying to get ahold of you all night, trying to make sure you were okay. Miles said you could barely walk straight when you left. They were worried you drove yourself off the road only to find out from me you don't own a car…no, you insist on walking!"

"Would you stop pacing!" she demands. "You're giving me a headache!"

"Do you realize how worried everyone's been?" I press.

"I told Dawn and Miles I was fine, and I was," she tells me. "There was nothing wrong with me when I left. And there's nothing wrong with me now. I didn't realize they'd be so worried."

"Why wouldn't everyone worry?" Does she think no one cares about her well-being? "Everyone has come to care a great deal about you in the short time they've known you." Can't she see that I care? That her well-being matters?

"I didn't mean for them to worry," she tells me, her voice softening.

"If you'd just answered one message…they've been trying to reach you since you left the party." I'm pacing again. Why wasn't she picking up her phone at least?

"Again with the pacing." She rolls her eyes and heads to her counter. Her bag is there. I'm about to ask what she is doing but I see her pull her phone out. "My phone's dead. I don't keep a charger here. I didn't know."

"If you'd planned on crashing here, why not have your charger?" I look at her.

"Because I hadn't planned on staying here," she tells me. "I intended to go home."

"Alone, again. In the dark," I add, shaking my head. I'm thinking back on the poor lighting of this town and how dark the roads are. She could've been seriously hurt.

"Yes, but I was tired so I came here," she says.

"So you weren't fine," I said. Was she lying? Was she trying to spare my feelings?

"I was fine," she insists. "I was fine but tired. What is your problem? What is with your third degree?"

"Everyone was worried," I tell her after a moment of silence. "*I* was worried." I need her to understand.

"I didn't mean to worry anyone," she whispers. She cautiously takes a step closer and places her hand on my forearm, much like the day before.

"Just, don't do that," I say quietly.

"I can't promise it won't happen again." I want to argue but she continues. "You have to understand, it's just me. For 10 years, it's been just me. I told you, I'm a creature of habit."

I'm trying to understand what she is saying. She didn't do this intentionally. I get it. And I'm starting to see that she doesn't realize there are many out there who genuinely care if she's okay.

"Your parents?" I ask.

"Never knew my dad," she says. "And Mom skipped town when I was young. Small towns suffocated her, I think." I think back to what Betty told me…about Lucy going through a lot. I'm starting to see just how much more there is to Lucy.

"What about your husband or boyfriend, or whatever?" She rolls her eyes at me.

"Is that your clever way of trying to determine if I'm otherwise attached?" she smirks. Admittedly, I'm embarrassed at my not-so-subtle approach to learn her status.

"It's just me, Vincent," she tells me and begins to walk away.

"Lucy," I start but she cuts me off.

"I'll call Dawn and apologize for making everyone worry," she promises. "I'll stop at the shop on my way back home."

"No sessions today?" I ask. Maybe if she's free, I can take her out. Make up for the rocky start?

"No," she says. "Day off for me today."

"Do you have any plans?" I ask. "Would you be open to…I don't know… grabbing some breakfast or something?"

"Are you asking me on a date, Vincent?" She looks surprised I'd be asking her to go out. I wonder why that is.

123

"Maybe?" I take a step closer. "Try as I might, I can't seem to stay away from you anymore. I can't seem to get you off my mind. I'd like to at least get to know you."

"I'm not sure whether I should be creeped out, flattered, or insulted." She laughs. I roll my eyes. I'm trying to be serious here. I'm trying to be…vulnerable.

"Be serious, please," She stops laughing. "I'm trying," I add.

"You're right, I'm sorry," she apologizes.

"So…breakfast?" I ask. "Or something?"

She's hesitant but I don't understand why. Does she not want to join me?

"I'm not really dating right now, Vincent." She's looking everywhere but at me.

"Lucy, if you're not interested you can say that," I tell her. "I won't' be offended." And I won't be. If she's not interested, then she isn't. But if there was a possibility that she was…

"Remember I told you…I don't lie," she reminds me. "So when I say I'm not dating, there's no smoke and mirrors."

"Does not dating mean you're not eating anymore?" I smirk and she glares at me. "Breakfast among friends?"

"We're friends now?" she asks, taken by surprise.

"Well, maybe the past few weeks were rocky," I admit. "But friendship is a good starting point."

"Friends," she repeats. She's thinking about it, I can see those wheels turning in her head. She looks cute when she's pensive. "Okay, yeah. But can we raincheck on the breakfast or something?"

"Yeah." I smile. "I'll go check in and let everyone know you're okay."

"I'd appreciate it." She smiles.

"I'll see you soon, Lucy," he says.

I'm out the door, sending Dawn a text letting her know Lucy is safe and sound in her studio. Lucy will likely be getting quite an earful from Dawn about the entire ordeal. And very likely getting chewed out about the car situation. Dawn isn't known for letting things go.

But I for one, I'm looking forward to the opportunity to get to know Lucy better.

CHAPTER 12

VINCENT, THEN

The next day, I'd promised Mom and Dad I'd stop by and finally make an appearance. Technically, I needed to stop in regardless and return the swatches and paint samples Mom loaned Dawn during the remodel of her shop.

"Anyone home?" I ask as I open the door and step inside.

"Out back!" I hear my mom call out. I pass through the hallway, through the kitchen, and into the green room out back. I'm surprised by the influx of boxes I'd passed along the way.

"You guys were serious about moving back to Beaufort, weren't you?" I laugh.

"Of course we were." Mom looks at me, surprised. She comes over to greet me properly. Which, by her standards, involves a longer than necessary embrace, cutting off my circulation. "Let me look at you!" She pulls away, looking me over.

"Mom, this is a bit excessive, don't you think?" I'm trying to move out of her hold, but she's got a grip on me.

"Well, if you came around more often, then I wouldn't have to do be this way," she rebuts. She's staring me down, analyzing in the weird way she does. "Something different about you."

"Nothing really changed, Mom." I laugh. "Work. The move. Same old."

"No, something's definitely different," she insists.

"If you figure it out, let me know." I laugh. "But here, Dawn is done with these samples. I wanted to make sure they made it back to you."

"Thank you." Mom smiles. "She said the pictures turned out incredible from the opening night."

My interest is piqued. Lucy finished with the pictures this week. So quick? "You look surprised," Mom notes.

"Oh? I just didn't realize Lucy could get them all done so quick," I tell her. Mom smirks at me.

"Lucy, huh?" Mom's eyeing me, making me nervous.

"Quit staring at me like that, Mom," I tell her.

"Am I making you nervous?" She laughs. "Or does the mention of this Lucy make you nervous?" Oh jeez. Was I really this transparent in my developing feelings for Lucy? "It is her! Vincent, you've finally met someone?"

"I wouldn't go as far as to say that," I tell her, an attempt to calm her down a bit.

"Well, how would you describe it? Because I can't begin to remember the last time the mere mention of a woman made you become so unhinged!" She's smiling.

"There's nothing going on," I tell her. "Lucy isn't dating anyone."

"Well, she could date you," Mom teases. "Then she'd be dating someone."

"No." I laugh. "She said she isn't dating at all."

"And you're leaving it there? Just like that?" She raises an eyebrow.

"Well, no," I admit. "I figure friendship is a starting point."

"The best relationships develop from friendships." Mom smiles. "What's she like?"

"She's incredible, Mom. She's beautiful, yes, but there's so much more about her." I sit down. "She's kind, talented, funny. She's stubborn as all hell. It's like everyone who meets her gravitates toward her, and she doesn't even realize it." Mom laughs.

"Oh, Vincent." Mom's eyes are tearing up. "She sounds incredibly special. And she must be to bring you back to life."

"I'm scared, Mom," I admit.

"There's no reason to be." Mom reaches out and takes my hand.

"But Charlie," I tell her. She understands.

"Sweetheart, she would want you to be happy," Mom assures me. "She'd want to you live your life. You're young and have so much more to experience and live for. And it does not mean you're forgetting her by moving forward."

"You don't know that." I shake my head.

"I know that for certain," Mom tells me. "Once upon a time I felt the exact same way as you when I lost someone dear to me. But I got the closure I needed."

"How's that?" I ask her.

"Well, I could tell you, but the skeptic in you doesn't believe in it," Mom teases.

"Oh god, Mom." I roll my eyes. "Someone fooled you too?"

"No." Mom is adamant. "I'm not naïve, sweetheart. I know there are people out there who will exploit your pain. I know it. I've encountered it. But the person who helped me? The real deal."

"I doubt it, Mom," I tell her.

"Well," she starts. "We're moving back to Beaufort. If that family is still around, maybe I can see if their family gift has continued to be passed down."

"Oh, an inherited gift, is it?" I ask. Of course, I don't believe a word of this. And if that family is still in town, I'd be curious to see who filled my mom's head with nonsense.

"You'll see." Mom laughs. "Will you be at the dinner tomorrow?" Shit, I'd forgotten.

"I'm not sure," I tell her. She groans. "I have to be on sight to oversee a project in Savannah. I'll try to make it but no promises, Mom."

"I understand." She smiles. "Do what you can. Even if it's just for dessert. We'd all love to see you."

"You got it," I promise.

And I do just that. I do what I can to get out of Savannah and head back to Beaufort in time to see everyone. I'd even thought if I got there early enough, maybe I could find and spend some time with Lucy. She'd rain checked our "dinner or something" but I sensed for her it was indefinite. And if I didn't get something concrete planned, I felt she'd be hiding behind her "I don't date" crap forever.

I pull up to the house, hoping I didn't miss it all.

"Hello? Mom? Dad?" I call out as I step inside. I make it through the house and into the dining room, looking around the room to greet everyone. I do a double take when I see Lucy. She's here? They invited her. Why wouldn't they tell me? I can't help the smirk forming on my face knowing I now don't have to track her down. And she can't avoid me now.

"Vincent, you made it!" Mom comes over to pull me into a tight hug. Here we go again with her cutting off my circulation.

"I'll go grab another plate," Lucy offers and gets up before anyone can stop her. She's headed for the kitchen. I say my hello's as I pass through and follow her in. I'm doing my best to ignore the knowing looks I'm getting from Kyle as I pass by. She turns around, plate in hand but I'm close. Maybe too close. She's anxious.

"Lucy," I greet her. "I knew we'd be getting together soon for breakfast or something, but if you'd just wanted to skip straight to meeting my family you could've just told me."

"You're funny." She rolls her eyes. "Your sister invited me. It would be rude to say no."

"If I knew you'd be here, I'd have tried to get away sooner to be here," I tell her. Though I wonder if she's comfortable with how open I'm being in divulging how I'm feeling. Should I not?

"Kyle said that actually," she teases. Oh great. I could only begin to imagine what they said about me while I wasn't here.

"Oh god, what else did he say?"

"Not much more than that," she says. "I'm good at changing the subject." I laugh. She is very good at that, I'll admit.

"I do wish I'd come sooner," I admit. I notice a loose strand of hair and can't help myself. I'm reaching out to gently tuck it in place behind her ear. I feel electricity surging around us. A force is pulling us together, and it's harder to fight it. I'm trying to fight the urge I suddenly feel to kiss her. She licks her bottom lip, and the movement catches my attention immediately. I'm leaning in…not thinking I could get much closer than I already was.

"Hey guys, what's taking so long?" Dawn suddenly barges in, and the trance is broken. I can't help but groan, frustrated by the interruption. Her eyes widen at what she just possibly interrupted. "I'm so sorry!" She's apologizing profusely. "Carry on!" she squeals and bolts out of the kitchen. I'll never hear the end of this now.

"Saved by the Dawn." She laughs nervously.

"Were we though?" I ask. Was she truly relieved we were interrupted?

"I don't even know to be honest," she admits. "But it is getting late. I should start to head out."

"If you're heading out, I'm driving you," I tell her. She's not walking. Not from all the way out here. "You'll argue. I'll argue. You'll get in the truck."

"Why are you so sure that I'll get in?" She's challenging me, narrowing her eyes at me.

"Because no one would enjoy the walk that waits for them this late at night in an area that's new…unless you come up this way all the time?" I meet her challenge.

"I really don't like getting in cars," she whispers. I don't fully understand it. Not yet. But I don't want her to feel uncomfortable.

"I get it," I tell her. "I may not understand why, but I get it makes you uncomfortable. I'll go slow, okay? Please humor me and let me do this?"

She looks uncertain.

"Alright, let's go," she says. At some point I'd taken her hand in mine, and I'm relieved she's yet to let it go. We're holding hands as we enter the dining room to bid everyone goodnight.

"Do you really have to go so soon?" Mom asks both of us.

"I want to make sure Lucy gets home okay," I tell everyone.

"We just bet you do," Kyle coughs under his breath. He isn't subtle. We heard him. He's made it awkward and earned himself a smack on the back of his head by Mom.

"Take some dessert," Mom says. She doesn't give us much of a choice in the matter. She's already packing up slices of cake—several in fact—for us to take.

The ride back is awkward initially. We're riding in silence. She's mainly staring out of the window.

"Did you have a good time tonight?" I ask. I'm hoping to break some of the awkward tension.

"I did." She smiles.

"Hopefully they didn't give you too hard of a time, "I tell her.

"It wasn't too bad," she admits.

"Not too bad?" I tease. I dread what they said when I wasn't there.

"Your family cares a great deal for you," she tells me, turning to look at me.

"They're just protective," I say. "But they can be extreme."

129

"I think they just want to see you as happy as they are," she says. "You're lucky to have them, Vincent."

I can't help but smile. I truly do feel lucky to have them.

"I didn't realize it was just you in town…" I told her. "That your mom left when you were younger."

"I don't remember her all that much," she admits. "Here and there a postcard will pop up, but I think they're intended for Gran. It's been 10 years since I got anything though. Gran raised me."

"Where's your Gran?" I ask.

"She passed away 10 years ago," she responds.

"Oh, I'm sorry!" I reach out to take her hand in mine, giving her a reassuring squeeze. It's all I can do while I'm driving.

"It was a long time ago," she tells me.

"I feel no matter how much time passes, it doesn't get easier," I say. I think of Charlie when I say this. Time doesn't make it easier. But I was trying. Or, starting to.

"You're right, it doesn't," she agrees. We finally make it to the pathway leading to her house. She hasn't made it a point to leave and neither have I. I turn the engine off and turn to look at her.

"What happened to her?" I ask.

"Car accident, "she says. "Though official reports confirm she had a heart attack before the accident."

"I'm so sorry, Lucy," I say. I recall Betty mentioning Lucy hasn't driven since the car accident. "Was she driving?"

"No," she says quietly. She takes a breath as she looks at me. She's bracing herself for what she's about to say next. "I was behind the wheel. We'd gone out driving, exploring different places for me to take photos of. It was a thing we did. She'd suddenly called out in pain or shock, I don't know…and lost consciousness. I'd seen something on the road. It all happened so fast. The car swerved—almost like something was pulling the steering wheel forcefully off the road and the truck went through the guardrail and into the river."

"But you made it out," I say. I'm almost saying this for my own sake.

"I honestly have no idea how I made it out," she says.

"You don't know?" I ask, surprised.

"I really don't," she admits.

"Maybe someone got to you? Before you were fully submerged?" I am thinking aloud here. I wasn't there so her recollection would be as good a guess.

"I was fully submerged." She looks away. "I remember being stuck. I remember the water completely entering the truck before it all went dark. Then I was laying partially in the river, partially on the grass, no one was there."

"You remember it?" I ask, shocked.

"Vividly," she admits.

"This is why you won't drive?" I suddenly understand. Her traumatic near-death experience has clearly made her fearful of getting into a car. It all makes sense to me now.

"Partially," she admits.

"And the other reason?" I ask.

"Truthfully I don't trust myself behind the wheel," she tells me. "I thought I saw something on the road. But they claim no one was there." There's silence. Neither of us said anything, possibly unsure of what to say with how serious of a turn our conversation went.

You are the dancing queen
Young and sweet
Only seventeen

We both jump, taken aback by the fact that not only is music suddenly blaring through the truck but that there's anything at all considering I had turned the truck off as soon as we pulled up. I'm too focused on the fact that of all things to be blaring, it's ABBA. AGAIN. What is with this song?!

"What the hell?" I ask, trying to push at the buttons to turn it off.

I'm trying to figure out how to shut it off when Lucy's suddenly out the truck and practically running up the pathway. Where the hell is she going? I'm rushing out, trying to catch up to her, calling her name.

"I need to get home," she tells me, not turning around.

"Wait." I finally catch up and lightly catch her arm. "Look, I know that was weird, but we don't have to end the night."

"You mean your truck doesn't usually start playing random music when it's turned off?" She's making a joke. Or I hope she's joking. She's joking, right? Was the truck turned off? I hadn't noticed.

"I wanted to grab my camera," she admits.

"And do what?" I laugh. It's late at night.

"What most people do with cameras…" she states as if it's the most obvious thing in the world.

"Far be it from me to disrupt creative processes," I joke. "But do you need to do this now? Look, Mom sent dessert, do you want to have some before we call it a night?"

"Raincheck?" she asks. But I don't want another raincheck. I want to make plans with her.

"How about tomorrow night I come by, and we hang out?"" I offer.

"You seem intent on getting into my house, Henry." She crosses her arms. But she misunderstood me.

"We can go anywhere, Lucy," I tell her. "I just want to spend time with you. Get to know you."

"As friends," she tries to clarify.

"It is a good starting point." I smirk.

"Okay fine," she agrees. And at that moment, the music stops. We both glance over at the truck.

"So weird," I say, shaking my head.

"Right." She shrugs. "Weird."

I'm eager for the next day to arrive as it means Lucy and I will finally spend time together. I can't tell if my inability to fall asleep in the urge for time to speed up already or if my sudden insomnia is at all related to Lucy sharing her past with me. What happened to her was tragic. And her story shook me to the core. I wasn't sure how much I'd believed her seeing something in the road. But I would be lying if I didn't admit my blood ran cold when she'd described the sudden pull of the steering wheel. It paralleled too close to the driver's story who had hit Charlie that night. What were the chances of something like that truly happening? Some forces at work conspiring. And to do what? I shake my head at the thought and berate myself for even momentarily entertaining the possibility of there being truth to such a thing.

Surprisingly, Lucy doesn't cancel on me, and we have an incredible time just talking and learning about each other. In fact, we begin to make it a point to connect by phone on days we miss each other or when I'm not in town.

I'm noticing the subtle changes overall in my day to day. I'm not as tense. I'm not as quick to anger. I'm hopeful. More and more I look forward to simply hearing from Lucy and how she's doing, trying my hardest not to be anxious at the thought of her walking alone when I'm not around. A few months had passed in this way. We were still in this limbo of in a relationship but Lucy's straight up denial of calling it what it was. It was cute how she tried avoiding it. But the reality was, we were in a relationship. Whatever made her hesitant, I respected her boundaries. And I didn't push any boundaries.

Eventually I told her about Charlie. Her compassion and understanding toward the situation, the lack of judgement, made me feel so much more strongly for her. I didn't think I'd feel this way about anyone again.

I'm in Beaufort for the day, hoping to catch Lucy and have a late lunch when Dawn calls.

"Double date tonight, brother dear," Dawn tells me. There's no greeting, nothing. Just demanding Dawn, as usual.

"I can cook," I offer. I know Lucy hates crowds. The reason behind it she'd yet to share with me. I sense there's a part of herself she's keeping from me, but I'm trying to respect that, with time, she'll let me in and stop hiding.

"Nah, let's go out!" Dawn says. I'm reluctant to agree, but I figure I can offer the idea to Lucy, and she can say no. "I'll send you the address."

"I'll talk to Lucy," I tell her.

"She'll agree." But before I can say more, she hangs up. I'm waiting in the courtyard for Lucy. She doesn't know I'm here. But her studio door is locked. I would've gone to her cottage but the "work in progress" sign is up, indicating she is here. I wait half an hour before the door opens and Lucy steps out with her client. Her client looked as though she'd been crying. I wonder what that's about.

Lucy notices me right away and smiles.

"Do you usually lock your door during sessions?" I ask.

"Every time," she tells me. "I like to respect their privacy." I follow her inside. Nothing looks out of the ordinary. I want to ask why her client was crying but I feel that's intrusive, so I don't.

"Did you want to grab dinner tonight? Dawn has been pestering me for a possible double date," I ask her.

"There's that word again." She rolls her eyes.

"What other way would you describe what we're doing?" I laugh but then realize I know exactly how she'd describe it. It's not funny anymore. "Never mind, I know how you would."

"You're not happy with me," she states. She's not asking.

"It's not that, Lucy," I assure her. "I guess I just don't understand what it is that holds you back. It's been an amazing couple of months. What's so different if there were real labels and exclusivity attached to it?"

She looks deep in thought, trying to find the right words to say. She's looking around, something catching her eye behind me. I look back, but there's nothing there. And she's back to focusing on me just as quickly. Odd.

"I don't have a good dating history, Vincent," she tells me. "I couldn't rely on those I've dated in the past."

"I don't think you need me to tell you that I'm not them, Lucy." I take her in my arms, offering her what I hope is a sense of comfort. "You set the pace for this, always. Hell, I'm easing into this as well for my own reasons, you know that. But I don't want to hide how I feel or what my intentions are." She tightens her hold on me, her gesture trying to convey the words she cannot speak. "Hey, how about a photoshoot?" I suggest. She'd yet to take a photo of me and while I normally prefer not to, it could be fun to lighten the mood. She looks at me, surprised at the suggestion and is again looking behind me at something for a split second.

"Alright, hot shot," she says. "Take a seat." She changes the backdrop.

"You know, one of these days we should set something up for new head shots for me and the guys. New marketing for the construction business couldn't hurt," I say. It's not a terrible idea.

"Whatever you want," she says. "Just let me know when and we'll make a plan." She starts taking some shots.

"Let's see…" I come over, leaning over her to see what she's got. I'm close. Her body stiffens for a moment, she's tilting her head in acknowledgement to something I'm not privy to. Her demeanor has changed, and I'm curious if she's okay. I could've sworn she did a side glare but at what, I have no clue.

"You okay, Lucy?" I ask her, making sure she's okay.

"I'm great," she tells me and continues showing me some shots she'd taken.

"Here keep pressing this button here." She shows me what to do and walks over to her desk. She's sorting through things as though she's looking for something. I wonder why she needs to do that now out of all times.

"Lucy, these are incredible." I smile over at her.

"Hey, Vincent," she says. "Would you mind grabbing me a coffee from Betty's?"

"Sure thing," I tell her, carefully placing the camera down. "Anything specific?"

"She knows my usual." She smiles.

I head across the courtyard to get her coffee. It's not a bad idea. I could use a cup myself.

I head into Betty's and, as usual, am greeted with her pleasant smile.

"Vincent, dear." Betty smiles. "What can I get you?"

"Hot coffee, small for me, and I'm told you know Lucy's usual coffee order?" I ask. Betty looks thoughtful for a moment.

"Is it one of those days?" she asks. I'm not sure what she means.

"Maybe," I tell her. She looks sad. It doesn't take long for everything to be ready and I'm heading back to Lucy's studio. Her back is to the door when I come back in, and I assume she's on the phone as I hear her say, "I know how this goes."

"How what goes?" I ask. She turns around to look at me. I noticed the AirPod in her ear. So she was on the phone, figures.

"Got to go," she says and takes the AirPod out of her ear. "Just a movie."

"Got your coffee." I handed it to her. She steps closer to take it and surprises the hell out of me with a kiss on my cheek. It lingers…the feel of her lips on my skin.

"Betty asked if it was one of those days." I laugh. "I wasn't sure what she meant but said maybe."

"It's one of those days," she confirms. Was she upset? Did the phone call not go well?

"Want to talk about it?" I offer, but she shakes her head no. "How about that date?"

"Why not?" She gives in. I guess we were going on a double "date" tonight. I was admittedly anxious, given the fact Dawn insisted on going out rather than staying in. Would Lucy be open to that?

I arrived to pick her up on time and am blown away by how incredible she looks.

"You look beautiful," I tell her, leaning in to give her a kiss on the cheek. Safe territory.

"Not overdressed?" she asks. She doesn't know where we're headed.

"Not overdressed," I promised her. "You're perfect."

"And you still won't tell me where we're going?" she tries again.

"Nope." I smirk. I led her to the truck.

"I don't think I've ever been on a date where I had no clue where it would actually be," she tells me.

"So you're admitting it's a date." I laugh. She rolls her eyes at me.

"Don't dwell on it, Henry," she tells me.

I open the passenger door for her when we finally reach the truck.

"Short ride?" she asks, hopeful.

"It's just outside of Beaufort, Lucy," I tell her. "I think you'll like it."

"Hmph," she grunts and crosses her arms.

The ride is calm. We enjoy the silence, and I enjoy the scenery.

"You know," I finally say. "I think I've just realized you won't look straight ahead."

She looked surprised.

"Just now?" she asks.

"Yeah," I admit. "Is it connected to your past accident?"

"I told you," she says. "I don't trust what I see when looking out a car window."

"Because you saw something on the road that night," I recall her saying.

"Right," she tells me. "Can you imagine if that happened again, even as a passenger, and I caused another accident by freaking out?"

"But Lucy," I start. I'm trying to find the right words. "They told you there was no one on the road that night."

"That they could see," she mumbles, but I heard her clearly and glance at her for a moment.

"You don't think you saw…a…spirit or whatever, do you?" I ask. She's not answering but I sense her staring.

"Or whatever?" she asks.

"You know what I mean," I say. We stop at a red light.

"I don't know what I think about that night, Vincent," she says truthfully. "Could it have been? Maybe. Could I have imagined it? They like to think so. I don't know to say one way or the other what it truly could have been."

"Lucy, you have to know that stuff isn't real," I tell her softly. The sound of a horn behind us startles me, bringing my attention to the now green light. I start on our path again. She doesn't respond. "Right?"

"I don't want to talk about this right now Vincent," she says, looking away. I feel maybe I've offended her. But I'm failing to understand how something like this would be offensive. We could have different beliefs, sure. But this felt different, and I wanted to understand.

"I'm sorry," I say. She's not looking at me. She's avoiding me, and I feel like an ass. A few moments later, I'm parking the truck. "I hope you like Italian food." I smile. She's smiling but it doesn't reach her eyes. She's forcing it. Was this a bad call?

"I love Italian," she says.

"It was Dawn's idea," I admit. "I thought we could do something together at home, in town. I know you prefer that. But she seemed to insist."

"Interesting and thoughtful of her," she says. "Shall we?"

I come around the passenger door to help her out and lead our way to the entrance where Miles and Dawn are already waiting.

"We're so glad you two could join us!" Dawn exclaims.

"Dawn, Miles," she greets. "Good to see you." She's staring at the doors to the restaurant like she's afraid of them.

"Shall we?" Miles offers. She's just starting at the doors, unmoving. I wrap my arm around her, bringing her focus back. She takes a shaky breath, and we go inside while Dawn checks us in for the reservation. Lucy's suddenly wobbly, losing her balance, and I catch her.

"Are you okay?" I ask. She's saying she is, but I can see she's not. She looks overwhelmed and like she's in pain. She's cringing and taking deep breaths. What the hell?

"Hello and welcome. I'm Hailey, and I'll be your waitress this evening," our waitress says. "Can I start anyone off with drinks?"

Dawn, Miles, and I order. Lucy's remained silent.

"I'm sorry, what was that?" she asks as we try to get her attention.

"Anything to drink?" Hailey asks.

"Water please," she tells her.

Eventually Hailey is back to take orders. But as soon as she's gone, Lucy's excusing herself from the table. She bolts to the restrooms. Is she sick?

"I should go check on her," I say.

"No, no," Dawn insists and stands up, not giving me more of a fighting chance. "This is all my fault. I'll be right back." She takes off.

"What's her fault?" I ask Miles, confused.

"No clue." Miles laughs.

Eventually they both come back, and the food is served. Lucy doesn't look any better.

"So, any plans for Thanksgiving, Lucy?" Dawn asks.

"I usually stay in," Lucy tells her. She's staring down at her plate but barely touching anything.

"Oh, say you'll join us this year?" Dawn pleads. Thanksgiving is over a month away.

"Don't feel like you have to, Lucy," I assure her, reaching out to take her hand, giving her a squeeze. I'm trying to silently express my concern. Maybe we should leave if she's not feeling well.

"Why wouldn't you want your girlfriend over for Thanksgiving?" Dawn asks.

"Lucy isn't my girlfriend," I say, though I wish it were not the case.

"Wait what?" Dawn asks. "You've been going out practically for months. I figured that distinction was applied."

"He just got me to agree to the fact we're dating," Lucy chimes in. I can't help but laugh. The admission. "What's meant to be will be."

"She'll come around eventually." I smirk.

"Lucy, is that you?" We all look to the side to see Clara, the owner of the florist shop in town. We have a town florist. Good to know.

"Hi Clara," Lucy greets her.

"How are you, dear?" she asks.

"I'm well, and you?" Lucy is being polite. You can tell it's a bit forced.

"Oh good, good," she says. She's awkwardly looking around the table and finally introduces herself. Though Dawn already knows Clara.

"You don't have your camera with you," Clara says suddenly. Why would that matter? I'm sure the restaurant has a photographer who circles around offering to take photos of the guests. She could go to them. Why Lucy?

"I'm out for dinner tonight, Clara," Lucy tells her. The kindness leaves her tone quickly. "I don't make it a habit of bringing my equipment."

"Of course." She nods in understanding, but I can see she wants to press the matter further.

"If you call the studio, we can set up a time for you to come in," Lucy states.

"Come, Clara," the gentleman with her urges her. He gets the hint. She does not. "Let's leave everyone to their meal."

"Right." She sighs. "I'll talk to you soon, Lucy." She's urged along.

"Well, that was odd." Miles laughs. "You really are in high demand, Lucy."

"What can I say?" She laughs.

"Do townsfolk truly think you'll bring your equipment with you when you're off the clock?" I ask, surprised by the incident. It was all bizarre.

"More often than you'd think," she tells me.

When we're done, we head outside, and Miles and I agree we'll each bring the cars around so the girls don't have to walk. While it's not too cold of a night, there is a breeze, and it looks like rain is coming.

Once more, we're en route. I can see a shift in Lucy the further away we are from the restaurant.

"You doing okay, Lucy?" I ask. "You seemed really out of it throughout dinner."

"I know, I'm sorry," she apologizes. "I really don't do well in crowds."

"You weren't kidding." I laugh. "But you're okay now?"

"Much." She smiles. And we sit in comfortable silence until make it back to the pathway to her cottage. She knows at this point there's no question of will I or won't I be walking her up. It's a given. We walk hand in hand together on the lit pathway to the door.

"I'd invite you in, but I do feel I should rest after tonight's exciting events," she says.

"You'll be okay on your own?" I double check. She stares at me, overcome with an emotion I can't quite place. But suddenly, I feel her tugging on my collar, pulling me down until I feel her soft lips form with mine.

I'm surprised at first but then respond immediately. I feel like my entire body is alight with an electric current. Feeling a bit bold, my tongue cautiously seeks entrance, and she grants it immediately. A fire erupts and we're closer together than I thought possible. My hand snakes around her waist to get her even closer. The other, on its own accord, weaves into her hair. I feel her arms secure their spot around my neck. We move together with perfect synchrony. Quite literally, I could kiss her forever.

Eventually, she pulls away.

"Well shit," she says, gasping for breath.

"Not very lady like," I tease her. "Not that I'm complaining, but what brought that on?"

"I just want to show you how much you mean to me," she tells me. "And how much it means to me how you've been there for me, being patient with me."

"Always, Lucy." I lean in to kiss her softly on the lips. "You should get inside, get some rest."

"Good idea," she says. Neither of us make a point to move away. We're stealing more kisses until I can see the exhaustion creeping in on her face.

Reluctantly, she pulls away and opens the door to step inside.

"Goodnight, Lucy," I tell her and start to walk back the lit pathway to my truck. I occasionally look back at her, smiling when I see she's looking my way. I realize, in that moment, that I may be falling in love with Lucy Adams.

CHAPTER 13

LUCY

I'm sitting in the studio with Helen. She helps run the town library—has done so for the last 10 years. I'd learned through the grapevine she had recently lost a close cousin. This week she'd called to set up a last-minute session *just because*. She doesn't know that I realize immediately what her true intentions are for this session. She's the last scheduled for today. She shares the same goal as the others I'd worked with today: connecting with a spirit. They don't say it—almost fearful—when I view them, the news that no one has come through. It's almost as though they believe it will happen every single time. They don't realize or understand it's potentially a good thing if no one comes through. It means their loved ones may have crossed over…they're at peace. And that disappointment I see on their faces sends one silent message—they doubt me.

It's the same with Helen, much to her dismay. No one has come through.

"You're sure there's no one?" she asks. She's doubtful, unsure.

"I'm sure, Helen," I tell her truthfully.

"But it worked when Susan came," she suddenly states. "Emma, too."

"What are you trying to say, Helen?" I place my camera down carefully to the side.

"How do I know you're not picking and choosing who to help?" she says. She doesn't look like she means what she is saying.

"Do you believe I'd lie and not share a message?" I ask, hoping she doesn't believe I would do such a thing.

"I'm not saying you would, Lucy," she says. "I don't know what I'm saying. Maybe Clara's confusing me."

"Clara?" I ask. I dread to think what she tells me next in connection to Clara.

"Yes...she's been pretty angry you haven't taken a photo for her," Helen shares with me. I try to watch my words. I tend to steer away from unnecessary drama. I'm uncomfortable hearing Clara's been saying unpleasant things about me...my abilities. It was very unlike her. She's usually very happy and kindhearted. Even after losing her loved one a couple months ago, she'd never acted in this way. Something wasn't quite the same with her and it made me uneasy.

"Right," I speak. I don't quite have the words. I'm not sure how to even process this information.

"Helen," I start. "As much as I want to, whether spirits come through or not is beyond my control. But I can say, if someone were to come through for you or anyone else, there is no reality where I would withhold that information. You deserve closure. Spirits deserve to be heard and to have their chance to move on and be at peace."

"So someone not coming through is not a bad thing?" She's hopeful.

"It could mean they're already at peace," I tell her. "I would never disrespect you or your loved ones in that way."

"I'm so sorry, Lucy." Helen looks down. "I don't know what's going on with you and Clara. But I'm so sorry it made me doubt you. So sorry."

I walk her out shortly after. I don't have much more to say. It would be a lie to say it was okay. It wasn't. It was offensive. It was hurtful. I felt betrayed. My feelings are mixed up all over the place. If I'm honest, it all feels too much and is weighing heavily on my mind.

I don't blame people for being skeptical or having doubts. But at the core of it all, I'm not posting neon signs inviting people to come to me if they want to connect with their loved ones who have passed on. People in this town who know my family's history and of my family's ability...they always seek me out. They come to me. They use me. "Exploit me" as Sarah had said. And I give them what they want even though I really would just like to focus on my business. But it all ends up circling back to my family legacy and my need to make sure I made my gran proud. How could I let her down—let my family down—by not being the connection between the spirit realm and the living? Who else could? Who else would not take advantage of the pain of others?

And then, I let my mind go there. To Betty's suggestion: my mother.

My mother...who had abandoned me when I was a little girl. I hardly remember her, if I am being honest. I don't know or understand the circumstances around her leaving. All I feel when it came to her was abandonment. I have no clue if she could do what Gran and I could. But I know the possibility was strong. And I can't help but wonder if the expectations and pressures of this town made her leave. But then why not take me with her?

Over the years, Mom would send occasional letters at times, but never addressed who they were for. To me? To Gran? I wasn't sure who she was sending them to. But it had been 10 years since a card came through.

I'd kept a box with all those letters and postcards at my house. I feel at the very least, maybe I should finally suck it up and go through all of it. Perhaps she isn't far away from Beaufort and I can finally reach out to her. Get answers?

I haven't thought that far ahead but figure there was always a starting point. And as I'm getting ready to lock up, my phone is vibrating, letting me know I have a message.

Might be able to come by before 5 if that works for you -Vincent

Crap.

For a moment, I forgot we had plans before Vincent left for Savannah.

Sounds good. I'll see you.

I worry as I walk home that I won't be able to hide how upset I truly am after today's events. How hurt I am. And I desperately want to confide in Vincent. I want him to know all about me. It's this that makes me realize that I need to tell him. But I fear as soon as I do, that'll be it for us.

The walk home feels like it went by faster than it normally does, and I have half an hour or so before he can get here. I figure I could at least find that box I'd hidden away and put it aside for later.

It doesn't take long—surprisingly—to find where I'd hidden it away. I put the box behind me so I can position everything back to its original place. I close the closet door and turn around to pick up the box of letters only to find it's not where I left it. Annoyed, I'm looking around trying to see where it moved to. I'm looking under the couch, in my bedroom, in the dining room. Nothing.

I move into the kitchen and see it. In the trashcan, protruding out.

"Seriously?" I say aloud. I don't know if I'm talking to Charlie or if I'm talking to Gran. Because whoever moved it isn't making themselves visible to me, and that's annoying as all hell. I try taking it out but am met with a strong force trying to keep the box in its new place.

"I think we know I'm just as stubborn!" I say through gritted teeth. "I'm not giving up."

The tug of war continues. Whoever is keeping this box from me isn't winning, but then I'm not either.

"Oh, come on!" I scream. "This is juvenile!"

"What's going on in here?" I hear Vincent laughing behind me. But I won't let his appearance deter me. If anything, I'm more determined than ever to get this box and hold on to it for the sole purpose of protecting it from another relocation.

"I didn't hear you come in," I say over my shoulder.

"I did knock, I promise," he tells me, coming to step to my side. "I heard you scream so I came inside thinking something was wrong. But it's a trash incident?"

"I'm trying to get the box out," I tell him.

"Why did you throw it out if you needed it?" He laughs.

"I didn't," I tell him. "It ended up in the trash can, but I need it out."

"Let me." He reaches over to grab it, and I figure, why not. Let him play tug of war for a while. I move around him and take a seat on the kitchen counter. He has a smug look on his face as though he thinks this will be super easy and he'll have it out in less than a second. But the smug look disappears when he's tugging and it's not budging. And quite frankly, it's an otherwise empty trash bag. So there was nothing for it to be stuck on. "What the hell?" he grumbles.

I cross my arms.

"Did you think it would be simple?" I laugh.

"Kinda?" He smiles but is unsure. He's confused. I look past him and see Gran. Ah, so not Charlie. Gran is keeping me from these letters. She's determined and focused with her arms crossed. "What's in the box anyway?"

"Letters and postcards my mother used to send over the years," I tell him. He looks surprised.

"She's kept in touch?" he asks. He lets go of the box. Gran looks smug, like she thinks she's won.

"She's sent letters. I've never opened them," I tell him. "But I intend on going through them one way or another." The second bit is more intended for Gran who doesn't look pleased.

"Why now?" he asks, coming over to me and stepping between my legs, placing his hands on either side of my waist. With Gran here, it feels weird to be in such a position. I try to ignore her. But it's hard. He can sense my discomfort and makes to move, but I stop him, wrapping my legs around him to keep him in place. I hug him and use this moment to raise a challenging eyebrow at Gran. She takes the hint, though, and vanishes. For now.

"I guess I'm hoping there's answers in those letters," I tell him as I pull back. He cups my cheek, offering me comfort. And I do feel comforted. For the first time all day, I feel at ease.

"You're looking to see why she left?" he asks.

"I just want to understand why," I tell him. "See what she was feeling that made her want to leave."

"You've never opened them before," he determines. I shake my head no.

"I never cared before," I admit. "I'm not saying suddenly I care and want to rekindle some mother-daughter relationship. But maybe reading those letters with give me some clarity."

"Do you want me here when you read them?" he asks.

"I think it's something I need to do on my own," I admit. However, I feel if I do get my hands on those letters, Gran won't be far behind and maybe...maybe she'll let me communicate with her once and for all.

"Should I leave?" he offers, though I can see he hopes I'll say no. And I don't want him to leave.

"I want you here as long as you're able to stay," I tell him. He's looking at me...I sense there's something he wants to say but isn't. There's much I want to say but am not. Which I know can't continue.

"Lucy," he whispers. I almost think I missed it. I look at him, curious. "I..." he starts but stops. He's second guessing whatever it is he wants to say. "I'm going to miss you while I'm in Savannah," he finally says. I smile at him.

"I'm going to miss you, too," I tell him, sincerely.

"I, um, brought some dinner with me in case you were hungry," he tells me, unsure.

"I'm starving." I smile at him. I barely had anything all day and didn't realize it until he mentioned food. He helps me down from the counter and turns his attention again to the trash can, leaning down cautiously to get the box. This time, there is no resistance, and it comes out easily.

"Huh." He stares at it. He's looking into the trash can itself to see what had the box stuck. "It's empty?" He turns to me, surprised.

"Yes," I tell him as if it was the most obvious thing.

"But..." He stops. He's looking back and forth between the box and the trash can. "Okay, that's weird. I thought the music stuff was weird...but this?" I came over to him and take the box.

"What music stuff?" I asked him.

"You remember that night I took you home and that one song from ABBA started playing?" He looks unsure.

"I do," I tell him. "Your truck was turned off. It's hard to forget that happening with no power for your car." I laugh.

"Right." He laughs as well. We're heading into the living room to get more comfortable. "Well, that wasn't the first time 'Dancing Queen' started blaring through my radio." He's got my attention now. That night in the truck was Gran. Her way of sending me a message—a message I had yet to figure out, to be honest. But I assumed it was because of me. But Vincent's experienced this on occasion when I wasn't around...what was Gran doing? What was she trying to communicate?

"I'd also had an incident with my hammer going missing," he tells me.

"Your hammer?" I'm confused.

"Yeah, that first night I drove you home. I was working at Dawn's shop and only called it a night because my hammer went missing," he tells me. "If it hadn't, I wouldn't have seen you walking alone at night and you probably would've stubbornly walked home alone."

I sit back and process what he's telling me. Gran's way of what? Bringing our paths together? I look around the room, but she's not in sight. Or is intending to keep herself unseen.

"You think it's weird, don't you?" he tells me. I've stayed quiet too long. It made him nervous. "It sounds crazy. You don't believe me."

"No, no," I assure him. "I do believe you. I'm not a skeptic, remember?"

"Well, I don't think spirits are behind it." He laughs. I frown. "What, you do?"

"Does it matter what I believe?" I ask.

"Of course, it does." He is trying to assure me. He's reaching for my hand. But I pull away.

"It doesn't matter if you think what I believe in is nonsense, Vincent," I tell him. I stand up and start pacing.

"Lucy, these things have logical explanations," he's trying to tell me.

"So what had my box stuck in the trash can, Vincent?" I ask. He remains silent.

"Ghosts aren't real, Lucy," he tells me. "Even if they were, they're dead. How could they move physical objects?"

"If they haven't crossed over, if their emotions are strong enough, if they're angry or confused enough, they build up energy over time and can manipulate objects," I told him. I'm being truthful. And I'm no longer hiding. He's staring at me.

"You say that as if you know this for a fact," he says.

"Have I ever lied to you?" I ask him. "Would I?"

"No, you wouldn't," he admits. "But this isn't something I can believe."

"Right, because you've been manipulated and fooled one too many times that if the real thing was presented to you, you couldn't bring yourself to open up to that possibility again," I say. He looks confused. I feel he's trying to think back to if he's ever openly said this to me. "The way you speak about psychics made it easy to read between the lines," I told him.

"My mom said to me once that there's a family well known in this town who claim to be able to communicate with spirits," Vincent says. I stop pacing and turn to look at him. Worried she'd told him before I could. "She said that a family member from that known family helped her a long time ago. That she knows she wasn't fooled."

"She mentioned it to me as well," I tell him. "The night of the dinner."

"I'd hoped to find out who this family was," he says. "And now I'm more curious because they've not only fooled my mother long ago, but you as well?"

"What?" I ask, offended.

"I get you're open minded and believe in spirits," he says. "We don't have to believe in the same things. But there shouldn't be people out there taking advantage of others, filling them with false hope and promises. What'd they promise you? Did they claim to reach your gran?"

I can't help it. Tears fill my eyes. Not for what I know will be lost but for its implications for me. About my family. I'm being open without quite literally spelling it out, and he doesn't believe in me.

"No one has ever connected with my gran," I tell him.

"They've convinced you somehow." He shakes his head, trying to figure it out.

Tears are now spilling over. He's on his feet, confused at why I'm crying, and is moving toward me. But I step away from him. "Don't come near me," I speak. He stops, confused.

"That family? The well-known family who can communicate with the other side?" I say through my tears. "That's my family."

He's frozen. He doesn't have words. He's processing.

"Your family," he says.

"Me," I add. I don't know what he's thinking.

"You…" he says quietly. "What are you saying?"

"I'm saying my family, for generations, have been able to communicate in some way with spirits." I'm wiping away my tears. "I'm saying that after my accident, my ability to do the same kicked into high gear and with the right *equipment* I have a way of communicating with them if they have a message to pass along. I'm saying I see spirits almost everywhere I go. That's my reality. My truth."

"Your truth," he repeats. "This is what you've been keeping from me?"

"What?" I ask, confused.

"I could tell there was something you weren't telling me," he says. I can't read his face. I can't tell what he's thinking. He looks detached. "I figured we're getting to know each other. With time, you would tell me. This was it?"

"Yes," I whisper.

"You were keeping the fact that you are just like all those others out there, exploiting the pain of others," he speaks. It's not a question.

"Excuse me?" I say through gritted teeth. I see movement in the corner of my eye and glance to see Charlie is here. And Gran is here. They both look at each other, then at me. They're worried.

"How many people have you fooled?" he demands.

"None," I tell him. He looks angry. "Let's be clear about something. I didn't ask for this." He scoffs, rolling his eyes.

"They all say that," he says. His eyes are full of hate.

"And you're going to listen," I tell him. "I didn't ask for this. I didn't know anything about this until after my accident. My gran never bothered to tell me, and yet after it happened, the people of this town suddenly knew more about what I'm supposed to be capable of doing than I was. But it's my reality. And as much as sometimes I wish I couldn't do what I can do, I've helped many people get closure. I wouldn't change that for anything."

"And how much do you charge, lying to people?" he pushes back.

"Nothing." More rogue tears are falling. I knew he wouldn't take it well. But I don't think my worst-case scenario could have prepared me for this. Quite literally I feel like my heart is being split in two, and it's hard to stay above the surface. "I don't seek people out. They come to me."

"Right." He rolls his eyes. "And I'm sure you want to tell me how you've supposedly seen my wife."

I stare at him. I look back at her. He notices. Of course, he notices.

"Oh please, you want to tell me that now, of all moments, she's here?" He puts his hands on his hips.

"I'm sorry," I say.

"I don't accept," he says, but I cut him off. I wasn't looking at him when I apologized. I was looking at Charlie. Because I warned her if he ever asked, I would not lie. She nods her head in understanding.

"I wasn't talking to you," I tell him. My eyes are now cold. I am aware where the two of us stand moving forward. "I was talking to Charlie."

"This isn't a game you want to play with me, Lucy." His eyes grow cold. Charlie moved from across the room to my coffee table, where my camera is. She's motioning for me to use it. I move to grab the camera. "What the hell are you doing? Now is not the time for this, Lucy."

I ignore him and snap a picture. I look down at it and then up at Charlie again. Only this time, I can hear her.

"I'm so sorry, Lucy," she tells me. "I knew he wouldn't take it well. But I didn't expect this."

"Me either," I tell her.

"You either what?" He's not part of the Lucy-Charlie conversation.

"He was always so, so stubborn." She shakes her head. "Tell him he never knew when to quit while he was ahead. I was always telling him that."

"She says you were always so stubborn," I tell him, looking down. I can't face him. "That you never knew when to quit while you were ahead."

"This isn't funny, Lucy," he tells me. But I won't look at him. Charlie keeps going.

"Tell him to get his head out of his ass. He's always wanted to believe this was possible. He's being presented with the real thing and an opportunity for a new love, and he's ruining it by running his mouth."

"I can't tell him that." I shake my head.

"Yes, you can," she tells me.

"Tell me what," he pushes. I look up at him. He looks so uncertain.

"Charlie says you need to get your head out of your ass," I tell him. His eyes go wide. I don't talk this way, he knows that. "She says you always wanted to believe this type of thing was possible. And she says you are being presented with the real deal and an opportunity for a new love and that by running your mouth, you're ruining it."

"That...that..." He has no words.

"That sounds exactly how I would have spoken to him, and he knows it," she tells me. "I never minced my words. I'm not sorry."

"She never minced her words," I tell him. "She's not sorry."

"How do I know this is even real?" Vincent is confused.

"I would have hoped you knew me well enough by now to know my intentions, in everything that I do, are genuine," I tell him. "That you would know that I understand your history with this very thing to know I wouldn't take it lightly by opening this door to you. That hurting you, especially with this, is not something I would do to you. Ever."

"This can't be real," he whispers.

"The night she died you told me she went out running," I tell him. He looks at me. "But that is all you told me about Charlie directly. She was wearing grey leggings and a matching top with her hair pulled up in a tight ponytail."

"Anyone could have looked that up," he back pedals.

"Okay," I agree. They could have, he's right. "You're right. They could have. But they wouldn't know she had an infinity tattoo on the inside of her left wrist."

"He was with me when I got it," Charlie tells me. "I was such chicken shit about it. I hated needles with passion. But I was determined to get it. So he poured me a couple shots of tequila before we went to the tattoo parlor." She's laughing. "I don't recommend that, by the way."

"She's telling me how much she hated needles," I explain. He doesn't understand why I'm suddenly laughing. "That she was so determined but so scared to go through with it, that you gave her a couple shots of tequila before you two went to the tattoo parlor." He gasps.

"How can you know that?" He wants to believe me, I can see it.

"Because Charlie told me," I tell him.

"You can really see her?" he asks, unsure. "You can hear her?"

"I can," I tell him. "She can hear you."

"I always thought I needed something like this, a way to connect with her one more time, and it would bring me closure," he says.

"But he didn't really need to reach me," Charlie says.

"She says you didn't really need to reach her," I tell him. I'm not sure what she means. "I'm not sure what she means, though."

"He's finally moving on," Charlie tells me. "He's finally happy. That's what I want for him."

"Is she saying something?" Vincent asks, unsure.

"Yeah." I'm looking back and forth between them. "That you didn't really need to connect because you're finally happy. Finally moving on and that's what she wanted for you."

I can't begin to imagine what this must be like for him in this moment. To finally have access to the one thing he'd been desperately searching for. The one thing that brought him constant disappointment and pain. Leaving a wound and only an instinct to be mistrusting and skeptical. He looks down. He looks lost.

"I hope he didn't royally screw his chances with you, Lucy," Charlie says, coming closer to me. "He wasn't thinking when he made those accusations. Please understand. Will you forgive him?"

"I don't know if I can," I tell her, closing my eyes.

"You don't think you can what, Lucy?" Vincent asks. I open my eyes to look at him. I'm fighting the tears which are threatening to form and spill over. He's taking a step closer to me but frowns when I back away. I need him to stay away from me. I'm doing this for Charlie. But also, because I promised myself, I would make sure to finally tell him this part of myself, hopeful he would accept.

"Well, you two are surely perfect for each other." Charlie rolls her eyes. "You two are so stubborn." I glare at her.

"Don't look at me that way." She laughs. "He messed up. Yes. And you don't need to be forgiving today. But don't shut that door. Also, your gran says your mother is in Charlotte, North Carolina. Audrey Adams." She vanishes, breaking the means of communication, and I'm left with just Vincent and that unexpected piece of information about my mother.

"Lucy?" Vincent asks.

"She left," I tell him.

"Left?" He's confused. "As in, crossed over or…"

"No, she's stubborn about crossing over," I tell him. "She just left. She's not here. I don't have more information to pass along."

"This wasn't the first time you've seen her," he surmises.

"It's not," I tell him.

"How come you never told me?" he asks. He doesn't look angry. I figured he would be.

"Because you were so receptive to me finally sharing this part of myself with you," I grumble, and he looks down. He looks regretful. "I didn't tell you because she didn't want me to. And I have to respect that."

"When did you first see her?" he asks.

"Dawn's grand opening," I tell him. "Came through in one of the pictures I took."

"I don't understand," he admits.

"I honestly don't think I have the energy to explain all of this right now to you," I tell him. "I think you should go."

"Lucy," he starts. He's figured out by now I need him to keep a distance. "I—"

"You need to get to Savannah," I tell him. "And I need to be alone."

"Lucy—" He steps forward, closer to me.

"No." I shake my head. "I really need you to leave. We can talk when you come back from Savannah. But right now, I can't be near you." I move to the door and open it, hoping he understands how serious I am.

Several minutes pass. He hasn't made a move to leave, and I'm still standing with the door open, hoping he finally takes the hint and just leaves. I won't look at him. I refuse. I'm barely keeping it together and am fighting back the tears I know are just waiting to push through. He broke my heart.

He must sense I'm not changing my mind because finally, he's moving to the door.

"Lucy," he starts as he crosses the threshold. I won't look at him. "I'm so sorry, Lucy." I say nothing, worried my words will betray me. He looks remorseful. I can see it. But right now, I am guarded and heartbroken. Ever so slowly, I close the door and finally succumb once more to the tears as I sink down to my knees.

CHAPTER 14

VINCENT

I am an idiot. I realize that.

I realize I've completely and royally just screwed up one of the best things that's happened to me in a long time. I'd insulted her. Offended her. Repeatedly. But more so, I recognized, too late, that I had betrayed her.

I could not even begin to rationalize everything. Everything I'd come to believe so strongly in my ever-failing search…everything I'd convinced myself so strongly…*that* was the fabrication. Lucy wasn't a fraud. I gathered that. I understood it. But I couldn't pull my head out of my ass long enough to wrap my mind around what she was trying to tell me. All that was playing in my mind endlessly were the ever failed attempts to connect with Charlie. The lies are all I could see, and they clouded what Lucy was trying to share with me. And now it was too late to take it all back. Regret was hitting me, hard. She couldn't stand the sight of me. She needed space. She needed me gone. And so, the one thing I could give her that she needed, was to leave. I didn't want to. How could I go to Savannah now? I couldn't focus on anything else.

I pick up my phone and call Tyler, our second lead on the current project, right away. On the third ring, he picks up.

"What's up, Vincent?" He's cheerful, in a good mood.

"I need to delay Savannah a day or two," I tell him. I don't greet him. This is urgent. I need time to fix what I surely just broke. "Can you be on site and loop me in until I get there?"

"Hold on." I hear some shuffling on his end. "What's going on? Are you okay?"

"Can you do this for me? Please?" I'm desperate.

"Yeah, man," he tells me. "I've got it handled, don't worry about it. What's going on?"

"I can't explain right now." And where would I begin? "But thank you. Seriously, Tyler."

"Don't sweat it," he assures me. "But let me know what else you need, and it's done, okay?"

"Thank you," I tell him and end the call. I'm headed to Dawn's. I knew she and Lucy had become close friends since moving to Beaufort. If there was any way I could begin to fix my mess, maybe she would help me.

When I get there, I'm surprised to find most of my family is already here.

"Dawn?" I'm knocking on the front door frantically. "Dawn?!" The door opens, and she's looking at me like I've lost my mind, no doubt caught off guard by my abrupt appearance and very likely state of disarray.

"What's going on?" she asks, stepping aside to let me in. "Are you okay?"

"I think I've just royally messed everything up," I tell her. I'm following her into the sitting room.

"Okay, you're scaring me." She pulls me to the couch and as nosy as my family is, of course they have gathered when they saw me. I look like a hot mess, no doubt. "What's going on?"

"I think I screwed up with Lucy," I tell her. "No, scratch that. I did. I screwed up with Lucy, and I don't think I can fix it."

"Oh boy," Sarah says, taking a seat in the love seat across from me. "How'd you screw it up?"

"I don't even know if I have words." I'm shaking my head, thinking back on everything that happened in the short time I'd spent at Lucy's. "I...she...Charlie...spirits."

"Slow down," Miles chimes in. "What about Lucy and Charlie? Did you say spirits?"

"Lucy can communicate with spirits..." I'm finally saying the words out loud. I'm trying to wrap my mind around how that even sounds, coming from me.

"No shit, really?" Kyle exclaims. I frown. He believes it at one go. Why could I not be more open minded with Lucy? She wasn't some wacko I'd randomly met. Even if I didn't believe this to be possible...I could have handled it better for Lucy. Miles looks surprised by this information. Kyle is stoked. And Dawn and Sarah look like this is old news. Did they know?!

"Wait, you knew?" I ask Dawn.

"Yeah, I've known for a while," she tells me.

"I just found out yesterday." Sarah shrugs. "It's legit, though."

"Well, you weren't so quick to believe it," Dawn reminds her. "You did give her a hard time."

"Of course, I gave her a hard time," Sarah says. "If she was ever going to tell Vincent about it, I wasn't about to let another possible fraud trick him. And she isn't a fraud. So there's that."

I groan, dropping my head in my hands.

"How many people know?" I ask.

"The entire town..." Dawn tells me. I looked up at her, surprised.

"It didn't seem like there was much option in that one," Sarah muses aloud. "Apparently her family goes back generations with this gift. So everyone just knows."

"And expect her to be at their beck and call 24/7," Dawn adds. "It's ridiculous the pressure they put on her."

"She didn't tell me any of this," I told them.

"Well, what did she tell you?" Dawn asks. "And why are you here and not with her? I figure you two would have a lot to talk about."

"She told me to leave," I tell them. "I didn't exactly...react well when she told me what she could do."

"You didn't believe her," Sarah guesses.

"Considering your history with this topic, I'm sure Lucy understood why it was hard for you to believe at first," Miles assures.

"Lucy understood that, though." Dawn shakes her head. "She's been trying to figure out how to tell you for the longest time. She was worried how you would react, knowing what you'd been through. She was afraid you'd think she was exploiting your pain and she'd lose you."

Shit. Shit. Shit.

She'd been wanting to be more open and honest with me. She'd been trying to protect me and find a way to approach this cautiously, and this is what I do? She put all her trust in me with her biggest secret, was vulnerable, and I accused her of being a fraud. The opposite of who she really was.

"How *did* you react?" Sarah asks, suspicious. I avoid eye contact. I'm embarrassed and ashamed. I was an asshole.

"Oh god, Vincent." Dawn gathers my silence and takes it for what it is. She understands I seriously screwed up. "What did you do? What did you say?"

"Besides calling her a fraud just like the others? I might've asked how much she charges while fooling and lying to people." I hang my head down in shame.

"Oh no, Vincent," Dawn says softly.

"I'm sure Lucy understood where you were coming from." Kyle is trying to find a silver lining. He's failing. But he's trying.

"Not with this one." Dawn shakes her head.

"How would you know?" Kyle asks. "Maybe there's still hope."

"There was a reason Lucy chose not to date," she tells us. "And her biggest reason of all is she can't be with someone who doesn't believe *in* her. But she let you in Vincent. I'm not sure how you're going to fix this one."

"She's stubborn," Sarah agrees. "Much like you."

"What made you finally believe her?" Miles asks.

"Charlie," I tell them.

"Oh, Charlie showed up again?" Sarah asks.

"You knew she'd been around?" I ask, surprised.

"I don't know much about before," Sarah tells me. "But I know she was enjoying the show between you and Lucy the other night." She giggles. My eyes go wide. She was there?

I think back to how intense Lucy's and my connection became the other night by the fire. And recall one thing leading to another, and we were on the couch until out of nowhere, Lucy screamed in what seemed like surprise. I didn't think anything of it at the time. I figured maybe I went too far too soon. But looking back, she'd been taken off guard and kept looking almost angrily over my shoulder. Could *that* have been why she stopped us? Because Charlie was watching?

"Charlie was watching. She was there?" I ask, surprised.

"Ooh, how much of a show did you two put on?" Kyle asks, wiggling his eyebrows up and down.

"None of your business, Kyle." I shake my head. "Focus, please."

"She was." Dawn laughs. "Lucy read her the riot act after."

"Why wait all this time to tell me she's been around?" I ask. "Lucy said Charlie didn't want me to know, but why?"

"Maybe because you never would have accepted things enough to open your heart to Lucy," Dawn says. "And Charlie wanted you with Lucy."

"She did?" I ask.

"Yeah." Dawn smiles. "But that doesn't solve the situation you're in now. Clearly, you believe it now. But not initially."

"It's a big thing to wrap your mind around, Dawn," I tell her. "But I handled it like an asshole. You should've seen her face. She felt so betrayed. She wouldn't let me come close to her."

I couldn't stand what I had done. The pain I caused her. I wanted to make it right. But was there anything to make it right?

"Maybe just give her some space?" Dawn suggests. "You're supposed to be going to Savannah, right? Maybe in a few days things will calm down a bit and you two can talk?"

A ringtone goes off—Sarah has a call. She excuses herself and leaves the room to take it.

"I put Savannah on hold for a couple days," I tell them. "Tyler's handling what's needed until I get out there."

"I can always go out there and handle it," Kyle tells me. "I know you're handling the main business in Savannah. But you wanted it that way before you had more of a reason to be here in Beaufort. Sarah is going to Charlotte for work in a

159

couple days for a week, I can handle Savannah while you figure out how to fix things with Lucy."

"You're sure?" I ask. "You're not a fan of the commute."

"I'll stay at your place while she's away," he says. "It's not a big deal."

"So, what'd I miss?" Sarah asks as she comes back into the room. If I'm not mistaken, she looks slightly worried after the phone call she just had.

"Kyle is going to handle Savannah for me so I can stay and make things right with Lucy," I clue her in.

"You'll be in Charlotte anyway," Kyle tells her. She looks nervous.

"I mean, it makes sense, we'd both be away for work," Sarah says. "But I don't think you'll have much chance to set things right with Lucy."

"Why's that?" I ask, taken back.

"Because she just called me," Sarah tells us. "She knows I travel a lot for work and asked the best ways to get to Charlotte without her needing to get behind the wheel of a car."

"Charlotte?" I repeat. What's in Charlotte?

"Yeah," Sarah says. "I told her I was leaving in a few days for work and offered her to just come with me. So she'll be out of town for a week."

"What?!" Dawn asks, surprised. "Lucy would never leave, even for a week."

"I'm sure she goes away for vacation here and there," I offer. Maybe she needs time away and will come back and all will be okay...

"No, she's got it in her head that people in this town need her, and she can't let them down," Dawn denies.

"These people in town can use a harsh dose of reality with how they treat her," Sarah says angrily.

"What do you mean?" I ask. "People in town love her."

Everyone's always been so friendly and happy whenever Lucy was around. They gravitated toward her.

"Yes, and they expect her to drop everything she's doing and start taking pictures, hoping she'll be able to communicate with whoever they're trying to communicate with," Sarah shares.

"Don't you remember the restaurant?" Dawn asks. "The woman was all put out because Lucy didn't have her camera?"

"Yeah," I recall. "She was glaring at Lucy the next day we were walking into town. All because she didn't have her camera. Why does she need her camera?"

"Because that's how they come through if they have a message," Dawn says. It makes sense now why she took her camera and snapped a random picture earlier today.

"So otherwise, she can't communicate with them?" Kyle asks.

"Directly, no I don't think so." Dawn shakes her head. "But she sees them. But she can't hear them clearly, and the camera helps make communication easier? Without it, it's constant distorted chatter. It's why she avoids crowds."

More and more things we'd encountered start to make sense. The crowds, how she'd been at the restaurant.

"Was the restaurant, I don't know, crowded?" I ask.

"Oh yeah." Dawn nods, looking sad. "She was pretty sick in the bathroom when I went to check on her. But she refused to call it an early night. Didn't want to ruin a good night out."

"That doesn't sound like a gift," Miles muses. "It sounds like hell."

"Maybe going to Charlotte will be good for her?" Kyle thought.

"People lose loved ones every day. I don't think leaving Beaufort will eliminate her ability to see spirits." I shake my head.

"But people outside of Beaufort don't know what she can do," Sarah points out. "She can get away from the pressure."

"But why Charlotte? Why now?" Dawn asks.

"When I was there earlier, she was planning on going through letters her mother had been sending over the years," I remember. "She was looking for some clarity. I don't know for what, but maybe her mother's there?"

"Guess we'll find out." Sarah shrugs.

"Maybe I should go too," I think out loud.

"What?" Dawn asks, surprised.

"I don't know if that's such a good idea, Vincent," Sarah says. "She didn't sound good on the phone. She sounded off. Now I get why."

"Good idea or not, it's going to take a miracle for Lucy to forgive me, let alone trust me after how I handled this," I say. "It's one thing to be skeptical, but I was an asshole. If this trip is in any way connected to her finding her mother, she's going to need me. And I want her to know I'm there for her no matter what."

"Okay, but can you get away for that long?" Sarah asks.

"Yes, he can," Kyle answers for me.

"I need to make this right," I say. "I have to start somewhere."

CHAPTER 15

LUCY

I feel as though everything is crumbling around me. I expected Vincent not to take the news about spirits and Charlie well. I did. I've seen firsthand how he felt about this very topic. I know what he's been through in trying to hold on to the possibility of spirits and communication with them being real, just to be disappointed. I understood how much it would take for him to take something he's so strongly believed for a long period of time and convince him he was wrong…that spirits and communicating with them was possible.

However, I never would have anticipated nor been able to prepare for the moment when he would accuse me of being like the countless others. I thought he knew me. The type of person I was. My character. I didn't think he would truly believe I was capable of such cruelty. Capable of lying and taking advantage of other peoples' pain. Did he really think so low of me? That was the part I could not overlook. The part that was crushing me.

I don't know how long I had been sitting on my knees on the floor. It should be uncomfortable, but I'm numb to any pain or discomfort. It's just too much. First the town. Now Vincent. I just can't stand it. It feels like too much, and I can't get myself back up from this massive hole I've sunken into. I need to get away.

I wipe away my tears and stand up. The couch is closer and looks inviting. The box of letters is on the coffee table. I make my way slowly, knees protesting from sitting on them so long. I stand and take a shaky breath as I stare ahead of me.

Gran.

Gran is back and seated in front of me next to the box on the coffee table. She's looking at me, sadness in her eyes. I sit up straight, wiping away more tears. I wasn't expecting her to finally make contact. We stare at each other for a few moments before I speak.

"If I use my camera, will you disappear?" I'm not trusting. My voice is hoarse from my crying. She shakes her head, indicating she will not disappear. And suddenly, I'm feeling nervous. It's been 10 years since I had a true opportunity to speak with her.

Hesitantly, I pick up my camera and take a picture. I glance at the picture taken—briefly—and then look back at Gran.

"Oh Lucy," she says. If I could feel her, embrace her, I'd be pulling her into my arms. But that was one barrier I could never make accessible.

"Gran." My voice breaks. I'm relieved she stayed. Relieved she's communicating with me. "What the hell!?" And I'm admittedly put out.

"Always a way with words." Gran laughs.

"I'm serious," I say. "What is with your disappearing act? Why have you been avoiding me?"

"Sweetheart." She smiles. "You haven't needed me."

"Please tell me you're joking, Gran." I look at her in disbelief. "Please."

"I know it hasn't felt that way," she says. "But this is how it was meant to be."

"But I did need you," I told her. "I still need you. Gran, all these years I've been trying to figure it all out. These gifts you say we have, how I even survived. How did I make it out of the water?" She doesn't make a move to answer. She just smiles at me as though I already have the answer.

"Not all things need to be explained, Lucy," she finally says. But I don't agree. And nothing makes sense. "Some things just need to happen as they were meant to."

"Gran, none of it makes sense." I shake my head. "I understood when I believed you had moved on. But 10 years later and you're following Vincent around? Why him?"

"There's something about him." She shrugs, and I think back to what Charlie said about me. "And he's good for you."

"Did you miss our falling out?" I look at her, confused. She'd witnessed it. She and Charlie—together, I might add, which was strange on its own—had front row seats to that showdown.

"He didn't mean what he said, sweetheart," Gran tells me.

"He meant it," I tell her. "He truly thinks I'm capable of lying in such a horrid way to people when they're grieving."

"Well." Gran looks sheepish. "I didn't say he was bright." I'm not laughing.

"It's not funny, Gran." I shake my head. "I should've just told him from the start. Before I stupidly got involved with him."

"Lucy, you don't mean that." Gran smiles.

"I do." I close my eyes. "It wouldn't hurt to lose him if I never got involved."

"You haven't lost him," she disagrees. "Don't be so quick to shut that door, sweetie. That will be your biggest regret. I promise you."

"I don't know how I can forgive him," I admit. "Or trust him."

"Right now, you don't." Gran nods. "But you will. Be open to letting him set things right. We don't always get it right the first time." She smiles at me and looks to the side, seeing the box of letters. "I really wish you hadn't kept these letters."

"Why are you so against me reading them?" I ask, remembering her trying to throw the box out.

"You've been through a lot, Lucy," Gran tells me. "You're hurting right now. I don't want you to be disappointed if the answers you're looking for are not the ones you're hoping for."

"You told Charlie she's in Charlotte," I say. Gran nods her head.

"She is," she confirms.

"Can she communicate with spirits? Is that what drove her away? Was it me?" I ask.

Gran takes an unnecessary breath. She's preparing for this conversation.

"In her own way, she can," Gran tells me. "But just as with you and I, her gift works differently. It made her world confusing at times."

165

"I don't understand," I tell her.

"Your mother could see spirits, communicate with them both in the waking world and dream world," Gran tells me.

"Are you saying they would come to her in her dreams?" I ask. She nods her head yes.

"And not always the friendliest of spirits," Gran tells me. "She seemed to attract dark entities. She eventually struggled with differentiating what was real and what wasn't. She truly believed they had a way of influencing those around her to do harm…to influence her to do harm, especially after you were born."

"So she left?" I ask.

"She left to protect you," Gran says.

"I thought maybe the townsfolk put too much pressure on her to help them," I admit.

"People of Beaufort have certainly forgotten what a blessing it can be to have someone who can help them the way you do," Gran says. She doesn't look pleased.

"So where is she?" I ask.

"In an in-patient psychiatric facility in Charlotte," Gran tells me, watching for my reaction.

"What?" I'm shocked.

"Our gifts can be a blessing, Lucy," Gran tells me. "But they can also be a curse."

"You're saying because of her gift, she's locked up?" I ask, not sure how to process this.

"I'm saying that as much as it pains me, your mother's gift did more harm than it did good." Gran looks down sadly. "And while I wish things were simple with our world, it's more complicated than you've ever encountered."

"Is this why you haven't crossed over?" I ask. "You're keeping an eye on her?"

"You always were perceptive." Gran smiles. "But she's not the only one I'm watching over. I want all to be safe and happy before I make my way over to the other side."

"All?" I'm confused. "You sound like Charlie."

"She's quite entertaining, isn't she?" Gran laughs. "Reminds me a bit of you."

"Right." I roll my eyes.

"Just be careful, sweetheart," Gran says. "I know there are things you need to do. Answers you are looking for. But be careful."

"You're being cryptic," I tell her. "Can't you just be a little more forthcoming?"

"Some things we need to figure out for ourselves." Gran smiles. "That's why I'm backing off when it comes to your mother."

"You'll be with me, though?" I ask, unsure.

"I'm always with you." Gran smiles. Not a moment later, Gran vanishes. Thus breaking the temporary line of communication I have with her. I had a feeling it would be the last. I close my eyes, trying to absorb everything into my memory. I want to hold on to this—the chance to have seen her again and speak with her again—for as long as I realistically could. Charlie had also told me not to close that door to Vincent. They were both so determined to make sure I didn't completely write him off. But how could I?

I open the box which contained the letters; there's fewer postcards than I had initially thought. And looking through them, they dated nearly 25 years ago, when she had just left. They're normal. Nothing too specific. But they also don't ask how I am or mention missing me. They're from various states around the country.

As the postcards diminish, the letters are the primary focus, and it's then I notice they're marked from a psychiatric facility in Charlotte. I'm seeing them go back 10 years at least. She'd really been in a facility all this time.

It's stupid. I know. But I want to go see her. I need to see for myself what has become of her. I want to see if she's lucid enough to converse with, learn from her what she had been going through which led her down this path. As Gran had said… for my mother, her gift had been a curse. What did it truly do to her?

But how could I legitimately get there without needing to get behind the wheel of a car myself to get there. I'm looking up different options…a flight, a greyhound? I'd never traveled outside of Beaufort.

I then remember…Sarah. Sarah had mentioned she travels a lot for work and is on the road quite often. Perhaps she could offer me some insight as to how to best get to Charlotte.

I pulled my phone out and dial her number. It's not long before she's answering.

"Lucy?" I hear her on the other end of the line.

"Sarah, hi." I clear my throat. It's still a bit raw.

"Lucy, are you okay?" She sounds concerned.

"Yeah, yeah, I'm okay," I tell her. "Is this a bad time?"

"Not at all, what's going on?" she asks.

"I, um, I need to go to Charlotte," I tell her.

"Okay?" She's unsure what my point is. I don't blame her. I'm cryptic.

"I really don't think I can get behind the wheel of a car to drive myself," I tell her. I don't have to explain.

"Right, no, I understand," she says. "I think I knew you didn't drive anymore."

"But I need to get to Charlotte," I tell her. "I know you travel a lot for work. Could you recommend a means of transportation?"

"Means of transportation?" Sarah laughs. "Lucy, I'm going to there for work. I'll be gone a week. Why don't you just come with me?"

"A week?" I ask. Could I go away for an entire week? How would people react to my being gone that long? Would they be angry? Would they be understanding? What about messages from their loved ones? How would my already scheduled clients handle my rescheduling their sessions? I'd never gone anywhere…

"Yeah," Sarah tells me. "Come with me. I think it could be good for you to go away."

"I…I'm not sure." I'm on the fence. Could I do it?

"If you're worried about the townsfolk, don't be," Sarah tells me. I can hear the seriousness in her tone. "Put yourself first here. You need to get to Charlotte. So go."

"When are you leaving?" I ask, taking a deep breath.

"Three days," she says. So soon?

"So soon?" I'm surprised and feeling nervous.

"Is that okay?" she asks. "I can see if I could delay…"

"No, no," I tell her. "Please don't do that on my account. I'll make arrangements at the studio. I'll go with you."

"That's great, Lucy," Sarah says.

"Where should I meet you?" I ask.

"I'll come meet you at the courtyard at seven in the morning," she tells me. "Does that work?"

"It does, thank you so much," I tell her.

"Lucy, are you sure you're okay?" she asks after a moment.

"I don't know." Tears fill my eyes again, but I'm in control this time. I don't know if Sarah and the others know anything about what happened between Vincent and me. And I certainly am not ready to dive into that conversation. I have no doubts she'll ask while we travel to Charlotte. But right now? I'm just not ready.

"Do you want to talk about it?" she offers.

"I don't think I'm ready to," I admit. "But thank you. I appreciate the offer."

"Anytime, Lucy." She seems unsure if she should let me off the phone. But if I have three days before I head to Charlotte, then there's much to be done. First and foremost, tomorrow morning I needed to head to the studio to go through the appointment book and start rescheduling. Then I could focus on packing.

For tonight, I'm calling it a day. It's been a mentally and physically exhausting day, and I just wanted to get some rest. I don't check my phone for messages. I don't trust myself not to be tempted to respond if Vincent has tried reaching out. Instead, I put the phone on the charger and jump into bed after getting myself ready. It's too early but that doesn't seem to be a factor because I'm out like a light as soon as my head hits the pillow.

The next morning, there isn't time to waste. I have calls to make. I grab my bag, the open box on the coffee table catching my attention as I'm getting ready to leave. I walk over and grab a handful of the letters I had stopped on. I figure I could take some with me.

"There better not be any missing," I say out loud. If Gran or Charlie are hanging around, they're not making themselves known. But just in case, I'm giving fair warning not to mess with my stuff again.

I take my time walking to the studio. I wonder if I'll run into anyone on the way—specifically I wonder if Clara and I will cross paths. On one hand I want to talk with her. But think against it because with how emotionally charged I'm feeling. I may not be as calm and collected as I try my best to be. I breathe a sigh of relief when I make it to the studio without disruption. I lock the door behind me.

I go over to my desk to go through the different appointments scheduled for the week ahead. I feel like something is off when it's mainly the most random headshots. Engagement shoots and family portraits are scattered throughout the month ahead. But somehow, this upcoming is mainly headshots and again, like earlier, for individuals who truly don't have businesses to market. I'm not one to judge…if they want headshots, they want headshots. But I sense it's more of an example of individuals in town utilizing my studio under the guise of hoping someone would come through. I needed to get away.

I call nearly all and successfully reschedule. It wasn't well received, especially when I would not provide a reason for the reschedule. I didn't find it appropriate or a need to share my personal business this way.

I feel better, at least, knowing the week is taken care of. And so, before I head back home, I take out some of the letters I brought with me and start looking through them.

None are addressed to anyone. But one is addressed from a couple months before the accident ten years ago.

The shadows are menacing again. They speak in riddles, invading each crevice of my mind. Don't you see them? Don't you hear them?

What was my mother going through? Just what type of spirits invaded her dreams? I wasn't naïve. I understood that just as we encounter spirits of our loved ones, that in the world of the unknown, other entities could linger. It's why I always tell people not to mess with things they don't know anything about…like Ouija boards. I, myself, had never encountered something dark…like a demon. I didn't discount the possibility things like this lurking around out there or hauntings…but I felt something kept that facet of the spiritual plane away from me. But what about my mom?

The letters are each of the same tone as the one sent 10 years ago. None are personal. At all. But then I got to one dated days before the accident.

Don't let her get in the car. Don't do it. Head my warning. They're circling. Gathering. Lurking in the shadows. They want her. Keep her away. Keep her safe.

I must have read and reread this letter 10 times, processing it. Who was she warning to stay out of the car? Me? Gran? Who was after "her"? Did they win? Was it Gran? Who needed to be kept safe?

I was so confused. I needed answers and was so thankful I had decided to head to Charlotte I would ask her about this directly myself.

I make a sign indicating I'll be away and place it on the door as I lock up. When I'm sure it's secure and in place, I turn only to bump into someone as I turn around. I don't need to know who it is. I feel who it is by the electric surge I feel go through me as we connect. It's Vincent. He's here, with his arms carefully bracing me to help keep me steady.

"I'm so sorry," he says. I don't look him in the eye.

"My fault," I say, shrugging out of his embrace. "I wasn't looking where I was going."

"Lucy." His voice is pleading. "Please. Please hear me out." I look into his eyes. I shake my head. I don't think I can do it. Gran's voice is in my head reminding me not to close the door to Vincent.

"I thought you were going to Savannah." I tilt my head to the side, remembering he was supposed to leave yesterday.

"Something infinitely more important came up," he tells me.

"I said I needed time," I remind him.

"And I get it, I promise I do," he tells me. "But I can't leave it like this. Not after how badly I know I ruined everything. I can't leave it that way. I can't wait. You're too important." I'm confused.

Before I could respond, I heard my name being urgently called. It's getting closer and closer. Our attention is pulled away from each other as Clara is rushing over.

"Lucy!" she exclaims, finally reaching us.

"Clara," I say. She's another person I did not want to encounter today. Not after Helen mentioned Clara's been talking about me to the townsfolk, putting doubts in their heads over her own vendetta. This behavior was so unlike her. I didn't understand.

"I was going to stop in and schedule a session with you, only to see your sign that you're going away." There isn't a question she's posing to me. And she grows frustrated when I don't initially respond. I can see Vincent eyeing her cautiously.

"Just where is it you are going that takes you away for a week?" she demands to know. "A week! Do you not realize there are people waiting patiently for you to decide to take a picture for us?"

I see Vincent glare at her.

"Where I'm going isn't really anyone's business, Clara," I tell her. "And I have no obligations to anyone to take pictures outside of the main purpose I do them: to help capture new memories."

"You *do* have an obligation to the people of this town," Clara insists. "What would your gran think of you ignoring the needs of the people of this town so you can selfishly go away?"

"I'm going to stop you right there, Clara." Vincent steps in. He's using himself to create a barrier between myself and Clara. "I think perhaps you are losing sight as to how lucky the people in this town are to have someone as real, true, and genuine as Lucy. There are people in the world out there who are frauds and make a living exploiting people like you to fool them into thinking they're the real deal. And yet you have the real deal in front of you...You really think it's appropriate to take advantage of her?"

Clara's eyes go wide. She's not used to people talking back to her.

"Why, I never—" She's in shock, and Vincent has cut her off.

"I wasn't done," he tells her. "I suggest if you want Lucy to be generous enough to do a session with you, that you back the hell away from her and think long and hard about what your next steps are going to be. Because over my dead body will I tolerate you speaking to Lucy the way that you are."

She's looking back and forth between us. I'm stunned to silence as well. Where the hell was all this coming from? Clara doesn't dare speak again. I'm not sure what look Vincent is giving her from my position behind him, but whatever it is, is enough for her to think again and leave us in peace. He waits until she's gone and out of sight before turning to face me.

"I'm sorry if I overstepped," he tells me, looking down, unsure of my reaction. I'm looking over his shoulder to where Clara had disappeared to briefly see Gran in the distance, smiling with pride at the display. She gives me a knowing look before disappearing. I shake my head. Meddler.

"You understand why I'm confused right now..." I finally say.

"I know, and that's my fault," he says. "But I would like the chance to make things right."

"Vincent, I'm going away for a week." I shake my head.

"I know," he says. I look up at him, surprised.

"What?" I ask, confused.

"Don't get mad," he starts. I'm intrigued. "I'm going with Sarah...and you."

My jaw drops. He's going where now?

CHAPTER 16

LUCY

ABBA's "Dancing Queen" is blasting in the truck as I see Gran and I belt the lyrics at the top of our lungs, laughing in the pure enjoyment of the moment. I'm here and I'm not. There's two of me, I realize, as I'm positioned in the bed of the truck, watching the last special moments between Gran and I before the accident.

Oh god, not again. I don't want to relive this again.

"Oh Lucy, thank you for today. It was so wonderful," I hear Gran say. I'm watching her from my spot in the bed of my truck. She's not looking at me in the driver's seat. She's looking in the rearview mirror, catching my eye. Me. In the bed of the truck. It's almost as though she knows I'm there watching.

"You say it as though we won't have many others, Gran," I hear myself say as I glance in Gran's direction, worried. "Are you okay?"

"I'll be just fine, dear," Gran tells me. I see her eyes are guarded. She knows something. They held secrets...something that she was holding back saying. "I've been meaning to talk to you for some time, Lucy."

"What's on your mind?" I turn the music off altogether, giving Gran her full attention while also minding the road.

173

"Your birthday is fast approaching," Gran starts.

"It does that every year, Gran." I hear myself laugh. I want to smack myself. It's not a time for laughing or making jokes.

"Don't be a moron! Pull over!" I shout from my spot. But just as with all the dreamscapes, no one can hear me. But I see Gran glancing at me. Does she know? How does she know?

"Yes, but you're turning 18," Gran continues, hesitantly.

"Eighteen's not that big of a deal, Gran," I tell her.

"Lucy," Gran started but stopped abruptly, a gasp coming from her lips as she moved her right arm to grab ahold of her left arm as though she's in pain.

"Gran!" I yell at the same time the Lucy behind the wheel yells in alarm.

"Gran?!" I'm looking in her direction, noticing Gran was now unconscious. *"GRAN!"* Lucy turns back to the road. And there it is. In that moment, something appeared on the road. A dark figure I can't quite make out. Chills run down my side. There's hate and utter darkness emanating from this figure. It has a purpose but what strikes me is it's not standing in the middle of the road. Was this not the thing that caught me off guard?

I'm determined to make this dreamscape more memorable, more purposeful than the rest. I'm jumping out of the bed of the moving truck, running toward whatever this figure is in the middle of the road. Jumping out doesn't faze me. I'm not truly here...I don't think. I'm looking at the figure ahead.

It doesn't look like a person. There is no true shape. It's extremely difficult to make out who or what this is, and I'm caught off guard when it suddenly turns to me. All I see is glowing red eyes. The energy coming off this thing is dark. It's consumed with hate. I can feel it emanating from this being. And I stop short on my run toward it in the middle of the road without realizing where I am standing. I'm staring at it, in shock and looking in the direction of my oncoming truck.

"MOVE!" I try to scream, try to give myself some warning. But I fail because the truck is suddenly swerving and blazes through the guardrail.

"No, no, no!" I'm running toward the accident, looking over the bridge as the truck is quickly being pulled under and into the water.

"Hurry, Lucy!" Gran is beside me. I turn to look at her in shock.

"Gran, what is going on?!" I ask.

"HURRY!" she urges, and I'm suddenly hitting the water going under, under, under until I'm at the door to my driver's side. I can see myself struggling to breathe. Gran is in the passenger seat, unconscious. I want to get to her. But suddenly, I'm seeing her peering in from the water, into the car on the passenger side. She's shaking her head at me, stopping me from even attempting what she somehow knows I am to do. She's pointing to me.

"HURRY!" I don't hear her, we're in the water. But I can make out her words, see her urgency as she's urging me to stop wasting time and act...

I startle awake, gasping for air. I'm so confused that initially I can't make out where I am. My mind is still in a haze.

"Is she okay?" I hear a voice ask. I was confused at first. Not sure I am or who I'm with. "Sarah, is she okay?"

Vincent. Vincent is asking if I'm okay. I'm taking deep breaths.

"I'm not sure," Sarah says, her voice filled with concern. "Focus on the road, Vincent."

"I should pull over," he says.

"We're five minutes from the hotel," Sarah tells him. "Focus on getting us there in one piece and then you can see for yourself if she's okay."

"What's going on?" I ask her, my voice raspy. I clear my throat.

"You scared the hell out of us, that's what," Sarah tells me. She's beside me. "You were asleep. You must have had some dream because you were screaming, thrashing, and then it sounded like you were damn near choking." I look at her with wide eyes. I recall before waking up the sensation of struggling against the water, trying to breathe. But how could that physically manifest? Was it not a dream?

"Where are we?" I ask, confused.

"We're almost at the hotel," Sarah tells me. "We're in Charlotte."

I'm sitting, processing, and trying to recall. Trying to remember.

"Lucy, do you remember us leaving for Charlotte?" Sarah looks concerned and glances up front to where Vincent is driving. And I do.

I do remember leaving. I remember getting everything in order. I remember arguing with Vincent over his insistence on going to Charlotte with us when things between the two of us were so far from okay. I didn't understand his sudden change in demeanor. I didn't understand his willingness to simply accept the truth after his harsh accusations. He'd tried explaining to me. But I wasn't ready to listen. And each day we got closer to leaving, we would argue over him coming.

I didn't *want* him to come. He said he *needed* to come. I didn't see how he could be there for me. He listed several insistent reasons as to why I *would* need him:

I'd never traveled outside of Beaufort. What if I'm overwhelmed? Who could I lean on? Sarah would be working.

I hadn't seen my mother since I was a toddler. What if it goes terribly? What if she refused to see me? Who would I lean on? Sarah would be working.

I didn't like traveling, especially in a car. What if I freaked out during the road trip? Who would I lean on?

I said I would be fine. I knew I could keep it together. But clearly, I was wrong.

I was not fine. That was not like dreams I'd ever had before. This was becoming too real. It felt as though I was truly there and fully capable of interacting with my surroundings. It was more than a memory. How could that be?

"I remember," I finally say. They looked relieved that I've finally said something after continued silence.

"We're here," Vincent says, pulling into a parking spot.

"I'll go check in," Sarah says. I want to protest. I would rather be with Sarah than Vincent, but I know it's useless to fight about it. And quite honestly, I'm feeling pressure in my head coming on that I don't care enough to start another disagreement that will lead us to an impasse.

Sarah gets out of the car. Vincent at that time has turned off the engine and is taking Sarah's spot next to me in the back. He reaches for my hand, but I pull it away. If not for any reason other than I am not ready to be touched. It's not personal.

"Do you have dreams like this often?" he asks. He's trying hard to mask the hurt on his face from my pulling away.

"Like this? It's the second time," I tell him.

"Is it always the same thing or different?" He's trying to understand how best to offer me comfort. I look at him.

"I've typically had recurring dreams of the night of the accident," I tell him. He looks pained to hear this. "But these last two have felt too real."

"What do you mean?" I can see his hand gripping the seat next to me. Like he's trying to fight the urge he has not to reach over and take my hand.

"Usually it's dreams, memories," I say. He nods his head, he's following along. "But tonight and before, it was like I was there. Like I was visiting and seeing the scene unfold. Getting perspective and interacting without being seen?"

"Can that…I don't know…be a thing?" Vincent asks, unsure.

"A thing?" I'm confused.

"I'm sorry, I don't even know how to ask or form the words," he apologizes. "I mean…given what you can do. Is it possible you *were* visiting? That you *were* there?"

"Well, I didn't time travel." I laugh. But I'm considering what he's saying with a new interest.

"Of course not." He laughs. "Physically you were here the entire time."

"Right…physically," I say, my voice trailing off.

"What are you thinking?" he asks.

"I don't know," I tell him honestly. "There's so much I don't know or understand. But what if there was a way for me to be there?"

"Okay, say it was possible," he says. "In what way? Astral projection? Lucid dreaming?"

"Astral projection?" I ask, taken by surprise. "How do you even know about something like that?"

"Why? Because I was a skeptic?" he teases. "It's because I was searching for answers in my failed attempts to connect with Charlie. Astral projection, lucid dreaming, different ways to connect to the spiritual plane, astral plane…it came up."

"This is too weird," I admit.

"What is?" he asks, curious.

"Hearing you of all people talk about this and these possibilities," I tell him. "That it's *you* who is even suggesting this can be a real thing."

"Lucy." He sighs. "I screwed up in how I reacted. I know I attacked you, your character, but please understand I know you are genuine and good at heart. I was just too clouded and lost in my past experiences and heartache to see and understand you. My mind went back there all at once, and I reacted without thinking. I'm sorry. And I know you need time to think—now not being that time given why you're in Charlotte to begin with—but I hope you can forgive me. You mean...so much to me. I can't lose you."

I close my eyes. I'm trying to hear his words. I'm trying to believe his words. He has no reason to lie to me. And I'm being open minded. As much as I want him. As much as I want to move forward with him...I can't seem to feel ready to take that leap and give him my full heart. It's still wounded.

"I just need time," I tell him.

"I know." He smiles sadly. "But I'm here for you. I'm not going anywhere, Lucy."

"Alright, ready guys?" Sarah is back bearing keys to our respective rooms. Vincent gets out and is quick to come around to my passenger door to help me out. On one hand, I don't want him to help me. But on the other, I'm admittedly a bit shaky still from that dream and don't trust myself to move without the possible support. I can feel my legs wobbling a bit as I step out and without thinking, I'm holding onto Vincent like he's my lifeline. The sensation that is present every time we touch is back in full force. It's nearly overwhelming. I let him guide me, not trusting myself as he leads me to what will be my room.

"Is it a good idea for you to be alone tonight?" Vincent asks.

"She won't be." Sarah comes to my side. "We're bunking together, isn't that right, Lucy?"

Vincent looks surprised. He's pleased on one hand, realizing I won't be alone. But there's a sadness present too as though he wanted to be the one staying with me.

"Right." I'm admittedly sad, too.

"I'll come by around ten-thirty tomorrow morning to take you to the facility, Lucy," Vincent tells me.

"Thank you." I give him a tentative smile and follow Sarah inside our shared room.

"He really hates that he's not the one in here with you." Sarah laughs after I've shut the door. I go over to the bed not claimed by Sarah and start going through my packed suitcase for something to change into as I get cleaned up. I smile at her and am entertained by how amusing she finds Vincent's evident frustration.

"I'll be right back," I tell her and head to the bathroom. I'm staring at my reflection and nearly flinch at how worn down I look. All that happened was my being in a car off and on during the road trip to Charlotte. But it looks like I'd been through quite an ordeal, and I can't help but think of the new variant of the nightmare I'd had before we got to the hotel.

I can't help but think back at what was so different this time compared to the last.

The shadow figure, lurking on the road with the red eyes...It was as though he could see me. Me. Not necessarily the me of that night but the me who was dreaming up the tragedy.

Me. Me being in the middle of the road, unable to seemingly be able to move out of the way to try to interfere or stop what was to come.

Gran. Gran, Gran, and spirit Gran. I could have sworn she knew my dream self was there in the bed of the truck watching the exchange.

Gran's spirit appearing on the bridge, telling me to hurry, and again in the water with me after feeling as though I'd been pushed in and rushed to the truck door and keeping me from attempting to save her. But what did that even mean?

I'm processing everything, feeling the pressure in my head building. I'm so confused.

And I can't help but think about Vincent's theories before Sarah comes back. I don't know much about astral projection or lucid dreaming, and I certainly have no idea if I could be capable of such things. Gran said I'd be capable of incredible things. Was this what she meant? But if my mom could connect and be influenced in her dreams to the spirit world, then was it possible I could interact in some way, shape, or form myself?

With astral projection, I don't believe I would be able to physically manipulate anything around me, even if I was suddenly in that place at that exact time. But lucid dreaming? I was aware...and if...big if...I got myself out of the water then manipulation of objects around me would be possible.

I shake my head at the thought.

What a stretch, Lucy, I think to myself. Shaking my head at the absurdity, I leave the bathroom once I'm ready and go to bed.

"All yours." I smile at Sarah. "Hey Sarah—" I call out, stopping her in her tracks as she heads toward the bathroom. "Thank you."

She smiles at me, nodding her head, and heads in to get herself together. I don't stay up much longer and find sleep welcomes me. Sleep comes easy. The night is more restless than the drive had been.

Sarah leaves early; she's got a busy workday and has a car arrive to pick her up. Vincent is prompt, showing up at 10:30 on the dot, bringing coffee with him.

"How'd you sleep?" he asks, searching my face.

"Well, thank you." I smile, taking the coffee he's offering.

"Are you nervous?" He leads the way to the car, opening the door for me.

"A little," I admit. "I don't think she'll even recognize me."

"You never know." He offers hope. But I know better. She hasn't seen me since I was a small child. We drive in a comfortable silence. I'm taking in the different type of environment I'm in. It's certainly not the small-town vibe Beaufort emanates. It feels good to see something new. To see sun for a change compared to the constant cloud cover and rain of Beaufort.

Twenty minutes later, we arrive. I'm staring at the facility, nervous suddenly.

"I'm right here with you," he tells me. I nod my head and slowly get out of the car. I get out before he can come around and help me get out. But I don't hesitate in taking his hand which he'd extended out for me. He looked surprised. I'm surprised. It was so instinctual to be with him. It was easy to gravitate toward him. He was my light.

We come inside, and I head over to a woman sitting behind a desk, busy typing on the computer. She hears me come up and looks up at me. She's weary.

"Visiting Audrey Adams," I tell her. She looks surprised. Genuinely surprised.

"Ms. Adams hasn't had visitors since she's been here." She's unsure. "I didn't think anyone was on the list."

"The list?" I ask, not sure what she means.

"You have to be on a patient's list of approved visitors to be allowed in to see them," she explains. She's typing on her computer. "Can I see your photo ID, please?"

I look in my purse, pulling out my wallet. I handed her my ID. Damn. I wouldn't be able to see her. I'm waiting for her to break the news to me that I won't be allowed in to see her because of the lack of authorization. But after several minutes, she hands me a visitor sign-in sheet and hands my ID back to me along with a visitor's pass.

I look at Vincent, surprised.

"He won't be able to go in the room with you," the woman shares, "but can wait right outside the doors until you've completed your visit. If you go through

Beyond

these doors, make a left and follow the path down. There will be an orderly to let you in. They've been notified to bring her to meet with you."

"Thank you," I say, genuinely. I'm following Vincent through the doors as we were instructed.

"You look surprised," he gathers.

"I didn't think I would be on the list," I tell him. "How could I be?"

"Maybe she made sure you'd be on there, in case you came looking for her?" he guesses.

"I don't know," I tell him. We make it to the doors, and there's a guard waiting for me. He's listing items I cannot bring in with me, and Vincent graciously offers to hold on to my things for me.

"I'll be right here," he tells me. I smile at him, appreciative of his support. I will never admit to him that he was right in coming. I'll never hear the end of it.

I look around the room at the various tables set up for those visiting. There's only a handful of others here. Spirits, fortunately, are scarce. I take a seat at the table in the middle and wait.

It isn't long before I hear the buzz of the door opposite me, and they are granting access to a petite woman with short, frazzled, strawberry blonde hair. It's in disarray. She's frail and pale, and her eyes are slightly sunken in. They show her where to go and she sits opposite me, eyeing me suspiciously. She's looking around the room, guarded. She's watching for something. What that something is, I have no clue. I don't see anything out of the ordinary.

"Do you know who I am?" I ask her. She's looking at me, trying to place me. She says nothing.

"It's Lucy," I tell her. Nothing. "Lucy…Adams. Your daughter." Her eyes grow wide.

"No." She shakes her head. "No, not here. Not safe. Red eyes. Red eyes. No face."

I'm confused. I look at her. I steal a glance back at Vincent who is watching. Whatever he sees on my face, he's concerned.

"I brought this with me." I take out the letter I'd found dated just before the accident and place it in front of her. "I only just opened it. I had to find you. What does this mean?" She's staring at the letter with wide eyes. She says nothing.

"Audrey, I'm trying to understand," I tell her. "This was before the car accident. This was 10 years ago."

181

"Ten years?" she asks, confused. "It happened? Did she get in the car? Did she keep her away?"

"Who had to be kept away?" I press.

"No, no." She shakes her head again. "Red eyes, not safe. Not here." I don't understand.

"Who was this warning for?" I ask again. "Me? Gran? Audrey, Gran died that night. Did you know she passed?"

Suddenly, Gran is seated to my side. The table had four chairs. One on each side of the square table. Gran is positioned in between me and my mom. I can't hear her. I don't have my camera, nor would I have been allowed to bring it in here with me. But I see her trying to say something, and I notice Mom cringing. She's cringing and trying to angle herself away from where Gran is positioned. And I realized. She sees Gran. She hears her.

"You see her, don't you?" I ask. Audrey's eyes snap at mine. That's the confirmation I need. I look at Gran; she is nodding her head, her way of acknowledging that, yes, in fact, Audrey can see her.

"Voices, so loud, screaming," Audrey continues. "Not safe. Should've stayed away from the car."

"That was 10 years ago," I tell her, confused. "We were both in the car."

"What?" she looks panicked.

"We were both in the car that night," I tell her. "It went into the river."

"But…you're here and alive…" She looks at Gran, albeit she looks terrified to look. "No, no…the shadow. He lingers. He watches. Takes. Not safe. The red eyes!" She's becoming hysterical, and I'm getting nervous. I'm looking at Gran who looks nervous as well and concerned.

"I don't understand," I tell her. I say it to both. The orderly is coming to get Audrey to take her away as they notice her become hysterical. I don't have a chance to say anything else before they've taken her, but a nurse comes over.

"I'm sorry," she says to me. "She's never had visitors, and we suspect she hasn't been taking her medication."

"You're medicating her?" I'm accusatory. Are they trying to make her think what she sees isn't real?

"She signed herself into this facility willingly years ago," she tells me, and I'm surprised. "If you come back another time, maybe she'll be more prepared for having a visitor?"

"I'm not from here," I tell her. "I'm only here for the week."

"Well, why don't you leave your number. We can update you on her status?" the nurse offers. I see Gran shaking her head no, advising me not to leave anything for them here.

"That's okay," I tell her. "I'll try to come again before I leave. Is she usually like this?"

"It's not the worst it's been," the nurse tells me. I thank her, and we each part ways. I made it over to where Vincent was anxiously waiting for me.

"What happened? Are you okay?" he asks. I shook my head and take his hand, leading him out of the facility. This isn't where I want to have this conversation.

He waits patiently until we're in the car and then is wanting some answers. But I can't help but think over the different things she had said to me. *He's watching. No face. RED EYES.*

And I think back to the shadow I'd seen last night in my dream. No face. No true shape or form. Just menacing red eyes glowering at me, watching me. Is that who she meant?

"Lucy?" Vincent asks, capturing my attention. "What happened in there?"

"I don't understand what happened in there," I tell him. "She wasn't making any sense."

"How so?" He takes my hand.

"She kept going back and forth about it not being safe. Saying something about a faceless shadow with red eyes, watching," I tell him, recalling our conversation.

"Who does she mean? Do you know?" he asks. I'm still thinking. Could it be connected. She seemed so surprised to see me…alive. "Lucy?"

"I'm not certain, but I think I might…" I tell him. "Last night in the dream, I was back there…that night of the accident. This time I'd seen what had been in the road."

"You mean the something that appeared out of nowhere?" he clarifies. I nod my head.

"In my dream I saw a shapeless black form with red eyes," I tell him. I have his attention. The hold on my hand tightens. "And it saw me."

"What do you mean?" he asks.

"I don't mean the me that was there that night...the night of the accident. It was focused on my truck, yes," I tell him. I doubt I'm making sense. "But I tried running at it, getting it out of the way. But I couldn't move from the middle of the road."

"The middle of the road?" he repeats. I nod.

"Then it looked right at me," I tell him. "Like it knew I was there, in the dream sequence. It wouldn't let me move. And the truck swerved, going over and into the water."

"But it saw you," he confirms.

"I think so," I tell him. "I really don't understand any of it. But what you were saying last night about astral projection and lucid dreaming got me thinking...if such a thing could be real...say it was. Say I was there. Say that shadow who saw me was the shadow my mom wrote about, warning about, and I was the person appearing in the middle of the road that night...what if it was me?"

"We're talking about the possibility that you were back that night somehow and you were there when the truck suddenly swerved uncontrollably and went through the guardrail," he repeated, processing, trying to understand. I nod. "So where does this shadow fit in? How did you get out?"

"My mom looked genuinely surprised that her letter wasn't listened to and said it was impossible for me to be there, alive," I tell him. "What if I was the one she was warning to stay away from the truck, and whatever menacing spirits she's been seeing was after me?"

"How would she even know that?" he's confused.

"Gran said my mother's gift worked differently...spirits she'd see day to day and in her dreams weren't always friendly. She said what she encountered had a way of influencing those around her to do harm...it's why she left, to protect me," I tell him. He's surprised. In avoiding him, I had yet to explain to him how it all worked for me, for Gran, for my mother.

"Demonic beings, those are the ones you're talking about," he clarifies.

"Maybe?" I say. "I've never dealt with this type of thing. I sound insane."

"No, you don't," he disagrees. "It's just...a lot. Let's say that is the case. Just for arguments sake. What does it mean?" I'm thinking.

"She said it was watching. That it wasn't safe," I tell him.

"Meaning what? That you're not safe?" He looks worried.

"I've been okay all these years." I sigh, not understanding. "I've never sensed anything menacing lurking in the shadows."

"But why would she think it wasn't safe then?" he asks.

"I don't know." I look at him. "I feel like in searching for answers, I'm walking away with more questions. I wish Mom was lucid enough to explain."

"What are you going to do? What do you *want* to do?" he inquires.

"I think I need to come back," I tell him, looking him in the eyes. "I think in a couple days, I should try talking to her again."

He's searching my eyes, looking to see if I'm sure. And I am. Whatever he sees there is enough to assure him in the next plan, and he smiles.

"A couple days then." He nods. "Let's get lunch?"

"Lunch sounds good." I smile.

CHAPTER 17

LUCY

I was anxious after visiting my mother. I wasn't sure what my expectations should have been going into it. So I hadn't imagined the possibility of her not being lucid enough to have a genuine conversation with me. There was more I didn't understand after the visit than when I first got here. And if I'm being truthful, Gran was right. Maybe I wouldn't like the answers to the questions I had. Because if there was any sense to what my mother was saying—and I did not believe there was sense to it—then what did it mean? That there was some dark presence out to get me? If it was out to get me...then why? Why me?

It made no sense. But then, not many things associated with my mother or my family legacy made sense at all.

I'm taking in the scenery as we're driving to find a place for lunch. It's incredible, what exists outside of my Beaufort bubble. Hell, the sun alone is a nice change compared to the constant cloud cover of Beaufort. It's also refreshing not being around so many who seem to want only one thing from me. I start to wonder why I hadn't explored seeing other areas sooner.

"You doing okay?" I hear Vincent ask, breaking me out of my thoughts.

"I'm not sure," I tell him honestly. "But I don't really want to dive into it and try to make sense of things."

"Any preferences on what to eat?" Vincent asks. I can tell this is his way to acknowledge and respect my need for a topic change, a distraction. I notice he's gripping the steering wheel.

"Not really," I tell him. "Have you ever been to Charlotte?" He shakes his head no. "We can be adventurous and drive around until something stands out," I suggest. He smiles, seemingly to like the idea.

"Next place we see, we stop?" he offers.

"Sounds like a plan." I smile. This was nice, I realize. Having him here with me. Supporting me. I want to mentally slap myself at how easy it is to just be around him and how quickly I'd been to take his hand in mine when we first arrived at the psychiatric facility.

It's not even five minutes before we're pulling into a parking lot of what looks to be an American bistro. He's looking at me, hopeful that our spontaneity was favorable, and I can't help but smile. He's out the door, coming over to my side to help me out. I can see he's debating internally with himself over whether he should offer out his hand like he did before. And if he did, I know without hesitation I would take it. But I don't dare initiate this gesture. A look of determination crosses his face…he's decided and is offering me his hand. There is uncertainty, I can see it. And I feel guilty because it's there because of me. But I'm trying. He's trying. And while all his actions and his support speak volumes, I'm not sure how quickly I can trust it yet. But forgiveness? Damn Gran and Charlie.

I take his hand and see the instant relief cross his face. I, too, am pleased to have been able to give him this.

It's lunch hour, and I'm quickly realizing how easy it has been to forget the world with Vincent. Crowds.

How crowded would this place be if we were to go in?

"What's wrong?" Vincent stops, having sensed a shift. I don't want to tell him. I don't want to ruin a good thing.

"It's nothing, let's go inside." I smile. I'm not sure what he's seeing on my face but after a moment, a look of understanding crosses his features.

"Should we go somewhere else?" he asks.

"Somewhere else?" I'm confused.

"Somewhere that isn't, I don't know, crowded?" he offers. "Dawn explained… why you avoid crowds."

"I don't know how…*crowded*…it is yet," I tell him. "Without going in, I won't ever know. But that's the case for me everywhere I go."

"So you brace yourself for the possibility," he says in understanding. And I truly wonder how he understands me so well.

"Exactly." I smile.

"What do you want to do?" he asks, letting me lead this.

"Let's go in," I tell him. He looks like he wants to protest but I continue. "If it's a problem, it looks like they have outdoor seating. It's okay." He's searching my eyes again, looking for any sign of my offering this just to please him. He must sense I am serious in my offer because he visibly relaxes, and we head inside.

I'm looking around, pleased to see it's not *overcrowded*. I sigh in relief at this and look up at him with a smile which he happily returns. The hostess is friendly enough, leading us to a private booth toward the back, leading to the outdoor seating. It's quite lovely.

Our waiter doesn't waste time. Not long after the hostess leaves us with our menus, he's over to our table reading off the specials and is taking our order for drinks. Vincent is glaring daggers at him as he walks off to get everything taken care of.

"Stare any harder and you'll likely leave a hole in the guy's back." I laugh.

"I don't like him," Vincent says, still looking in the direction the waiter went.

"You don't even know the guy." I look at him, bewildered.

"He's got a look about him," Vincent says. "And a wandering eye." I look at Vincent, amused.

"Why, Vincent, was he checking you out and it made you uncomfortable?" I tease. He quickly looks at me, then shakes his head in disbelief, realizing I was joking.

"You're funny." He rolls his eyes.

"And you've got nothing to be jealous of," I tell him. "He's being friendly." Vincent looks like he wants to say more but thinks better of it. But I'm finding I want to know what he wanted to say.

"I really appreciate you coming with me," I finally tell him. I didn't want to admit to him that I was happy he came...not after the endless arguments we had over the issue during those three days.

"Really?" He quirks his eyebrow.

"Yes," I tell him. "Really."

"Hmm," he muses.

"What?" I look at him curiously.

"Nothing, nothing." He shakes his head.

"You want to say it." I glare at him. "Go ahead."

"That I was right?" he asks. I don't respond which amuses him further. "I just wanted to be here for you, Lucy. I'm glad it turned out to be the right call."

"I just wanted space," I tell him honestly. "After everything, I just needed to think."

"I understand," he tells me. "And I'm sorry I didn't give you that space."

"You're not." I laugh. He looks sheepish. "I get it, though. And I appreciate what you're trying to do."

"Alright, here we go." The waiter returns, offering us our drinks. I look at his name tag—William. I'm sure he'd introduced himself earlier when we first sat down but quite frankly, I wasn't paying much attention. "So what'll it be?" he asks, though I can see he's mainly focusing on me. I can see, now that I'm paying closer attention, two things. The first, he does have a wandering eye, and I'd rather he not be here because his intense gaze is bordering on uncomfortable. The second is the spirit following closely behind him trying to mutter words his way but neither William nor I can make out what they're saying. I look away, toward Vincent quickly, trying to keep my attention solely on him. Because if the spirit realizes I could see him, he'll try to make contact only to quickly grow frustrated when they realize I don't understand them. And my gear is in the car.

My focus is on Vincent. Vincent's focused on William, glaring at him. And William's probably still focused on me which would explain Vincent's glare. I kick him from under the table to get his attention. He grunts but makes no further indication that he'd just received a hefty kick under the table. But the noise is enough to bring William's focus on Vincent.

"I'll have a double cheeseburger, medium well," Vincent huffs at William.

"And for the pretty lady," William says, but I'm not looking at him. I can see the spirit from the corner of my eye.

"I'll have the same," I tell him. Vincent looks surprised. I can sense William is still standing there, longer than necessary. I stand up suddenly, catching them both by surprise and move to sit directly next to Vincent rather than across from him. From Vincent's position, William would be headed in the direction behind us when he finally took the hint and moved on. I wouldn't have to fight the temptation to keep an eye on this spirit and calling unnecessary attention to myself.

Tentatively, Vincent brings his arm around my shoulder, and I immediately lean into his embrace. It's comforting.

"I think we're good here." Vincent looks at me a moment longer, before bringing his attention back to William who finally nods.

"Of course," William says and quickly heads the opposite direction to hand the order in to the chef.

I immediately breathe a sigh of relief, sinking further into Vincent's embrace.

"You saw something, didn't you?" he finally asks. I look at him, surprised.

"How could you know?" I ask.

"I'm paying attention." He smiles sadly. "You reacted similarly when we went on that double date with Dawn and Miles. I didn't understand it then, but I can see it. There's a noticeable shift when you're seeing…something."

"I didn't realize I was so obvious," I mumble.

"I don't think it is," he assures me. "But I…I care very much for you, Lucy. And so, I pay close attention. What did you see?"

I'm staring at him for a time, searching for his face. He's sincere. Genuine and curious.

"There's the spirit of an older gentleman with him," I tell him. "He seems frustrated. Wanting to tell him something, but William can't see or hear him."

"But you can?" Vincent's confirming.

"I can see him," I tell him. "But hear him? Not clearly enough to know what he's trying to say."

"What do you mean?" he asks. He looks confused. But so am I? He seems as though he'd received a lowdown from Dawn, but I don't know how much she'd told him. "Dawn told me a little bit about it. But I don't get how this all works."

"Oh," I say, surprised. "Without my camera, I can't clearly communicate with spirits, but I can see them. Without it, it's all static and garbled. So when there's so many in one space, it's sound and stimulation overload. It's disorienting for me."

"So when you use your camera, it does…what do you think?" he inquires.

"I think it thins the veil between the spirit realm and ours, allowing for the communication to come through clearer. Like it brings us both to the same frequency," I explain.

"That doesn't sound like something easy to have figured out," Vincent muses. "When did you realize that's how it worked for you?"

"About a month after the accident, I'd turned 18 and went back to the bridge," I tell him quietly. Ever so slightly, I wasn't sure if I'd imagine it, Vincent's hold on me tightened. I look into his eyes and he's looking at me with a look I can't quite define. It's not the first time he'd given me that look.

"Do you remember what happened around that time?" he finally asks, clearing his throat.

"Yeah," I say, hesitantly. He's being patient with me. He's not pushing. "I went back to the site of the accident about a month after it all happened. I don't even know why I went. I just felt compelled to go there of all places and I brought my camera. I don't really go anywhere without it." I chuckle.

"I did notice that." He smirks.

"But I found myself going over to down to the river," I tell him. "To the spot they'd found me. I remember I took a picture of the bridge—where the truck broke through the guardrail—from that perspective. I'd been looking at the pictures, just to see how the lighting was…if I needed a different lens…and there was Gran one moment in the picture and the next, standing next to me, talking to me."

"So you take a picture, maybe a spirit shows up in the picture and then you can hear them?" He's thinking it through.

"They appear in the photo briefly," I tell him. "When I develop the film or adjust the digitals, there's nothing there. But yes, that's how they come through. And usually if they have a message."

"And you got to see your gran." He smiles at me.

"I did," I say. "She wasn't that helpful though…I never knew I could do this. I'd always thought I'd see things here and there. But I was like you once, skeptical of believing if the supernatural could be real."

"And then one day it was." He nods.

"Seeing sometimes truly is believing." I shrug.

"Was she able to move on…after communicating with you?" he asks.

"For the last 10 years, I truly believed she had crossed over," I tell him.

"But now you don't?" he asks, confused.

"I know she hasn't," I say. He's looking at me questioningly. "That first day we met? When Dawn brought me into the studio to check it out for possible promotional photos?"

He's remembering.

"Yeah, I remember," he finally says. "You'd looked like you had seen a ghost. You dropped your bag."

"Yeah, well, that's because I did see a ghost," I tell him. "My gran."

"What?" His eyes are wide in surprise.

"Yeah, she was hanging around you," I tell him. "But every time she'd catch me looking, she'd disappear."

"Why me though?" he asks, confused. "Why not you?"

"That day I finally told you what I could do, she came to me. She came through when I used my camera," I told him. "Said I didn't need her all these years. That things happened the way it was meant to."

"But that doesn't answer why she'd be hanging around me," Vincent says.

"I don't know how that woman's mind works even in the afterlife." I laugh. "But she'd made it known at times she was there."

"How?" He looks surprised.

"Before the accident, Gran and I were blasting and singing along to ABBA's 'Dancing Queen'" I tell him. Once more he's got a look on his face that I can't quite decipher. "You and I heard it turn on in your car that one night," I remind him.

"That wasn't the first time that had happened," he whispers. Now I'm the one confused.

"What do you mean?" I ask.

"I mean, there were times before that day and after where that song would either start playing on my radio or just in Dawn's studio," he shares. "I didn't get what it was about that song or how that was happening."

"But you brushed it off because of the obvious." I nod in understanding. "I wasn't there so I can't say for sure if it was Gran. But I wouldn't put it past her."

"So she was there that night in the truck," he surmises.

"Yeah." I nod. "She was there. And today with my mom. She was there."

"Does it ever get confusing?" he asks, suddenly. But I know and understand what he's asking me.

"Sometimes," I admit. "Sometimes it is hard to differentiate what's real versus what isn't. But with spirits, you can sense what they're feeling. At times, I can feel what they're feeling, and I know. It's become easier over time. But not in the beginning."

"It sounds exhausting," he whispers.

"It is," I tell him. "Sometimes, depending on how strong the spirit, I feel drained after the connection is gone."

"Here we go." We both jump. William's back and caught us both off guard. He places our meals in front of us. I look up to thank him, seeing the spirit lingering just behind him shaking his head and pulling at his hair in frustration. I'm curious and wish very much in that moment that I could make the connection and help this spirit. William notices my gaze and looks behind his shoulder, to see if there's something that caught my attention. But he can tell nothing is there. "Everything okay?" he asks.

"Yes, sorry." I shake my head and look over at Vincent.

"If you need anything, just let me know," William says and walks off

"What is it?" Vincent asks.

"Whoever the spirit is, he's frustrated that he can't connect with William," I tell him. "He was pulling at his hair."

"You want your camera so badly right now, don't you?" He smiles at me. He's not teasing me, I can tell. He's in awe of me?

"I really, really do," I admit. He laughs. "I just want to help spirits feel at peace so they can move on instead of being stuck in this limbo."

"Does it have to be your equipment?" he asks.

"What do you mean?" I ask him.

"Well, is there something special about your camera equipment? Was it passed down from your family, like your gift was?" I shake my head no. There was nothing special about it. "So why does it need to be your camera? Why not the camera on your phone?"

I look at him with wide eyes.

"It never occurred to me to try," I admit.

"No better time like the present." He shrugs.

"How awkward would that be." I roll my eyes. "Hey dude, just testing out the lighting, you don't mind me taking your picture, right?"

"You never know, he seems taken with you." He laughs. I start to roll my eyes but then have a thought. Vincent's caught by surprise as I stand abruptly and am pulling my phone out of my pocket.

"What are you doing?" He laughs.

"Smile for the camera." I laugh. I'm lining up my shot with my phone to take of Vincent. To anyone, it just looks like I'm snapping a regular photo. Maybe even being a typical tourist in their eyes. But I've angled the phone in such a way that William is more in the shot than Vincent. He's looking over in my direction, curious about what I'm doing. But I'm focusing on the spirit with him, and the spirit realizes in that moment that I can, in fact, see him. I take the picture quickly so I can take the attention off me.

"Moment of truth," I say as I look at the photo. My eyes go wide when I see the spirit appear in the photo before appearing by my side. I quickly take a seat in the booth.

"Did it work?" Vincent asks but at the same time he asks, the spirit is asking if I can see him.

"Yes," I say. I briefly glance at Vincent but turn toward the spirit of the man sitting beside me. I'm answering both.

"How can you see me? How can you hear me?" the spirit asks me.

"It's just something I can do," I tell him. Vincent's about to ask—mostly likely ask what I'm talking about—but the look I give him tells him what he needs to know. That I'm not communicating with him in the moment. I'm interacting with the spirit.

"Well, thank the stars." He looks relieved. "I'm Mitchell. Mitchell Wilkins. William's father."

"Hi there." I smile at him. "Lucy."

"Lucy." He smiles back. "I need you to tell my moron of a son that he needs to quit this job and go back to school. My Willy was going places. "

"Um." I take a breath. "Mitchell, does he *want* to be in school?" I look at Vincent apologetically. I should feel weird doing this in front of him, but strangely I don't. And the look he's giving me right now? He's not judging or weirded out.

"He does," Mitchell urges. "There was a mix up in his paperwork for a scholarship he had at state. But I took care of everything just before I had my heart attack. I had the paperwork in my brown leather jacket. And the moron packed it up today in a box to give to goodwill. You need to stop him. Tell him to check the pockets and get his ass back to the admissions office to reinstate his scholarship."

"I can do that," I smile at him. He sighs in relief as he thanks me, then vanishes. I look at Vincent and smile, reaching over to my plate and grab a French fry.

"Sorry about that," I tell him. "I didn't think the camera on my cellphone would actually work."

"I wouldn't go shouting it off rooftops around Beaufort," Vincent teases. But then his face grows serious. "No, really, don't tell them you don't need specialized equipment."

"Not everyone in town is like Clara." I smile sadly. "The townspeople have always been kind. Have you ever noticed the crime rate is nonexistent?"

"I have, actually." He smiles sadly. "I think, however, if you asked Dawn or Sarah or even Betty, they'd disagree with you about the townspeople," he tells me. "Do you take photographs because you genuinely love the art or because of the expectations of the town?"

"Honestly, I love art and wish sometimes it can be just about what I love," I tell him.

"You'll never have that in Beaufort, Lucy," he tells me.

"I never ever considered leaving Beaufort, for obvious reasons," I share. "And I'm not saying I'm ready to just up and jump ship, but I'm loving the aspect of the endless possibilities beyond Beaufort. And..." I pause, not sure how to share the next part.

"And what, Lucy?" Vincent asks. He reaches over to take my hand, assuring me that I could confide in him.

"And I may have looked into different photography contests to put some of my work out there for exposure," I tell him.

"That's incredible!" he exclaims. "Did you hear back?"

"Not yet," I tell him. "I haven't told anyone about it."

"I'm glad you told me." He smiles and squeezes my hand gently. I nod my head, content that I'd shared this with him. We take some time to eat our food. By now, mine's gone cold but I don't care as much. We're just about ready for the check, and Vincent flags William down to let him know. We pay him, telling him to keep the change but I stop him before he walks away. He's hopeful for a moment until he glances at Vincent. Not sure what look Vincent's giving him, but that hopeful look is gone just as it came.

"William," I start. "Listen, there's no way to say this so I'm just going to rip off the Band-Aid." He looks confused.

"Say what?"

"That box you put together with your dad's things for Goodwill this morning? You need to go back through it before you drop it off and find his brown leather jacket," I tell him. His eyes go wide.

"How did you—" I cut him off.

"Not done," I tell him. "Your dad fixed whatever mix up was going on with your scholarship. He arranged everything the day he had his heart attack. But the paperwork is in that jacket. Get that paperwork, go to the admissions office, and get back to where you're supposed to be."

William's eyes are wide in disbelief. He's looking back and forth between me and Vincent. Not sure if he should or shouldn't believe what he's hearing.

"I'd listen to her," Vincent tells him. "You may regret it if you don't."

"Yeah," he whispers. "Do I want to know how you know this?" I shrug but give him a reassuring smile.

"Good luck, Willy," I tell him, intentionally using his father's nickname for him. "And don't forget to get that paperwork." He nods his head, understanding. He looks like he's in shock over the ordeal. I take Vincent's hand and lead him out of the restaurant.

"Well, that was eventful." I laugh as we make it back to the truck.

"It was incredible." He smiles at me.

"It doesn't happen often. Me giving a message to someone who doesn't know what I can do," I say aloud.

"If you ever left Beaufort, it may happen more than it does now," he muses, and I agree with him. If that were to ever happen. He opens the door for me to the passenger seat and there's that look again. I don't understand it and it's quite off-putting.

"What's that look?" I ask him. "I can't figure it out."

"Look?" he asks, confused.

"I'm not sure sometimes if you're weirded out by what I've been sharing with you…between what I found out about that night from my mom, to how it all works, and then actively interacting with a spirit in front of you…you've had a look about you. Like there's something you want to say but aren't saying it."

"You're very perceptive," he muses.

"I've been told that." I shrug. "So what is it? If it bugs you or you don't believe it, I need to know. I won't judge."

"I'm afraid if I tell you, I'll scare you off," he admits. I'm slightly surprised. How bad could it be? It couldn't possibly be worse than how he initially handled finding out about my gift.

"You don't scare me," I say, challenging him. He steps closer, very little space is between us and my breath catches.

"You sure?" He smirks, leaning closer. I'm not backing down. He can see it in the look on my face.

"Positive," I tell him with determination. "I can handle it." He's searching my eyes. I'm not sure what he's looking for.

"I…" he starts. He pauses a moment before gathering whatever courage he was searching for. I'm bracing myself for something horrible. "I am so in love with you, Lucy Adams."

CHAPTER 18

LUCY

I felt like I'd lost all touch of reality. I'm not sure how long I stood there, shocked, at hearing the most unexpected words from Vincent. But clearly, however long it was taking me to process was too long because he'd manage to guide me into the passenger seat and was already starting the truck. Silence filled the truck. My mind simply can't fully wrap around those words he'd shared.

He's in love with me?

He's…in love with…*me?!*

The revelation alone makes me feel a way I've never felt before. Entirely likely because I'd simply refused to open my heart to anyone in such a vulnerable way. And how could I?

These years I felt as though I was a gimmick…a hot commodity to be exploited…to the previous failed attempts at relationships. And after the way I'd acted toward him…shutting him out, not trusting him…despite it all, he's in love with me? He wants me. Me.

As that sinks in, I'm realizing my brain is mush and my inability to be coherent just probably ruined everything. For all I know, he likely thinks I hate him or something worse with how hard I see him gripping the steering wheel out of the corner of my eye.

But it's not the case. And I want to shout to him that I love him too. Because of course I do. Yes, he reacted terribly. Questioned my very being. And I'd been so focused on how much that tore me apart that I wasn't focused on how hard he was clearly trying to show that not only did he believe in me, but he cared for me so deeply that the thought of me putting myself into hurtful situations was something he couldn't do without being by my side...supporting me.

It's this realization of how deep my feelings for this man truly go and self-admission that affirms in my heart that I truly do forgive and trust him.

He accepted me as I am.

He believes in me.

He protects me.

He cares for me.

And everything he's doing was practically screaming those facts to me. I'd been so blind.

I'm mentally slapping myself for taking so long to realize my feelings. I'm mentally slapping myself for sitting in silence, letting him believe his feelings were not reciprocated. I want to say something. Why am I not saying anything?! What is wrong with me?

"We're back," he tells me silently. I can hear the sadness in his voice. I look around, not sure what he meant when he says we're back because I'd been so lost and absorbed in my mental processing train that I'd missed the entire ride from the bistro back to the hotel.

He doesn't wait for my response. He continues, as the gentleman he is, despite thinking I hate him, to come around to the passenger side to help me out of the truck.

Say something, you idiot! I'm internally yelling at myself.

I take hold of the hand he's offered. I'm letting him guide me to my room.

Silence.

Come on, Lucy, just tell him how you feel! I'm at war with myself, trying to muster up the courage to be as vulnerable with him as he was with me.

We come to a halt. I look up, confused. I'm realizing we're standing in front of my hotel room. Neither of us is making a move to part nor are we making any attempts to speak.

Beyond

The awkward silence is too much. I finally get the key card out. Sarah isn't back yet, I realize.

"Sarah isn't back yet," Vincent notes. I look at him.

"I think she mentioned she won't be back until late," I whispered.

"Right." He nods his head. "I think I remember her mentioning that."

Once more—silence.

Come on Lucy! I'm screaming to myself.

"Well, if you need me, you know where to find me." He offers me a smile. It's strained. I did that.

STOP HIM, YOU MORON! I'm screaming at myself and on instinct, my hand shoots out to grasp his as soon as I realize he was moving away to head back to his room. I've effectively stopped him and at the same time confused him. He's looking at me questioningly. He's waiting for me to say whatever it is that caused me to stop him.

But I don't have the words. I'm terrified to say them out loud.

But I also cannot let him leave. It would quite literally be my biggest regret if I let him go.

And so I do the only thing I can think of aside from saying the words I know I feel. The hold I have on his hand tightens, and I throw myself at him, pulling him down toward me. For once, I don't think, and I don't give him time to question. Instead, I plant my lips to his in a hungry kiss.

I can tell I've caught him off guard. At first, he's not responding, and I worry I made the wrong call. I'm about to pull away when I feel him start to reciprocate. He kisses me back, winding his arm tightly around me as the other is weaving into my hair. And this is everything. We've thrown caution to the wind and are finally giving in to this pull we've felt toward each other for months. We're fighting for dominance. I want to get closer. The fire igniting inside of me is too much to ignore.

We pull away for a moment. I stare at Vincent, trying to catch my breath. His lust-filled gaze stares back. I see awe and wonder mixed in with his current emotions. But that momentary pause is enough to allow his doubt to begin to seep in. I can see it. The uncertainty. And again, I'm reminded that my utter silence doesn't explain this sudden development.

"Vincent," I whisper.

"You don't have to say anything." He smiles sadly.

"No, I do." I move forward, my arms lifting to find their resting place on his shoulder. "I love you," I tell him. Saying it out loud causes a feeling of elation to surge through me. I'm on cloud nine. I said it. I said it!!

It's his turn to go speechless. He's frozen in front of me, unsure how to process the words. I want to laugh. It's comical.

"See?" I giggle, I can't help myself. "Hearing it isn't quite believable the first time, is it?" I place soft kisses up his neck, following up his jawline to the corner of his mouth. When his arms circle my waist once more, I know he's finally waking from his momentary brain freeze.

"I...you..." He's trying to find his words. "You love me?"

"Of course, I do." I smile at him. "I'm just so sorry it took me the entire ride back to the hotel to process what you said. But I love you. So much."

His lips are back on mine. I'm moving backwards after feeling for the doorknob of my hotel room and fumble with the key card to open it. He follows me willingly. I hear the door slam as we enter the room. He must have kicked it shut. I suddenly feel the hardness of the door against my back.

Neither one of us has paused or come up for air. The need is mutual, and we are both falling, falling, falling and allowing this feeling to consume us well into the night. Some time later, I'm feeling content as I lay safely enveloped in Vincent's arms as I start to drift off to sleep.

I hear ABBA's "Dancing Queen" blasting once more as I'm back standing in the bed of my truck. Gran and I are singing at the top of our lungs, enjoying our time without a care in the world...without knowing what is about to come. My presence here feels more real to me. There's a new level of awareness with each increasing visit to this dreamscape. I don't understand it, but there must be something pulling me here. I'm determined to make this count while it lasts.

"Oh Lucy, thank you for today. It was so wonderful," I hear Gran say. I'm watching her from my spot in the bed of my truck. She's looking in the rearview mirror, catching my eye, much like the last time. I'm almost certain she knows I'm here. Why is it she can see or sense me but the other me is oblivious? Is it connected to our abilities or the lack there of in this moment of my life?

"You say it as though we won't have many others, Gran," I hear myself say as I glance in Gran's direction, worried. "Are you okay?"

"I'll be just fine, dear," Gran tells me. I see her eyes are guarded. She knows something. Of this I'm certain. It's written all over her face. "I've been meaning to talk to you for some time, Lucy."

"What's on your mind?" I turn the music off altogether, giving Gran her full attention while also minding the road.

"Your birthday is fast approaching," Gran starts.

"It does that every year, Gran." I hear myself laugh. I roll my eyes at myself. I could throttle this version of me for being too self-centered to pay attention to what's going on around her.

"Don't be a moron! Pull over!" I shout from my spot. But only Gran catches my eye and focuses on me.

"Yes, but you're turning 18," Gran continued, hesitantly.

"Eighteen's not that big of a deal, Gran," I tell her. Gran's gaze is intense in my eyes. There's an acceptance in them.

"Lucy," Gran started but stopped abruptly, a gasp coming from her lips as she moves her right arm to grab ahold of her left arm as though she was in pain.

"Gran!" I yell at the same time the Lucy behind the wheel yells in alarm.

"Gran?!" I'm looking in her direction, noticing Gran was now unconscious. "GRAN!" I notice the dark figure appear in the road, and I'm enraged. Whatever it is…it must have played a role in not only what happened to Gran but to the truck as well. Gran was perfectly healthy. I could not believe her heart would suddenly just give out unless there was some unknown malicious force influencing the circumstances. It shouldn't have taken me this long to think logically about this.

If I'm going to keep materializing and engaging within this dreamscape, I might as well be more purposeful in what actions I am allotted. I'm jumping out of the bed of the moving truck, running toward whatever this figure is in the middle of the road. Jumping out doesn't faze me. I'm not truly here…I don't think. I'm looking at the figure ahead.

It doesn't look like a person. When it suddenly turns to me, it doesn't catch me off guard. Not this time. It doesn't scare me. I won't let it intimidate me. All I see is glowing red eyes. The energy coming off this thing is dark. I stop in the middle of the road, glaring back at it with hate. I can't let it win. I just can't. I turn back, seeing the truck approaching.

"MOVE!" *I try to scream, try to give myself some warning. But I fail because the truck suddenly swerves and blazes through the guardrail. I glare at the figure. I hear its sinister laugh as it thinks it has won. But whatever force previously held me back is no longer in control of me. I feel stronger than before and confident in what I can do.*

"No, no, no!" I'm running toward the accident, looking over the bridge as the truck is quickly being pulled under and into the water.

"Hurry, Lucy!" Gran is beside me. I turned to look at her in shock.

"I knew you could see me!" I exclaim.

"HURRY!" she urges, and I'm suddenly hitting the water going under, under, under until I'm at the door to my driver's side. I can see myself struggling to breathe. Gran is in the passenger seat, unconscious. I want to get to her. But Gran's spirit appears opposite me, staring from where her physical body is submerged in the passenger seat. She's shaking her head at me, stopping me from even attempting what she somehow knows I want to do. She's pointing to me.

"HURRY!" I don't hear her, we're in the water. But I can make out her words, see her urgency as she's urging me to stop wasting time and act...

I startle awake, practically falling out of the warmth of the bed and onto the floor. Just as quickly as I've fallen, Vincent startles awake and is up and rushing out of the bed and over to me to help me.

"Lucy." He puts his arms around me and lifts me up, gently setting me back on the bed. "Are you okay?"

"I think so," I whisper. I'm still processing everything. It amazes me that just a few months ago a dream like this shook me to my core so strongly I'd fought off my re-emerging panic attacks. But now? There's confidence in myself I never realized I had. I don't know when the shift happened, but it did. And these dreams no longer terrify me. If anything, I'm starting to see the truth behind Vincent's theories of my ability to somehow truly be able to interact within the dreamscape. Lucid dreaming.

My gran had told me there was more to our abilities than I could begin to imagine. But without guidance, there was no one to help me figure it out. All I'd been truly aware of was my ability to communicate with spirits. But the rest—whatever that may be—was a mystery to me. Could it be that *this* is what Gran had in mind? Could she do this?

"What happened?" he asks, worried. "That nightmare again?" I nod my head. "Do you want to talk about it?" I appreciate that he isn't pushing me. I can sense he wants to know, but he's letting me set the pace. I look up into his eyes, seeing the concern all over his face. Where could I even begin?

Before I could process to share what I'd encountered, the door suddenly opens and a scream fills the room.

"Oh my god, my eyes!" Sarah shouts. "Ever heard of a 'DO NOT DISTURB' sign?"

I stare at her, surprised at first. But then I roll my eyes and stand up from my place on the bed.

"It's not like we're naked. Relax," I tell her. She looks between the two of us. Me, wearing Vincent's T-shirt. He is wearing nothing but his boxers. It could've been a more awkward situation had she come back an hour ago.

"Well, I'm thankful to have missed the show." She snickers and closes the door behind her. Rather than leave, she's helped herself inside and is setting her things down. "I'm not the only one who missed the show…right?" There's amusement in her tone as she clearly remembers the last time Vincent and I attempted to share an intimate moment.

"No bystanders," I grumble, crossing my arms. "This time."

"It's not that funny, Sarah," Vincent mumbles. "Do you mind?"

"Do I mind getting comfortable in my hotel room after a long day of meetings and presentations? Not at all," she smiles at him innocently. He wants to be annoyed; you can tell he's really trying but he fails. "Besides, I want to hear about how it went?"

"That's private, Sarah," Vincent chastises as he stands up to get his jeans. He looks over to me, offering me a smile.

"You're on your own for a shirt," I tell him. "I call dibs on this one." I point to the shirt I'm wearing.

"Keep it." He laughs, shaking his head.

"As entertaining as I'm sure *that* would be, I meant how it went with your mom." She rolls her eyes at us.

"Oh that," I say, moving to take a seat opposite her at the small table.

"Yes, that," she says, but amusement she once had is gone. She's taken on a more serious tone. "I take it that it didn't go very well."

"I just have more questions than I was able to get answers," I tell her. "She made no sense. She wasn't coherent at all."

"But they said she was off her meds, right?" Vincent adds.

"They're medicating her?" Sarah asks, surprised.

"I guess." I shrug. "She checked herself into the facility 10 years ago. Just before the accident."

"So what now?" Sarah asks.

"Well, we're here a week," I say. "I figure we can give it a few days while they try to get her back on her medication and then try again."

"You really want to go back? You're sure?" Vincent asks.

"I'm positive," I tell them. "I...I had another dream of that night."

"Again?" Sarah asks, worried. "Does it seem they're becoming more frequent?"

"A bit..." I admit, taking a moment to think about it.

"I wonder why that is..." Vincent muses aloud.

"Maybe my mom has some of those answers..." I speak.

"Your incoherent mother?" Sarah looks unsure.

"I didn't say she would definitely have the answers." I roll my eyes.

"She likely won't," Sarah says.

"Well, I can choose to be defeatist, or I can be optimistic and see where that path takes me." I cross my arms.

"We support whatever you want to do, Lucy." Vincent comes over to me, wrapping his arm around my shoulders in comfort.

"Of course we support you," Sarah says. "Please don't misunderstand me. I just don't want you getting your hopes up only to be let down, again."

"I get it." I smile at her, though I know the smile doesn't reach my eyes. I try my best not to let the seeds of doubt invade my thoughts.

"Well, I'm a total buzzkill." Sarah sighs.

"Eh, you always were," Vincent jokes, trying to lighten the mood. "Should we maybe call it a night?" He looks at me, hopeful. He doesn't need to say out loud what it is he's thinking. I sense he's silently trying to gauge where we each will be calling it a night. Together or apart.

"You can see yourself out, Vincent." Sarah stands up with an amused smile on her face. He doesn't make a move to leave. "You'll see her in the morning lover boy, go." She laughs. I laugh too. He really doesn't want to leave…or…leave alone, rather. I got up to walk him out. "Oh no no, she stays here." Sarah stops me.

"Relax." I sigh. "I'm walking him out."

"Fine." Sarah grabs her bag. "You better be here when I get out. We have much to discuss!" She heads to the bathroom and slams the door behind her.

"You know she just needs to get her third degree out of her system, and she'll leave us alone." I chuckle.

"Is it bad that I don't want to sleep without you beside me?" He looks sheepish.

"No, it's not." I smile. "But if I grant her this, we might be able to get away with changing the sleeping arrangements for the rest of the trip."

"She's stubborn, you never know." He laughs. "Will you be okay?"

"I think so," I assure him. "I know you want to know more about the dream… but I think I need to visit with my mother and hope it brings some sense to things. Right now, I'm confused and need to process on my own."

"But you know you're not alone in this anymore, right?" I feel his hand gently caress my cheek. I lean into his touch.

"I know." I smile. "I'm not shutting you out. I promise." He smiles and leans in to kiss me gently on the lips. But the moment our lips touch, the energy between us once more feels charged, and our kiss quickly intensifies.

"Do I need to get an ice bucket?" Sarah suddenly emerges, causing us to break apart. "I passed the ice machine not far from this room…I promise I'll get a bucket."

"I'm leaving, calm yourself." Vincent shakes his head. He gives me one more quick kiss before he's out the door and headed just a few doors down to his own room. I close the door and turn to glare at Sarah.

"You really know how to ruin the mood," I tell her, making my way over to my bed.

"Oh, I'm the least of your worries." She laughs as she pulls her phone out and starts dialing. My eyes go wide. I realize who she might be calling.

"Please tell me you're not calling her," I say. I wish I could say this surprised me.

"Oh, yes…yes I am." She laughs.

"Do you have any idea what time it is?" Dawn's voice fills the room.

"Wake your pretty ass up, lady." Sarah laughs. "You'll never guess what I walked in on…"

The third degree over what events transpired between me and Vincent went on well into the night. Hours. Partly because certain things were none of their business and I refused to divulge such private and intimate details. But damn were they determined.

We'd decided to wait a couple days before heading back to the psychiatric facility to see my mom. It would be my last attempt before heading back to Beaufort. Vincent and I gradually moved my stuff into his hotel room, little by little so Sarah wouldn't initially notice. She didn't have a problem with it. She was actually very happy for the both of us, underneath her third degree. She enjoyed messing with Vincent too much to drop the act. But within two days it was determined I'd be staying with him for the remainder of the trip.

And it was amazing using this time to just be the two of us and continue to get to know each other. Especially with no more secrets in the way. It was peaceful and his presence was calming to me. My confidence—generally—continued to flourish and any doubt in myself, my abilities, and the uncertainty created by these nightmares started to wash away. Vincent's presence in my life had an overall positive effect that was welcoming.

We toured Charlotte. We explored parks and did private tours in the wineries, choosing to avoid the museums just in case they were *crowded*. Vincent thought it would be funny to sign up for one of Charlotte's most haunted ghost tours. He just barely managed to dodge the book I'd thrown at him at the mere suggestion.

"Too soon?" he'd teased me. I was glad he found it amusing.

But finally, the big day had arrived. We'd just parked outside the psychiatric hospital and waited a moment.

"You're not as squeamish riding in the truck like before," Vincent says aloud on the way there.

"I'm still not comfortable," I tell him.

"I said not *as* squeamish." He laughs.

"Yeah, yeah." I shook my head and started to head out to the building.

The same woman from a few days ago is seated behind the visitor's desk. She doesn't look surprised to see me. Though she's not as friendly as when I initially arrived. There's a dark energy I'm sensing from her, and it catches me by surprise. Vincent takes my hand in encouragement. He doesn't know why my demeanor has slightly shifted.

"Visiting Audrey Adams," I tell her, much like a few days prior.

"She's not suited for visitors today." She hadn't bothered to check with the clinical staff. Something else was going on and it was confusing.

"Can you check, please?" I press. Her irritation seems to be escalating quickly. "I won't press. If it's a no, then I'll go. But here's my ID, like before, just in case."

She stares at me before finally reaching over to take my ID. For a moment, our hands touch. And in that moment a surge of energy passes between us, and a glazed look clouds her eyes. When I move my hand away, she blinks repeatedly, as though gathering her bearings. I look at Vincent in confusion. He's equally confused. The woman lets out a shaky breath.

"Are you okay?" I ask her. She shakes her head before finally focusing on me.

"Never felt better, actually," she says. Relief is overcoming her features. "You're visiting Audrey Adams."

"I am…" I tell her. "But she's not suited for visitors?" I double check.

"Did I say that?" She looks confused.

"Yeah…" I'm equally confused. She couldn't remember what she had said not two minutes ago?

"That doesn't seem right." She shook her head, confused. "Let me get everything processed and let you know what her status is." I nod my head and move to the side to stand with Vincent while the woman gets the paperwork processed and makes a phone call.

"You saw that, right?" I whisper to him.

"The complete 180 after you touched her?" he whispers back. "I did. What did you do?"

"I didn't do anything," I say. Did I? "I don't think I did…"

After a few moments, she hangs up the phone and calls me back up to the desk to formally sign in.

"If you just go through those doors down that hallway like before and have a seat, they'll escort her in," she tells me. "Your friend here won't be able to go in with you, I'm afraid."

"It's okay." I smile at her. I reach to take my ID back, careful to avoid contact this time.

"I'll be out here." He kisses me softly.

I follow as instructed through the double doors and take a seat at the same table as before and release a shaky breath I hadn't realized I'd been holding. I'm sitting, patiently waiting and realize as I look up that I'm not alone. But this time, I have more company than I'd expected. Gran...and Charlie. I look at them both questioningly. I know I can't hear them, but I'm very confused.

I hear the buzz of the door ahead and look up to see my mother coming through the doors. I'd hoped the few days might change her demeanor with them figuring out her medication. But she looks equally confused as she was then. She's hesitant to approach the table. She's trying to focus on me and me alone. But I can tell she sees the company we have, and it's unnerving her. Her eyes are wild, and carefully, she sits down. She's cringing in either direction, not sure how best to get away from Charlie or how best to get away from Gran. I don't know how best to help her without them leaving us alone. But something tells me they need to be here and sending them away would be a grave mistake.

"Audrey," I start. She looks at me cautiously. "I really need your help."

CHAPTER 19

LUCY

I could tell she wasn't comfortable, and I hated adding to her discomfort.

"Audrey, please," I beg. "I just need some answers. Do you remember writing this?" I take out the postcard with the warning I'd found. She looks at the paper and starts shaking her head. I look back and forth between Gran and Charlie. I could see Gran is saying something. I know my mother can hear her, but I can't.

"Not here." She shakes her head adamantly. Her fingers are tapping on the table in an unsteady, nonsensical rhythm. "No, not safe. Red eyes."

"Whose red eyes?" I press. "Who were you warning to stay away?" The rhythm with her fingers on the table picks up in tempo.

I gently take hold of her hand to offer her a sense of comfort and ease. And the moment we connect, I feel a similar surge of energy as I had with the woman at the check in desk. My mother's hands stop moving frantically. She stops fidgeting. Her eyes cloud over in a momentary Zen-like state before she shakes her head. I don't let go of her hand. And she returns the gesture as I feel her hold on mine tighten.

"My god." She lets out a shaky breath. I look at her in awe. She suddenly seems coherent, and any sense of discomfort or uncertainty is washed away. I look at Gran in awe. She's looking back at me with pride. I'm not sure what this means. And Charlie has a knowing smile plastered on hers. Not being able to fully hear them has never been more annoying to me. Whatever shared secret they had, I wanted to be in the know.

"Are you okay?" I ask, confused. I try to release my hand, but her hold tightens. She refuses to let go. I don't fight it. If this helps her, I won't deny her comfort.

"This." She takes a breath. "This is the quietest it's been in nearly 10 years." She looks around, taking in her environment.

"I don't understand," I tell her. She looks at me confused for a moment, then looks at Gran who seems to be filling her in on something I'm not privy to.

"You don't know just how talented you are, do you?" she whispers in awe. I shake my head.

"I'm just trying to get some answers about your warning about that accident," I tell her. She looks down at the letter.

"How much do you know about my…abilities," she whispers the last word.

"I barely know about mine, let alone what you could do," I admit to her. She looks at Gran a moment.

"Wait, you can't hear them?" she asks suddenly.

"Not without them coming through on film," I tell her.

"But you see them." She doesn't ask. I nod. "Oh Lucy, there's so much you don't know."

"Whatever you can tell me would be helpful," I tell her. "Starting with this warning."

"It was warning your gran to keep you out of the truck," she tells me. "I was trying to warn her to keep you safe."

"You knew about the accident?" I ask her.

"I kept having a recurring premonition about you dying," she admits in a whisper. "Ever since you were a young girl, it kept recurring. But your gran was never in the truck with you." She looks at my gran with tears in her eyes.

"But why?" I ask. "I don't understand."

"Everything has to be balanced in this world," she tells me, whispering as she looked around cautiously. "Ying and Yang. Good and Evil. One doesn't exist without the other."

"Right." I'm not sure what she's implying.

"Lucy, not all things that go bump in the night like that there are such powerful forces of light," she tells me. "Darkness wants to snuff out the light. Especially those destined for greatness."

"Are you saying there are dark forces that were intentionally trying to kill me?" I ask, shocked. She nods her head. "But why?"

"Because you are incredibly talented, Lucy," she tells me. "You don't realize how much positive energy and light you emit just by existing. And the number of people you help and spirits you help cross over? You're an incredible force of good. The other side doesn't like it."

"But I survived," I whisper.

"You were very lucky," she says. "I'm so happy you did. Not all people targeted by these forces get as lucky." She looks pointedly at me, then Charlie. I look at Charlie, surprised.

"Wait, Charlie?" I ask, in shock.

"Her death wasn't an accident," my mom whispers. "That driver didn't happen to black out. He was manipulated. These forces are capable of dangerous things." Is that it? Is that the connection of what drew Charlie to me? The force that caused her accident is the same force that tried to eliminate me?

"Gran said sometimes these beings would visit you in your dreams, confusing you? Manipulating you?" I ask. My mom nods her head.

"They've never left," she admits. "They're always there…in my head. It isn't safe for you to be around me for too long. You're a threat to them."

"So how are you lucid enough right now, I don't understand." I look down at our hands. She squeezes my hand tightly again.

"It's you." She smiles. "Incredibly powerful in emanating your light, forcing the darkness away."

"You're saying I got rid of the darkness influencing you?" I ask, confused. I didn't understand.

"If the darkness is there, unnaturally manipulating a being, you have the ability to expel it with your touch. If you couldn't, you and I would not be having this conversation right now," she tells me. "Simply by existing, goodness follows you. Followed our family."

"Wait," I back track, confused. "You're not saying our family's mere presence is why Beaufort is literally the boring, uneventful town that it is?"

"It's been a working theory," she shares. "Never proven. We simply never leave."

"But I'm here," I point out. She stares at me, not saying much more. It leaves much question in the air about what ripple effect my leaving town may or may not have created.

"I don't know what I expected to find out when I came back here," I admit to her. "I can't say *this* is what I would discover. What about my nightmares?"

"Nightmares?" she asks.

"I've more recently started revisiting the night of the accident. It's almost like I'm there, interacting with the dreamscape." I pause. She's listening intently. "I've seen the dark figure with red eyes." Her eyes grew wide.

"Has it seen you?" she demands to know.

"I think it has," I tell her. She looks worried.

"Has it hurt you?" she presses. "In the dreamscape, what happens?"

"When I first started having these interactions, I felt frozen in my spot. I couldn't do anything to interfere or stop the truck from going into that guardrail and into the river."

"It saw you," she says. She's thinking. I can tell her mind is going a million miles a minute.

"Eventually I'd be able to break through the force and Gran would appear," I continue and glance at Gran, who is avoiding looking at me. She's sheepish. I'm not too sure, given I can't hear her, but I'm suspecting her spirit really did appear to me in the dreamscape. "Then I would wake up. But now it's different."

"Different how?" she asks. She's hanging on to every word.

"It's seen me," I say. I know this for a fact. "But it doesn't have a power over me. It couldn't keep me in place and stop me from interfering within the dreamscape anymore."

"It hasn't been able to control you…or influence you?" she asks in amazement. I shake my head no. "What's changed?"

"What do you mean?" I ask.

"These dreams started picking up in frequency the same time something in your life changed. Whatever this something is, it's making you more confident in yourself, what you're capable of…overall YOU are stronger…they don't like it, Lucy," she warns me. "If they succeed in killing you in that accident, a great deal of good you've done and will do will be erased. And it would tip the scales toward the darkness."

"But I make it out," I say. "Don't I? It's already happened, and I *am* here."

"With the increase in these dreams, it seems they're trying to go back and get the job done," she tells me. "Whatever you are doing, whatever is changing in your life, they're going to get one window to try to change events, and you must not let them." She's grown serious.

"Time's almost up," an orderly calls from behind my mom. I panic. I don't want to leave. What will happen to her if I left?

"I can't leave you here," I tell her. "What happens the moment I let you go?"

"You have to, Lucy," she tells me. "I'm safer here, where no amount of influence from them causes true harm to others. *You* are safe with me here."

"I don't know what to say," I admit. "I don't know what to do."

"Don't doubt yourself," she tells me. "Whatever you've been doing recently to get them so nervous, keep doing it. And if you find yourself in that dreamscape again, trust your instincts. They won't fail you." I nod my head.

"Will they ever leave you alone?" I ask, hopeful.

"Perhaps one day." She smiles. "And if that day comes, I know where to find you."

"Alright, let's go." The orderly comes over. He's surprised to see my mother so calm and collected. The complete opposite to her norm.

After a moment, she finally let go of my hand. It doesn't take long before I see the confusion rush back in, and the chaos existing in her mind from whatever influencing forces tormented her rushes back.

"No no no no." She shakes her head in a frenzy. "They're angry. So angry. Stay away. Get away!" she urges. They quickly take her back, getting back to a more secure location where they likely will sedate her. Tears form in my eyes. I look once more between Gran and Charlie. They wait a moment before nodding their heads in acknowledgement toward me and vanish.

Releasing a shaky breath, I stand up. I put the postcard back into my pocket and make my way back out toward the area Vincent was waiting. Once I'm through the doors, he's instantly in front of me, embracing me. We wait until we're outside and back in the truck before either one of us says anything.

"Can we go somewhere?" I ask. He looks at me, worried.

"Drive around or did you want to go somewhere specific?" he double checks.

"There was that one park with some hiking trails we'd been meaning to check out before leaving tomorrow morning," I tell him. He looks at me for a moment, wanting to ask what happened. But he knows to wait.

The drive itself feels like it's taking forever. I'd never felt more uncomfortable in the truck since I'd started willingly getting in and traveling with Vincent. So much of what I'd discussed with my mother kept circling back on replay in my mind. And then there's Charlie. I didn't expect to learn what I did. She was never meant to leave this world early. And if there had been a way to keep those dark forces at bay, she would maybe still be here. With Vincent. And he and I would never have met or became what we did. I didn't know what to grieve for. How would I tell him this?

I don't realize the truck has come to a stop until I feel Vincent's hand in mine. He's slow in his movement, not wanting to alarm me. I look at him, tears in my eyes. How do I tell him this?

"What happened?" he asks. He doesn't press me, but he's not going to let me shut him out either. "Was she not able to get you the answers you need?"

"I don't even know where to begin," I tell him. A rogue tear escapes and trickles down my cheek. He's quick to wipe it away.

"Was it worth it, going back?" he asks, trying to create a good starting point.

"Yes," I admit.

"So she was coherent? Helpful?" he asks, hopeful. I let out a shaky breath.

"Not at first," I tell him. "But eventually, whatever darkness was invading her mind cleared. It was probably the most coherent she's been in years."

"What happened?" he asks again. He's intrigued. I look down at my hands, recalling what she'd told me about my touch and expelling anyone who is actively influenced by dark forces. I never knew this. How could I? The town never had anything bad happen...

"I took her hand in mine," I whisper, still looking at my hands.

"Like you did the woman at the check in," he recalls. I abruptly look at his face. I'd forgotten about that interaction. And then recall how she'd been acting when I first got there days ago. And Gran's silent warning to not share any information with her. I then recall her demeanor when we arrived today. When our hands momentarily touched, I remember the energy and the evident shift in the woman's attitude and behavior. Could she have been influenced by dark forces? Just how many of them linger around the different parts of the world?

"Exactly like that," I tell him. "And everything changed. She was clear headed. Coherent."

"Do you think it's something you did?" he asks, cautiously.

"According to her, it was," I tell him. "But there's so much I don't know, and I can't stand it. My mother whose been absent most of my life knows more about what I'm capable of than I do." He takes me into his arms into a tight embrace, offering me a sense of comfort. How was I supposed to be fully confident in my capabilities if I didn't know the full extent of what they were?

"What else did she say?" he asks, still holding me.

"It'll sound insane," I say into his shirt.

"Not to me," he promises. I look back to stare into his eyes.

"Are you really the same guy I met all those months ago who was so skeptical and grew angry at the mere mention of spirits?" I smile sadly.

"I believe in *you*," he tells me. "I love you." His words are soothing and give me courage.

"I love you, too," I tell him. He kisses me a moment before pulling back. Distracting him won't work.

"You won't distract me easily." He chuckles. "Whatever you learned is troubling you. Talk to me."

"She said with everything in life, there's always a balance. With every good force, there's also bad," I tell him. He nods his head. "Well, sometimes the bad forces don't particularly like when good prevails and they try to influence others to…snuff out that light…so to speak." He's listening intently.

"So the night of the accident, who was she warning?" he asks.

"She was warning my gran to keep me away," I tell him. "She'd been having premonitions of my death since I was a little girl. She never had one where I'd made it out."

"But you did." His hold on me tightens, a self-assurance that I am in fact with him.

"I did," I assure him. "I will. I think I will."

"What do you mean?" He's confused.

"I really don't know, it's so confusing," I share. "But she thinks the sudden increase of the nightmares where I'm visiting these dreams is not a coincidence. Something in my life has changed and maybe put me in a better position than the dark forces want me to be in. So they're trying to go back and make sure it never happens."

"They were trying to kill you," he repeats.

"Maybe somehow still are," I whisper. "But she said my gran was never in the premonitions with me."

"But she was…and she passed away from a heart attack," he says.

"I don't think it was a heart attack," I admit to him my suspicion. "She was perfectly healthy."

"So what do you think happened?" he asks.

"I think her being there might have worked against her but against them at the same time," I think aloud.

"What do you mean?" He's confused.

"I mean, she was never meant to be there," I tell him. "Not according to all my mother's visions. But she was. So maybe that force saw the opportunity to eliminate her from the equation too."

"You think it killed her," he determines. I nod.

"But I don't think it accounted for how powerful of a spirit my gran could become," I tell him. "And I think she was there in spirit as soon as the truck hit the water."

"Do you think she got you out?" he asks. I shake my head no.

"I haven't figured that out yet," I say. "But I think she played a larger role than I ever realized in my surviving." I look down. I need to tell him about Charlie.

"There's more, isn't there?" he guesses. I nod my head. "You can tell me."

"I don't know how you'll take it," I admit. "It' about Charlie." He stares at me blankly.

"What do you recall about her accident?" I ask him. "You said a driver blacked out? Hit her while she was out running one night?"

"Yeah, he tried pushing unknown medical cause for a blackout and memory loss. He didn't remember how the car lost control and ran her off the road at a pedestrian crossing," he says robotically.

"Knowing what you know about this crazy world you've found yourself tangled in with me, do you still believe it sounds insane?" I ask, cautiously.

"I haven't given it much thought," he says. "Why would any dark forces intentionally try to hurt her? She was a good person." A slight realization of what he'd just said to describe her resonates with him.

"An amazing person," I agree. "Destined to do incredible things."

"It wasn't an accident," he surmises. "That's what you're telling me."

"From what my mother said…from what Charlie may have told her…it wasn't." I look at him carefully to see how he's processing what I'm saying.

"Charlie was there?" he asks.

"She and Gran," I tell him. "But you know I can't hear them. I don't know what they were telling my mother."

"But your phone." He steps back.

"Vincent, phones aren't permitted in the guest area," I remind him. "You know that." He pauses a moment, then nods his head, remembering. "I think it's the same thing that tried to kill me that night." I drop that bit of information. He looks at me. I can't read his expression.

"The connection," he notes. "Why Charlie was drawn to you initially?"

"I don't know," I tell him truthfully. "She's never been very open about it. She's cryptic." A slight chuckle escapes him.

"That's Charlie alright." He laughs a moment.

"I'm sorry," I tell him.

"For what?" He looks surprised.

"This might change things, no?" I look at him cautiously. He steps back over to me, holding me once more.

"It's a lot to process," he admits. "But Lucy, it's not your fault what happened to Charlie. This doesn't change anything between us. But we do need to figure out what your dreams mean to make sure you're truly safe from all this."

"I agree." I smile at him. "I'm sorry my world isn't normal."

"I'm not," he admits.

219

"Evil forces are afoot to try to get your girlfriend," I tell him, squinting my eyes. "What about any of this is appealing?"

"You," he says simply. "The details don't matter. Only you do."

"Flattery won't get you anywhere," I tell him, laughing. He pretends to look disappointed.

"I think I can get you to come around." He laughs, placing kisses on my neck, gradually moving up along my jaw until he reaches the corner of my lips. He stops there, teasing.

"Nope, not going to work." But it's totally working. How this man gets me to turn to mush so quickly is beyond me.

Since he's come into my life, he's infuriated me, confused me, admittedly hurt me, but he's also made me the happiest I'd ever been. For the first time since the accident, I didn't feel alone. Before him, there was no one else besides the townsfolk who knew me. But even then, none truly knew me. Not the way Vincent does. Each passing day with him, the less alone I felt. And consequently, the stronger I felt.

It's then I realize. That's the one very big, very different factor that has changed in my life that my mother may have been referring to. Vincent. Even his family. Their presence and influence on my very state of being, helping me grow and become stronger and more confident in myself and the endless possibilities life had to offer me that I never allowed myself to even entertain before him.

"What is it?" he asks, noticing the change. I look at him in awe. There was nothing else that made sense to what would've caused such a change. Nothing.

"It's you!" I exclaim.

CHAPTER 20

LUCY

"It's you!" I exclaim. He looks at me both surprised and confused.

"What's me?" he asks.

"You're what's different in my life," I say aloud. He's still confused. "I'm sorry, I know this doesn't make sense. But I can't help thinking back to what my mom said back there. About something happening in my life…something that's now different that these dark forces feel threatened by."

"And it would be me?" he clarifies. "My presence in your life?"

"It's the only variable that's changed…that's changed me," I tell him. "You. Your family. Everyone."

"Changed you…is this a good thing?" He's unsure.

"From my perspective, of course it is," I assure him. "But to them, maybe not? Think about it. Before, I was alone. I've had only the townsfolk for the last decade. My gift all but isolated me from everything because of the fear of how disoriented I'd feel in crowds and because I never knew what someone's true motives were for getting involved with me."

"But you're not alone anymore," he caught on.

"I'm not alone anymore," I repeat, smiling at him. "I've never felt stronger, more confident or unafraid in what I'm capable of. Maybe this is why its power over me in the dreamscape is starting to fail…"

"Whatever it is that's making you stronger to go against it and win, I'm a supporter, you know that." He smiles at me. But he's worried too. I can see the worry in his eyes. "But what if you're wrong about this?"

"Maybe I'm reaching," I admit. Any guess would be as good as the other. "But what if I'm right?"

"What would that mean?" he asks.

"More questions I have no answer to." I bring my fingers to my temple to try to rub away the headache I'm starting to feel come on.

"One step forward," he says.

"Three steps back?" I finish for him. He laughs. "I just know that whatever it is that's happening, I don't think I should be afraid of it. How can I be when I know I have you?"

He looks at me a moment before placing a gentle kiss on my lips.

"Will you think less of me if I admit that I'm afraid?" He looks down, not wanting to meet my eyes. I bring my arms around his neck, getting closer to him. I placed my hand gently on his cheek. He leans into my touch.

"How could you think that?" I ask sadly. "I think I'd be more worried if none of this phased you. It's not exactly normal."

"I just don't think I could survive it," he admits, looking into my eyes intently. "If anything happened to you, I don't think I would survive something like that again."

"Nothing is going to happen to me," I promise him.

"You don't know that," he whispers.

"I promise you," I tell him. "I promise you I will keep digging to try to figure this out. I won't give this thing that kind of satisfaction. And I won't let it get away with hurting Charlie."

We stayed in the park another hour, holding each other, processing but trying to get our minds off everything. The ride back home was uneventful. For this, I was thankful. I certainly wasn't interested in a repeat dreamscape encounter I had had when we were heading into Charlotte. Dawn was waiting outside my cabin when we arrived. She didn't want to waste a moment getting caught up on the entire trip. I think she was more curious to see if Vincent and I had cleared the air and made up. Only to drop the news of all our other discoveries.

"This could've waited another day, you know," I tell her as we're walking up the path, bags in tow.

"No, it can't," she rebuts. "I can't believe you live out in the middle of nowhere. I got dirt on my shoes." Dawn shakes her head in disbelief.

"It's quiet." I shrug. "And it'll come off, relax."

"And if anything were to ever happen, you're in the middle of nowhere with no one around to help you," she points out.

"It's Beaufort," I rebut. "Nothing happens here."

"Well, you've missed a lot," she tells us as we make our way inside.

"What do you mean?" I ask, confused. "Did someone finally get a speeding ticket? I bet the sheriff would be excited over that." I laugh.

"A speeding ticket would be mild compared to the uptick of craziness that's been going on in the week that you've been gone," Dawn says. Vincent and I exchange a glance.

"What's been going on?" I ask, serious.

"There's been a series of break ins, hit and run accidents," she shares. "Some people in town have been uncharacteristically malicious."

"That can't be right." I shake my head in disbelief. "It's Beaufort!"

"You're telling me none of this has ever happened at any time in all the years you've lived here?" she asks, not believing me.

"That's exactly what I'm telling you," I respond. "Even before I was born… this town has not had as much as a speeding ticket so much as a person spouting cuss words. Now you're telling me I'm gone a week and chaos ensues?"

"Maybe what your mom told you about your family and not leaving town actually has some merit?" Vincent says.

"No one has ever tested that theory," I tell him.

"But didn't your mom leave town?" Sarah asks, confused.

"Yes, but Gran and I were still around," I point out.

"Right, of course." She nods.

"This doesn't make sense." I stand up and start pacing. I can't sit still.

"What exactly did you find out?" Dawn asks. "What do you think is going on?"

"Can you maybe sit down?" Sarah asks. "You're making me dizzy with your constant pacing."

"Sorry." I sit down, sheepish.

Vincent and I spend time recapping what happened when I'd visited with my mother the second time. From the interaction with the woman at the check in, to Charlie and Gran's presence, to everything my mother told me once she was coherent enough to have a conversation. When we're done, they sit in stunned silence. They're not sure what to make of the information.

"This is so bizarre." Sarah shakes her head, trying to process everything we'd shared.

"That's putting it lightly, I think," I tell her.

"I don't get how you can be so nonchalant with all this craziness you've discovered," she adds. "How can you be so calm?"

"As opposed to what?" I ask her.

"You just found out literal dark forces have been trying to kill you." She looks at me bewildered. "That they likely caused Charlie's death. I'd be freaked out."

"You *are* freaked out," I point out.

"Because this is all insane," she says. Dawn nods her head in agreement.

"Of course it's insane," I agree. My life certainly hasn't been normal for a decade. I situate myself in the back.

"How are you so unaffected by all of this?" She looks back at me.

"I'm good at compartmentalizing?" I ask, trying to make light of it. She rolls her eyes at me.

"I'm not kidding." She takes a breath.

"I know you're not," I assure her. "But as insane as it all is, it makes the most sense out of anything else I could've come up with."

"But why now?" Dawn wonders aloud. "What's changed in your life? Your mom said whatever it is, it's putting you in a position they don't particularly like."

I look at Vincent. We exchange a look, and I think back to our conversation earlier at the park.

"I have a theory," I tell them. "And maybe I'm reaching at straws. There's so much uncertainty with all of this. Even to me."

"What's your theory?" Dawn asks.

"Vincent," I tell them. They look confused. "Vincent. You guys…your family…you're all what's different in my life now."

"But isn't that a good thing?" Sarah asks, confused.

"I think that's the point," Dawn chimes in, realizing what I'd meant. "What's more threatening than a beacon of light being at their strongest, with a full support system?"

"Well, it's just a working theory," I add.

"But I agree with you." Dawn smiles. "It's the only thing that makes sense."

"As if any of this makes sense," Sarah mumbles under her breath. "Okay, so what does she do now?" Sarah asks, looking around the room.

"What do you mean?" I ask, confused.

"This dark force is threatened by you. Might be legitimately trying to get rid of you and is what, influencing the town?" Sarah shares her thoughts out loud.

"I don't know about that," I admit. "But what do you suggest? I try to find it on my own and battle it out?" Now I'm not one looking at her as though she's crazy.

"Absolutely not," Vincent chimes in.

"I wouldn't even know how to do something like that," I say. "I'm not seeking anything or anyone out."

"But it's not going away," Dawn adds.

"No," I agree. "If anything, the dreamscapes are getting more frequent. I'm sure I'll encounter it sooner than later."

"Maybe if you figured out why they're becoming frequent…" Sarah shares.

"That would be helpful actually," I agree.

"Is there anything significant about this time of year?" Vincent asks. And I'm thinking again. I'm up once more, pacing. With everything that's been going on in my life, it was easy to lose track and just be in the moment. I don't realize until I see my calendar hanging on the wall across from me what month we're in.

"Oh my god," I say, as realization hits me.

"What is it?" Vincent asks, coming to my side.

"With everything going on, I barely realized we're already in October," I admit. October 17th, to be exact.

"What's significant about October?" Dawn asks, curious.

"The accident," I tell them. They look confused. "The accident happened on Halloween, almost 11 years ago." Their eyes go wide.

"You never told us..." Dawn pouts.

"I hardly think those details matter right now," Vincent dismisses.

"But maybe it's connected," Sarah adds. "The frequency in your dreams as you're approaching the anniversary of the accident. That's two weeks away."

"Right...the accident where this force quite literally was or is trying to get you out of the way?" Dawn says aloud.

"Maybe," I agree. "As crazy as it sounds, it strangely makes sense."

"But what does this mean?" Vincent asks, worried.

"It's all theory," I say again. I'm trying to downplay it, but if I'm honest, this theory feels all too real. I don't think we're reaching here. I think we've hit the nail on the head. And if we're right, that's critical information I've never had before. I feel empowered having this information rather than fearful.

"Let's stop saying it's theory at this point," Sarah says.

"If it's not theory," I say.

"It's not," Sarah interrupts. I roll my eyes.

"Then it means more encounters are inevitable. And maybe my chance at making sure it doesn't win will come in two weeks," I admit.

"What if it wins?" Vincent asks, worried.

"It won't win," I deny.

"But what if?" he presses.

"I'm here, aren't I?" I ask, looking around the room seeing everyone's' concerned faces. "If I'm here right now it means I won. I made it out somehow. Something pulled me from that truck."

"You're not afraid?" He interlocks our hands together, looking down.

"If I were afraid, then I'm giving it what it wants," I tell him. "I made you a promise that I intend to keep."

"You better," he whispers before leaning down to kiss me. It's easy to momentarily forget we have an audience. But we're pulled back to reality when someone starts to clear their throat.

"You two are just too cute." Dawn squeals as she runs up from her seat on the couch and pulls us in a hug. I always knew she was too hyper for her own good.

Only Dawn would go from doom and gloom to sunshine and rainbows at the drop of a hat.

"I'll add you for another plate for Thanksgiving dinner," she says matter of factly.

"How can you be thinking about Thanksgiving right now?" Vincent asks, taken back.

"How about we get through Halloween first, yeah?" I suggest.

"We will," she says. "You will," she clarifies.

"Right," I agree.

"Why don't we give Lucy some time to unpack?" Sarah suggests.

"But she's been gone a week," Dawn pouts.

"I think you're all caught on the week's events." I laugh awkwardly. "But I do have an early day tomorrow before sessions are set to resume."

"Just be careful around town," Dawn reminds me. "Not everyone has been themselves."

"I'll keep an eye out, thank you." I smile.

Vincent stays the night with me after everyone leaves. I'm silently thankful he was so insistent on not leaving me alone. Even in the handful of days of rooming with him in the hotel, I'd quickly felt the need to have him beside me at night. I welcome the comfort and security his presence gives me.

We walk into town together, heading straight to Betty's for coffee. Nothing seemed out of the ordinary at first glance. There are customers early in the morning but otherwise not too *crowded*. But walking into Betty's proved a different story. Betty was usually so down to earth, warm, and friendly. No matter how early in the day, it was like she only had one way about her.

But walking into the bakery this morning shows a very different Betty. There is a slight sunken look to her. Like she'd had trouble sleeping. She is also arguing with a customer early in the morning. This is very unlike her. I can even see Claire standing cautiously a distance away from Betty to avoid a confrontation.

After much back and forth, the customer turns and runs out.

"Betty, hi," I greet her cautiously as we approach the counter.

"And what do you want?" she asks aggressively. There is no greeting. She barely looks me in the eye.

"The usual?" I ask.

"And you expect me to keep straight everyone's USUAL around here?" she practically screams. This is not the Betty I know. I'm very concerned. I'm looking around, not sure how best to respond or what the best course of action would be. I briefly catch a glimpse of Gran beside Betty behind the counter.

"Gran's here," I whisper to Vincent. I'm looking back and forth between Betty and Gran. I can't understand her, this is a given. But I'm trying to best understand what she's trying to silently convey to me. A thought occurs to me, and I take a chance.

"You know, Betty," I redirect the conversation. "I think there's something on your hand there, if you don't mind…" I don't give her a moment to react before I'm reaching over across the counter and take her hand in mine.

The familiar surge of energy returns, along with a glazed over momentary look in Betty's eye. And I know. In that moment I knew that whatever was going on with Betty had everything to do with some dark force trying to influence her and snuff out the wonderful light that she was. If there wasn't a force influencing her, whatever this ability of mine was simply wouldn't work. My mother had been very clear.

Betty releases a shaky breath, and a brightness returns to her eyes. She's confused, yes, but I can see the change in her demeanor. I can see the relief on Gran's face, worried for her dear friend.

"Oh Lucy, dear," Betty exclaims in excitement after a few moments pass. "You're back! Hello, Vincent! The usual for you two?" Betty has no recollection of her previous interaction with me and likely anyone else who she might have crossed paths with. Claire looks confused from her spot near the corner, but she approaches cautiously to help start the order.

"The usual please." I smile. She gets started on our orders. As she keeps busy, I turn to Vincent.

"Was that what I think it was?" he asks.

"Yes," I tell him.

"What happened to her?" He's in disbelief.

"Besides being somehow influenced by something otherworldly while I was out of town?" I rebut.

"I don't think there is a besides-that scenario," he says sadly.

"I don't understand how in just a week of my being gone, something like this could even happen," I say aloud. "Just how many others do you think are affected?"

"I'm not sure." He shakes his head. "But you're back now. It'll be okay."

"Will it?" I ask in doubt. "Does this mean I can't ever leave?"

"I'm sure it doesn't mean that," he tries to assure me. "Maybe whatever is going on is tied to this dark force you've been dealing with. If it goes away…then maybe you can leave if that's what you wanted."

"Too many maybes," I grumble.

"Here you go!" Betty chimes in, bringing us our orders. "Oh, I can't wait to hear all about your trip!" She steps around the counter, allowing Claire to take over, and we move to the side to catch up a moment.

"I'm sure there will be plenty of time to catch up." I smile at her, happy to see she's okay and seemingly back to her old self. "How have things been here?"

She's about to answer then pauses. She looks confused.

"I actually don't remember the week much, it's such a blur." She laughs. "Must have been quite the week."

"Do you feel okay, Betty?" I ask her.

"Never better, dear." She smiles. "Here you go!" She hands Vincent and I our orders and turns to the next costumer. The entire encounter is very surreal, and frankly, leaves me worried for the others in town.

"Come on," Vincent urges me out toward the courtyard. I'm hesitant to leave Betty's. "She'll be okay," he adds.

I allow him to lead me out, though I steal several glances back to make sure Betty truly is alright. I see she is. But I'm concerned. Who wouldn't be? The courtyard itself isn't busy and bustling as much as the café is. Dawn hasn't opened her boutique yet. I take note of Clara's floral shop as well. Closed. Usually she's the first of us in and ready for the day. I figured she'd jump at the opportunity to approach me, knowing when I'd intend to be back. But she's nowhere in sight.

"Flower shop's closed," I say quietly.

"What?" Vincent looks around.

"Clara's usually the first one of us in, ready to start the day," I point out. "Do you think she's okay?"

"Why wouldn't she be?" he asks, turning back.

"I don't know," I admit, taking a deep breath. "Who knows who else has been acting weird since I left town?"

"But she was acting strange before you left," he points out.

"True," I agree.

"Are you okay to work today?" he asks.

"I'll be okay." I smile. "Don't you have to travel back to Savannah at some point and check in with your team?"

"I do." He looks apprehensive.

"Don't say you don't want to." I laugh. "I know you're the boss and all, but you have to go. You have to make sure everything's on schedule."

"Kyle's had it," Vincent points out.

"And his wife just got back from being gone a week," I rebut. "Go relieve him and let them have some quality time together. I'm sure they'll be appreciative."

"It'll only be a week tops," he promises.

"Even if it takes longer, I'm not going anywhere," I tell him. "I'll be okay."

"It won't be longer. Not if I can help it," he says with certainty. "Keep me in the loop, please?" he asks.

"Always." I smile at him. "Now go. The sooner you go the sooner you get to come back." He laughs before leaning down to kiss me.

CHAPTER 21

VINCENT

I absolutely hate, with a passion, that I have to head back when so much was starting to unravel with Lucy. I know she's right. I know on a rational level that I can't just abandon my responsibilities and the business. But out here, I feel useless in not being able to help her. What can I do from here? Nothing. That's what.

Kyle was clear. Everything had been going well. The initial plan of being away a week seemed reasonable.

"I heard things went well in North Carolina," he greets me, trying to fight the grin off his face.

"I'm sure you've heard plenty." I shake my head. "Your wife talks too much."

"She means well." He laughs. "But really, I'm glad things have sorted themselves out for you and Lucy."

"Me too." I smile.

"I'll be honest, I thought she'd make you fight for it longer." He laughs and manages to dodge my right hook.

"I'm lucky she didn't," I say and leave it at that. "Let's just keep things going on the same schedule. I said I'd be back at the end of the week."

"Yeah, Sarah filled me in on what's going on," he said, suddenly serious. "I'll tell you one thing. Your life will never be boring with Lucy."

"Be serious." I glare at him.

"I am." He chuckles. "I'm sorry. It's just funny how things turn out. You, the most skeptical one of all, are thrown in the middle of trying to figure out how to keep your girlfriend safe from legitimate dark forces who hate that she's a strong beacon of light and want her gone. Tell me that's how you thought things would turn out for you."

"It's definitely keeping me on my toes," I admit.

"But she's worth it, just the same," he says. He doesn't have to ask. I look at him.

"She most definitely is," I say.

But the week didn't turn out as good as it had when Kyle was here without me running the show. It's like everything that could go wrong, did go wrong. First there was a delay in the materials by three days and the clients were adamant about sticking around to make sure we were ready to go the MOMENT everything arrived. They hate delays. From their perspective, I sympathize. From a business standpoint, I sympathize and want to make sure our clients were satisfied and appreciative of being prioritized. From my personal standpoint, I was in hell. Delays in materials can't be avoided. These things happen, and we work with it. But then, as one problem was resolved, another arose.

The water valve burst while we were gone with no rhyme or reason. The clients themselves were unsure how it happened. Twice. No one was on site when it happened. And so this delayed the installation of materials. We installed new PVC pipes and that allowed us to continue. Then the clients went away for two days and supposedly the spare key they would leave for us went missing, so we could not gain access into the home. But it was all too suspicious.

Something was legitimately intent on keeping me away from Beaufort. And the more that came up, the angrier I would get. And the more worried for Lucy I became. She and I spoke every day. She was doing well. Jumped right back into the flow of business. She had no issues with the townsfolk, not that she shared. She'd even noticed things improve within the town just days of her return.

But I could sense there was more. I could sense she was nervous without even having to say it. I'd kept in touch with Dawn, especially since she was trying to convince me to convince Lucy to attend the Halloween party she'd decided to put together at the last minute. She'd said it would be a good distraction for Lucy to be surrounded by those who loved her on a day that brought her tragic memories. But I wouldn't push her. If she wanted to make an appearance, I would do everything in my power to be there.

Dawn clued me in on little things she'd observed. Like the fact that Lucy now made it a point to avoid going home to the cottage late at night. I was thankful for that. But she used to be very headstrong in her belief nothing was afoot, and it was safe. So it felt there was more to it than she simply wanted to go home early.

The day before Halloween, I was still stuck but adamant that even if it was late tonight, I'd be on my way back to Beaufort.

"This is getting a bit ridiculous," I tell Lucy on the phone. We'd connected on the phone before a client session she had lined up.

"It can't be that bad." She laughs. She has no idea.

"Babe, one time a water valve bursting is an unfortunate incident, but a second in the same location that we'd just fully repaired with all new PVC pipes…that's intentional," I press.

"So which of your guys is messing with you?" she asks, trying to control her fit of laughter. I knew it wasn't any of the guys. They knew better.

"They know better than to mess with our work," I insist.

"Vincent, it'll be okay." She's comforting me. It's working. "Kyle said he'd get there to reprieve you tonight. You'll be back before the party tomorrow. It'll be okay."

"I just want to be there with you already." I sigh. I'm frustrated.

"I'd love that too," she admits. "I may or may not miss you."

"May or may not?" I laugh. That's great.

"That's the best you'll get out of me, take it or leave it," she says matter of factly.

"I'll take what I can get," I tell her. "I promise I will be there this time."

"I know you will," she says with confidence. She's distracted from a moment by something on her end of the phone. "Vincent, I have to go. Your sister just walked in," she says.

"I'll talk to you later," I tell her. "Tell Dawn I said hi."

I continue working, determined to try to get done today and leave. But of course, another hiccup. I check the time and see around this time, Lucy would be closing to head back to the cottage. I took the chance and gave her a call. She answers almost immediately.

"I've missed you," I whisper to her. Hearing her voice brings me a sense of calmness I've been missing these weeks apart.

"I've missed you too," she tells me. She's walking to the cottage, I can tell.

"I'm sorry I keep getting delayed," I apologize.

"That's okay," she assure me. "What's one more day, right?"

"I was hoping to have been able to make it back tonight," I admit. "I really tried."

"Let me guess, another hiccup?" She assumes correctly.

"Yes," I grumble.

"Something really is keeping you from coming back." She laughs. She's kidding but I'm convinced. And it's part of what is making me anxious to get back. I don't like the idea of whatever is causing this is doing so with the intention of keeping us apart.

"What's wrong?" I ask her. I could sense something is bothering her.

"Your sister tried getting me to come to the Halloween party," she says. But that isn't it.

"That's not it," I disagree.

"You know me too well." She releases a shaky breath. "You're not even here, and you can tell something's amiss."

"I certainly like to think so," I tell her. "What happened? Nightmare again?"

"No," she denies. "It's been quiet on that front. I had someone come through during a photo session today," she says. She has my full attention.

"Did it not go well?" I ask.

"No, it went fine, as far as these things can go," she admits. "But they had a warning to pass along to me."

"A warning?" I sit up from my current position, hanging on to every word. "They're threatening you now?"

"No! Not at all." She's assuring me. I take a deep breath, and release it in an effort to, calm down. "They're warning me that spirits talk. And to be careful."

"To be careful," I repeat.

"That's all he said," she says.

"Sarah's right, you are very calm with dealing with these types of things," I think aloud. "I envy your ability to do that."

"What's the alternative?" she asks. "Halloween is literally right around the corner. If something's going to happen, it's going to be soon, right? Why else would that warning come through now?"

"I'm starting to really dread Halloween," I admit.

"I am too," she shares.

"But you'll be okay," I tell her.

"I will be okay." She had to be. She promised. And if I knew anything by now it was that Lucy, above all else, kept her word.

I'm bummed to be off the phone, but a new level of determination hits me to get things done. And I'm making a good time. I'm triple checking everything and as soon as Kyle makes an appearance, I'm getting my things to start the drive to Beaufort.

Lucy and I had exchanged messages about my meeting her at the cottage to walk her over to the party. But she insisted for me to just go straight to Dawn and make myself useful and help set up. We agreed tonight she'd finally be staying at my place. Personally, I didn't care where we stayed so long as we were together. But if she preferred this, who was I to deny her? I made it with enough time to be able to effectively help Dawn start setting up. I was even ordered to pick up additional refreshments and pick up the catering to feed the town. Mom and Dad were helping with decorations. Dawn had enlisted the help of all of us, and luckily Kyle was the only one safe from a Dawn on a mission.

"What, no floral arrangements?" I joke as I returned with every time successfully crossed off on my list.

"I tried," Dawn says as she and Sarah come over to grab the different trays.

"What do you mean you tried?" I laugh. "The floral shop is within walking distance."

"Yeah, but Clara has been completely M.I.A for the last couple weeks," Dawn says.

"Whatever you said to her must have really resonated because she's been really avoiding Lucy," Sarah said, walking past me.

"Avoiding her?" I ask. That's odd. "That doesn't sound like a Clara thing to do. Why suddenly give up the chance to work with Lucy?"

"How would I know?" Sarah asks. "I would not read too much into it. It's probably not a big deal."

You are the dancing queen
Young and Sweet
Only seventeen

ABBA's song suddenly is blaring through the courtyard, and I freeze on the spot. A chill goes down my spine. It's that song. *The* song that'd been taunting me when Lucy and I first met. The same song that had been playing when Lucy and her gran were in that car accident.

"Who put that song on?" I call out.

"Nothing's plugged in," Miles calls from where the sound equipment was being set up. "I don't get what's going on." A sense of dread overcomes me. Something isn't right. I'm searching for my phone. I need to call Lucy. There should be enough time to catch her before she leaves and have her wait for me. She shouldn't be walking by herself.

"Where's my phone?" I shout in a panic. I can't find it.

"I'm not sure. What's going on?" Dawn comes over when she realizes something is very wrong.

"I can't find my phone, call Lucy, please," I beg her. "Tell her to wait for me to come get her." Dawn doesn't waste a moment. She's on the phone and calling Lucy. But the line keeps ringing and ringing. And the song in the background keeps getting louder. I look over at Miles in a panic, trying to see if there's even the slightest chance something is simply malfunctioning with the system.

It's then I feel my eyes are playing tricks on me. Standing by the sound system is an elderly woman who I recognize from a dream I'd had months ago. She'd appeared to me in a dream I had had standing in a field of tulips. I'd never seen her in my life, except for in this dream. And again when Lucy had shown me a picture of her gran. She's looking at me very intently. She's determined and wants to make sure I'm paying attention.

"Quit gawking and hurry!" she shouts, clear as day. And I'm taking off without questioning it. I hear Miles and Dawn yelling for me to wait, not understanding what it is that is going on. I'm running through the courtyard in the direction of where I knew Lucy would be coming from and in the distance, I see her. I stop for a moment, feeling relieved. She is okay.

"What is going on?!" Dawn catches up to me.

"Something just isn't right." I turn to look at Dawn and Miles, who were now with me. The sound of a car suddenly blaring in the distance catches our attention, and we turn to look in the direction Lucy had been coming from. She'd been crossing the street. There's a sedan which has materialized seemingly out of nowhere, and it has its sight set on Lucy. I'm instantly brought back to the night of Charlie's accident and her being run down. This time, I'm actually here, and I need to get to Lucy. She's realized in the same moment that the car is gunning for her. She's running toward us. Miles and I take off toward Lucy to get to her in time. She tries to move out of the way, but the car follows her. She's the target and there is no avoiding the collision. All too quicky, with an unnatural speed I watch in horror as the car rams into Lucy, sending her flying into the air. I could hear the sound of the initial impact followed by glass shattering. The car is driving past us. I am too focused on Lucy and her body rolling on the ground until she's stopped to get a plate number. I'm running toward her, careful not to move her. There's a deep gash on her head and who knows what other damage is left from the accident. Dawn is screaming, she is freaking out.

"Call an ambulance! Hurry!" I shout to Dawn. Lucy's eyes are glazed over. She's trying to look around. I'm not sure what's she's looking for but just as quickly, she loses consciousness.

"Is she breathing?" Dawn is crying. She's trying to dial her on the phone, but her hands won't stop shaking. I carefully feel for a pulse.

"Her pulse is faint. Did you call?" I urge. She's nodding her head.

"I called your dad, he's coming." Miles is now beside me.

"I can't lose her. I can't." I shake my head. I'm looking around, searching for help. I'm making sure not to move her. I'm utterly helpless.

I can't lose her.

CHAPTER 22

LUCY, THEN

Vincent went to Savannah not long after we returned from Charlotte. He's only meant to be gone a week, leaving us another week to really dive in and try to get more answers as to what supernatural forces may or may not have been secretly plotting against me. He'd been confident the work trip would be quick. Kyle had positive feedback, and everything was on track. But the reality was very different. It seemed each day Vincent had been a step closer to coming back to Beaufort, something would go haywire, and he'd been stuck that much longer. We had one day left until *the* dreadful day. I'd teased him that his presence caused such a disruption. But he wasn't entertained by it. He just wanted to get back and was waiting to line schedules up with Kyle if he had to again. But since returning, there were no dreamscape recurrences. I wasn't sure if that was a good thing or not.

Customers continued to come in for sessions. They'd taken genuine interest in my time away and if I'd enjoyed myself. No one knew the true reasoning behind my leaving town, nor did they need to know. But their interest was appreciated. No one jumped back into the sessions with any expectations other than the premise of the shoot. Even Emma had stopped back in during the week. She'd been doing much better after her encounter with Johnny. There was an evident change in her.

It was refreshing and a welcome change.

In the short days I'd been back in town, whatever influx of break ins had all ceased. There was a returned calmness to the overall feel of the town that seemed to be lacking when we first came back. And even through the calm, I felt uneasy walking around alone at night. I never felt uneasy before now. I didn't want to tell Vincent about how I'd been feeling. Instead, I'd made it a point to make it back home before nightfall. Light felt safer.

Clara had turned up the day after my return. However, she hadn't made her way over to set up a session which was surprising, considering she was obsessive over it in the weeks before my departure. I wasn't sure if she was acting out of spite or if maybe Vincent's reality check had hit a nerve. Regardless, she kept her distance. Avoided eye contact with me any time we crossed paths.

"This is getting a bit ridiculous," Vincent says. We had connected on the phone before a client session I had lined up today.

"It can't be that bad." I laugh.

"Babe, one time a water valve bursting is an unfortunate incident, but a second in the same location that we'd just fully repaired with all new PVC pipes…that's intentional," he presses.

"So which of your guys is messing with you?" I ask, trying to control my giggles.

"They know better than to mess with our work," he presses.

"Vincent, it'll be okay," I assure him. "Kyle said he'd get there to reprieve you tonight. You'll be back before the party tomorrow. It'll be okay."

"I just want to be there with you already." He sighs in frustration.

"I'd love that too," I admit. "I may or may not miss you."

"May or may not?" He laughs.

"That's the best you'll get out of me, take it or leave it," I state matter of factly.

"I'll take what I can get," he says. "I promise I will be there this time."

"I know you will," I tell him.

I hear the door to the studio open. I don't look over to see who it is. I already know.

"Vincent, I have to go. Your sister just walked in," I tell him.

"I'll talk to you later," he tells me. "Tell her I said hi."

"Will do!" I end the call. "Hey, Dawn. Vincent says hi," I say, tuning to look at her.

"How did you know it was me?" she asks. I hear the shock in her voice. "Wait, is that one of your abilities…are you telekinetic? Can you read my mind?" I stop what I'm doing and look up at her, straight-faced.

"I think the word you're looking for is *telepathic*," I say. "And no. Only you walk around with this town in those god-awful death traps for shoes."

"They're heels, and they're adorable," she rebuts, placing her hands on her hips.

"Death traps," I disagree.

"You'll come around eventually," she tells me.

"Don't count on it," I tell her. "How can I help you today?"

"I'm hoping to convince you to come to the Halloween party tomorrow." She smiles.

"Seriously?" I ask, surprised. "I thought we'd been over this." She'd come up with this idea days after our return from North Carolina. She didn't care that she had little time to pull something together for the entire town. Her parents were coming and had always gone all out to celebrate the holiday. They didn't want this year to be any different.

"Don't you want to see everyone?" she presses. "Mom and Dad haven't seen you since the dinner a couple months ago."

"Halloween and I don't have a good history," I remind her.

"I know, I know," she assures. "But won't it be a welcome distraction?"

"Crowds…the impending confrontation with evil forces…and you want me to go to a party?" This feels like a bad idea. Terrible idea.

"Okay, you have a point," she admits.

"It's good you're doing this though," I tell her. "The townsfolk love Halloween. I'm sure you'll have a great turn out."

"But you won't go, will you?" She looks at me sadly.

"I'm not sure," I tell her. "We'll see."

"I'll take what I can get." She laughs. "Do you want anything from Betty's?"

"I think I'll grab something on my way out," I tell her.

"I noticed you've been leaving at a more reasonable time this week." Dawn takes a seat across from me. "No more late-night strolls."

"Did you share that with your brother?" I look at her.

"It might have come up," she admits. "Don't look at me like that. He's been worried about you."

"I talk to him every day," I say in surprise.

"And that's not going to stop his worrying." Dawn laughs.

"I get that," I agree. "But what will you tell him that I haven't already told him?"

"Well, apparently the not walking at night alone thing anymore," she points out.

"It wasn't a secret." I roll my eyes.

"I know." She smiles. "But it's something I've noticed."

"Should I be creeped out with you watching me so intently?" I squint my eyes at her. I hold up my hands, wiggling my fingers. "Do I need to use these?"

"I'm not being influenced by anything." She pushes my hands away, laughing.

"I know." I laugh. "You're still too bubbly for your own good. But stop watching me. It's creepy."

"I'm just making sure you're okay," she assures me.

"Noted." I roll my eyes. "And appreciated. Creep factor aside."

I move from my spot to start getting different back drops ready. I'm making sure the studio is ready for when the client intends to come pick it up in the upcoming days. Vincent's supposed to come back tomorrow, and I'm excited for the reunion.

"Are you all set for today?" she asks.

"I actually have one more session, and I'll start heading out." The moment the words leave my mouth, my next client comes in. She looks unsure as she enters the studio.

"Am I early?" she asks. Stacy was her name. She'd booked a session a few days ago for headshots as she'd changed professions recently, entering real estate. For business marketing, she needed to get some things in the works quickly. I knew her from around town and had seen her occasionally over time.

"You're right on time," I assure her. "Dawn, I'll check in with you later?" Dawn nods and excuses herself politely.

"So, real estate?" I ask Stacy.

"I was looking for a fresh start." She smiles. I nod my head in understanding.

"After you." I show her to the area I had set up for her for the backdrop. We went over a few different options, trying to gauge her vision for her photos. Once everything was in place, I went over to lock the front door to minimize distractions and maintain her privacy…just in case.

"What should I do?" she asks.

"Whatever feels natural for you," I tell her. "Did you bring outfit changes?" She shakes her head no. I smile. "That's okay. We can start with some head shots, then we can stage the space based on how you envision any full body shots."

"I think head shots are okay," she says quietly. I can sense she's not entirely comfortable. With her lead, I start taking some different shots from different angles. I move the lighting to reframe the space. It's turning out good, and she's gradually becoming more and more comfortable as time passes in the shoot.

"I don't know why I was so nervous," she admits.

"I'm not a fan of getting my photo taken either." I laugh.

"But you're a photographer." She laughs.

"I know." I smile. I look at some of her photos on the camera once all is said and done. It's then I see an elderly man in the photo next to her. A moment later, he's next to me and has a grim look on his face.

"It's not the photos making her nervous," he tells me. "It's me. I can't help it."

"Um. Stacy," I start. "You know from around town what I can do…besides photography?"

Her eyes grow wide. "Someone's with me, aren't they?"

"I'm Philip, her grandfather," he tells me. "My passing was recent; the family is still processing."

"Your grandfather is here," I tell her. Her eyes widen, tears fill but do not spill over.

"Why do you think you're the reason she's nervous, Philip?" I ask him.

"I don't know what I'm doing," he admits. "But spirits talk. I think I'm making her nervous…me hanging around her."

"Was there a reason you were hanging around?" I ask, nodding my head in understanding.

"I've been trying to figure out a way for them to know I'm okay," he tells me. "Sudden passing or not, I did have my affairs in order. If you tell Stacy to look inside my mattress, everything they need is there for them. Everything." Inside?

"Stacy," I start, thinking of way to best convey his message. "From my understanding, your grandfather's passing was rather sudden?" She nods her head. "Sometimes even for spirits it's a hard transition to process. They can get confused.

He's been around trying to let you all know he's okay. But to also go look inside his mattress. That everything you need is there."

"Inside?" she asks.

"That's what he said." I shrug. "But he's okay. He'll be okay. And so will your family." She smiles at me. I look over at him and he looks nervous. "Was he a nervous nelly type of guy? Would you describe him that way when he was around?"

"Quite the opposite, actually," she tells me, wiping away a rogue tear. "He was full of life, very outspoken. Didn't shy away from anything." That was interesting for me to hear. He's looking at me, as though he wants to say more but isn't sure if he should.

"Spirits talk," he says, cautiously. I turn my head to the side, trying to understand what he's trying to say. He's looking around. "And you have to be careful."

"What?" I ask, taken back.

"Is everything okay?" Stacy asks. I nod to her, reassuring her.

"You have to be careful," he warns. "There's more happening on this side of things than you can imagine. And it's not all good things. Be careful." He stares at me intently but with fear in his eyes before he vanishes. It was as though he was fearful of saying too much.

"He's gone," I tell her. She's looking confused. I'm confused too. It's the first time I can't be certain if a spirit truly crossed over or high tailed it out of here. "I'm sorry, it's never happened before where a spirit took a moment to share otherworldly happenings with me," I admit to her.

"But he's okay?" she confirms.

"He is," I assure her. "And don't forget…inside the mattress." She nods her head in understanding. "I'll get these developed and ready for you in the next week, as discussed. We'll take care of everything once it's all ready for you."

About an hour after she leaves, I get ready to close the studio and start to make my way out. I'm caught by surprise the moment I lock up, my phone goes off, and I smile. Vincent has good timing.

"I've missed you," he whispers as I accept the call and hold the phone to my ear.

"I've missed you too," I tell him. I started my walk back to the cottage, enjoying that in some sense I had Vincent with me. Even if it wasn't physical.

"I'm sorry I kept getting delayed," he tells me.

"That's okay," I assure him. "What's one more day, right?"

"I was hoping I to have been able to make it back tonight," he tells me.

"Let me guess, another hiccup?" I assume.

"Yes," he grumbles.

"Something really is keeping you from coming back." I laugh. I wasn't convinced of this at first. But now, now I am getting concerned that other forces may be at play to keep us separated.

"What's wrong?" He can tell I'm not quite myself.

"Your sister tried getting me to come to the Halloween party," I tell him.

"That's not it," he disagrees.

"You know me too well." I release a shaky breath. "You're not even here, and you can tell something's amiss."

"I certainly like to think so," he muses. "What happened? Nightmare again?"

"No," I tell him. "It's been quiet on that front."

"I had someone come through during a photo session today," I tell him. He's listening intently.

"Did it not go well?" he asks.

"No, it went fine, as far as these things can go," I admit. "But they had a warning to pass along to me."

"A warning?" His voice grows serious. "They're threatening you now?"

"No! Not at all," I assure him. He releases a breath, seemingly calming down. "They're warning me that spirits talk. And to be careful."

"To be careful," he repeats.

"That's all he said," I tell him.

"Sarah's right, you are very calm with dealing with these types of things," he says. "I envy your ability to do that."

"What's the alternative?" I ask. "Halloween is literally right around the corner. If something's going to happen, it's going to be soon, right? Why else would that warning come through now?"

"I'm starting to really dread Halloween," he admits. I'd taken the turn at the stop sign and am entering the lit pathway up to my home.

"I am too," I share.

"But you'll be okay," he tells me. His confidence in me gives me assurance I didn't know I needed. I smile.

"I will be okay."

That night, I slept horribly. I ache in the morning once I'm up and getting things ready for the day. Dawn continues her efforts to get me to join, at least for a small time, at the Halloween party and I think, why not. Why be alone waiting for something when I can be with those who love me and want to support me? Vincent was trying to make it back to come meet me at my home directly, so that we could walk over together, but he was held up in traffic. Vincent was hesitant to let me go anywhere alone. Though I'm not sure what the concern was with walking around town.

The real fear was what would happen once I'd fallen asleep, right? And while my sleep was shit, I at least had no nightmares. Tonight, I planned to stay overnight at Vincent's place. We figured we had been staying at mine all this time. A change in scenery was welcome. I pack an overnight back and glance over to the envelope on my desk that had arrived the day before. I can't hide the excitement over the news I had to share with Vincent about the photography contest I'd entered a while back. The news finally came. And it was share worthy. I place the envelope inside my bag and check to make sure everything I need was in order.

As I'm heading out the door, I hear my phone start to go off. I debate turning around to answer it but do not want to delay seeing Vincent. I've missed him, I admit it. Call me a sap but I missed my guy. I let it ring and lock the door behind me. It is a very short walk back into town from the cottage. It is not fully dark out, not yet. I felt comfortable doing this walk alone. What could really go wrong during that short walk? I had been confident that nothing would.

And how right I wish I was. I'd made it out of the lit pathway and onto the street to head the short blocks into the town. It's when I'm finally on the road that I get an odd feeling as if I'm being watched. Goosebumps form up and down my arms. I stop for a moment and look around. I don't see anything unusual, otherworldly or otherwise. But usually, my fight or flight instincts are on point, and something is telling me to pick up the pace and get to where I know Vincent is. I start walking again, checking the road to make sure all is clear before walking to cross and get to the other side. I'm not far from the courtyard at this point. I could see Vincent, Miles, and Dawn up ahead, running in a panic toward me. Close but not close enough. Their panic is concerning but as they see me, they stop. I can see the relief in their features as they see me. There's a moment of relief for me as well knowing they were headed my way to meet me. I release a breath I didn't realize I'd been holding. I was probably getting worked up over nothing.

My focus is reaching my destination until I hear the sudden uproar of an angry engine not far behind me. I turn around and just barely make out a woman behind the wheel of a sedan barreling toward me. I start to run but with every zig, the car zags. Until finally, it reaches its target, smashing into it. It's me. It's all so surreal how the entire incident unfolds. I feel the hardness of the material of the car as it initially rams into me. I feel and hear the hard glass of the windshield as I smash directly into it, shattering it beneath my weight. I'm airborne until I hit the ground hard and roll, roll, roll until the momentum gives and my body comes to an abrupt halt.

I ache. All over, I can feel a heaviness and excruciating pain overcome my body. There's an instant pain radiating from my head. My vision is blurry. It's hard to see at first but I know the sedan which came barreling toward me, hitting me, has taken off. Of that I'm certain. I hear screams and panic in the distance, gradually getting closer, but the heaviness intensifies, and I'm suddenly so tired. I feel myself being pulled away from consciousness.

As the screams get closer, I let the darkness pull me under.

I'm standing. No longer laying down, which surprises me. I'm looking around and realize I'm back. Back in what appears to be the dreamscape but it feels different than before. I feel I have a more concrete presence here. I figure I could dwell and panic on why I'm feeling this way or I can focus on the inevitable. ABBA's "Dancing Queen" blasts in the background. How I ended up back here this time, I'm not sure. But I'm here. And this must be my last chance to figure out what truly happened that night. I may not have another chance. Not if I recall what happened moments before I ended up back here. I'm very aware that my head hurts. I put my hand to my head trying to shake off this sensation of heaviness. Whatever this being's plan in eliminating me is, it tried to weaken my state of being. I can't help but wonder if it knew where I would potentially end up. It had to have been plotting this all along. Maybe this is what Philip was warning me about. If I could just hold on, I could maybe get through this.

"Oh Lucy, thank you for today. It was so wonderful," I hear Gran say. I'm watching her from my spot in the bed of my truck. She's looking in the rearview

mirror, looking at me, and she now looks worried. She can see I'm injured, unlike before. There's a difference in her awareness of my presence.

"You say it as though we won't have many others, Gran," I hear myself say as I glance in Gran's direction, worried. "Are you okay?"

"I'll be just fine, dear," Gran tells me. I see her eyes are guarded. "I've been meaning to talk to you for some time, Lucy."

I don't hang around to listen to this conversation. Not again. I don't need to put myself through listening to my own nonsense when I need to figure out how to prevail against this dark entity. I'm jumping out of the truck and running toward where I know this figure is undoubtedly waiting. It thinks it will win. But I won't let it. No matter the outcome, I won't let it win.

"Gran!" I hear the yelling coming from the truck.

The figure is there, as expected. It's menacing, and its glowing red eyes are alight with a fire it never had before tonight. I stare straight at it, challenging it. Its efforts to intimidate don't go unnoticed. I couldn't let it prevail.

"You think you're going to win," I taunt it. I ignore the growl it emits in anger. "You won't!" I scream as I turn around and run toward the truck that has already crashed through the guardrail and is being pulled under quickly.

"Hurry, Lucy!" Gran is beside me. "You can do this, hurry!"

I don't even question it anymore. Somehow, someway, I am determined to prevail against this entity. I must hurry. I sense my physical self doesn't have much time. Neither version of myself has time. I'm suddenly hitting the water going under, under, under until I'm at the door to my driver's side. Gran's spirit is with me, guiding me, supporting me. I look at her from my place at the driver's door. I don't have any tools to pry this door open, nor do I have the tools to shatter the glass. She's starting at me intently, pointing at the version of me that's fighting to be able to breathe.

"HURRY!" I don't hear her, we're in the water. I can make out her words. I sense her urgency as she's urging me to stop wasting time and act. And so, I do.

I act. Unsure where it comes from, confidence emerges from within me. Somehow, the door is opening into the truck. It's a fight against some unknown force and the pressure of the building water. Once I'm in, I have no resistance from the seatbelt and we're off. I gather myself, and I'm swimming against the water toward the surface. I'm pulling myself up and out and trying to get over to the edge of the river. Even if I don't have enough strength to get myself fully out, partially is still a win against the intentions of this dark force. I can feel myself draining of energy, and I don't know how much time I have before I'm pulled out of the dreamscape and back to whatever awaits me. I only manage to get myself partially out of the water, and I check to make sure I'm breathing. I sigh in relief that I am and stand to look up at the bridge in triumph.

The dark figure stands there, looking at what has transpired. Its red eyes continue to glow the angrier it gets as it realizes it has failed. Whatever window of opportunity it thought it had in eliminating me this night, is gone. I won. I hear its sudden growl as it's realizing that its efforts have been in vain. I look down at myself and at Gran who is also standing over me, protecting me. I take notice of a force of light emanating from her, cocooning around me in a protective barrier.

"I knew you could do it." She smiles at me.

"Why can I understand you?" I ask her, in slight panic. I have no gear...am I dead?

"Don't panic." She laughs. "The rules in this space don't apply when you're not visiting in your physical form," she assures me.

"This doesn't feel the same as before," I say aloud. I'm looking around, realizing by now I'd be fading out, waking up. But nothing is happening.

"Oh, sweetheart." Gran looks at me. I see the same guarded look in her eye as I had tuned in when I appeared back in this dreamscape. "I'm afraid it's not the same as before. But it's what was needed for you to act as bravely as you did to save yourself."

I'm not entirely sure what she means. In the back of my mind, I feel a permanence to this position I've found myself in.

"I'm not making it out here, am I?" I ask.

"You could." She looks at me sadly. "It isn't up to me, dear."

"Is it over?" I ask her.

"Oh, Lucy." She looks at me sadly. "It's never really over."

Her words sink in. I'm processing as best I can and still, I don't fully understand. The dark figure is nowhere to be found. A feeling of relief and triumph overcomes me. I can breathe freely in a way, given the unique predicament I have found myself in. I want to wake up. I pinch myself. Nothing happens. I look back down to where gran had been protectively positioned but she is now gone.

In fact, everything has faded. And what was once a dreamscape of a horrific memory in my past has begun to transform into a place of light, emanating warmth, and serenity. I don't know where I am, not really. It takes me some time to fully process before it truly occurs to me. Was I never going back?

"*Well shit,*" *I mutter aloud. It can't end like this…*

The End…?

Printed in the USA
CPSIA information can be obtained
at www.ICGtesting.com
LVHW020822201124
797036LV00012B/351